HOSTAGES TO FORTUNE

Persephone Book N°41
Published by Persephone Books Ltd 2003

First published 1933 by Jonathan Cape Ltd.
© 1933 The Estate of Barbara Hodges
('Elizabeth Cambridge')

Reprinted 2008 and 2020

Endpapers taken from a 1933 hand-printed
linen designed by Edwin Parker for the Silver Studio
© MoDA, Middlesex University

Typeset in ITC Baskerville by Keystroke,
Tettenhall, Wolverhampton

Colour by Banbury Litho

Printed and bound in Germany by
GGP Media GmbH, Poessneck on Munken Premium

ISBN 978 1 903155 318

Persephone Books Ltd
59 Lamb's Conduit Street
London WC1N 3NB
020 7242 9292

www.persephonebooks.co.uk

HOSTAGES TO FORTUNE

by

ELIZABETH CAMBRIDGE

PERSEPHONE BOOKS
LONDON

PUBLISHER'S NOTE

'He that hath wife and children hath given hostages to
fortune; for they are impediments to great enterprises, either
of virtue or mischief' wrote Francis Bacon (1561–1626) in his
essay 'Of Marriage and Single Life'.

'Elizabeth Cambridge' published *Hostages to Fortune* in
June 1933 and it was The Book Society Choice for that
month; we have chosen to publish it exactly seventy years
later. But, wrote the *Saturday Review of Literature* reviewer
that summer: 'Let me say at once that I do not believe that
sun-bathers and sea-shore nymphs will in any considerable
number select this book as a beach companion. It is something to be read and relished in an armchair at home. Its
taste and intelligence call for corresponding qualities in
the reader. For this author has successfully attempted an
extremely difficult literary feat: she has essayed simply to
describe the day-by-day life of a middle-class English family,
living in narrow circumstances in an Oxfordshire village; and
in doing it she has drawn an all but faultless picture of what
has sometimes been described as the "lost generation" . . .
I have no hesitation in describing this book as in many ways
the most remarkable, and one of the best written, that I have
read in a long time.'

CONTENTS

HOSTAGES TO FORTUNE

PRELUDE

CHAPTER ONE

I

'Is it a girl or a boy?'

'It's a nice little girl.'

'I . . . thought it would be.'

Catherine lay still. Through the slats of the blind she could see the hard white light of early morning; the bars were like a ladder. Black, white, white, black . . . was the white the rungs of the ladder or was it the space between? A white ladder, or a black ladder?

Water splashed. The voice of the newcomer, hoarse and uncertain, rose and fell, broken by deep, sobbing breaths.

A girl. An anticlimax. A girl . . . after all that! Oh well, William would be pleased. A 'nice little girl'. That was nurse, standing up for another woman.

'Can I see her?'

'Not yet. I'm just giving her a bath.'

Catherine closed her eyes. She wondered if being born hurt as much as giving birth. Somebody pulled up the blind and opened the window. Instantly the room filled with the smell of slaked dust. It had been raining in the night, but the morning was windless, damp, and fresh. An early tram clashed and rattled down the hill, the overhead wires sang as it passed. Out in the Sound a tug hooted. The tide must be falling now . . . all down the coast over miles of brown rocks, the gulls screaming in the pale June morning.

A girl. But who wanted girls, now, in the middle of a war? Catherine had never believed in the equality of the sexes. Women simply did not have the same chance as men. Nature had seen to that. If you wanted to produce a human being at all, it was only common sense to want to produce the kind of human being that was going to have the best time.

Best time? The expression was the wrong one. Surely? What did she mean by the best time?

She thought of the last morning on which she had seen the sun rise in summer. They had been coming home from a dance, five in a cab, singing. A jolly dance. The only refreshments had been iced coffee and strawberries and cream. Between dances they had walked about the steep, moonlit street below the houses. She had worn a grey silk dress trimmed with golden beads, her shoes and stockings were golden.

Girls had that sort of good time, but she hadn't meant that.

She opened her eyes. Nurse was standing over her, the baby held upright against her shoulder, like the bambino on a Della Robbia plaque.

Catherine stared. So that was her baby. Baby? Babies

were sleepy, amorphous, unconvincing and ugly. This creature was not amorphous, it was not even ugly. It stared at life with bright, unwinking eyes. Its underlip was thrust out, tremulous, indignant.

'My word,' Catherine thought. 'That's not a baby. It's a person.'

She looked at nurse. Nurse had not observed the phenomenon. She was presenting, proudly, a nice little girl.

Catherine freed one arm from the bedclothes.

'Give her to me.'

'Sure you aren't too tired?'

Catherine shook her head. Her body was tired. She felt as if she had just dragged herself ashore, breathless, from swimming in a rough sea . . . beaten and tingling. But her mind felt clear, bright and cool.

The child was warm. Warm as a puppy. Like a puppy it nosed and wriggled, feeling with its lips along the bare flesh of Catherine's arm. Catherine touched the mouse-coloured fluff on its head, stroked the place where it ran out into a gleaming film of golden hairs.

The poor little beast . . . with life, and a bath, and clothes all thrust at it at once. Catherine's heart warmed to her daughter. She sighed contentedly, closing her eyes and letting her body go slack.

'Don't take her away,' she said sleepily.

The thing's feet pushed against her side, it wriggled and grumbled, still full of its grievance against life.

Love, deep, impersonal and compassionate, welled up in Catherine.

'She won't lie still with you,' nurse said, scooping Catherine's daughter expertly out of the hollow of Catherine's arm, and marching off with her to the fireside.

Catherine opened her eyes angrily. Wasn't the child her own, then . . . after all these months? Hers? Well, not nurse's anyhow.

'Hi!' she called ruefully. 'You've stolen my baby.'

Nurse looked at her over her spectacles.

'You go to sleep,' she said. 'You don't know when you're well off. You'll have more than enough of her before you're done.'

II

Catherine's sister took the same line.

'Now you've done it!' she said. 'Now you'll never have another quiet moment.'

Catherine grinned agreeably but didn't answer. Her mouth was full of pins. She was re-trimming a hat with a piece of lace, some dark green tulle and a pink rose. Nurse had objected to the hat trimming. She said that the pins would get into the bed and prick the baby, and that in any case Catherine ought to be making flannel petticoats for her daughter. But Catherine knew that William might be home on leave at any moment. He would expect her to look attractive, but would not want to spend money to achieve that result. She hoped that he would be taken in by the hat.

'You can sit there and smile if you like,' Violet went on, 'but you've taken up something this time that you'll have to go through with . . . whether you like it or whether you don't.'

She sat down on Catherine's feet at the end of the bed. Her lap was full of parcels. Her coat and skirt were faultlessly cut, her summer blouse was fresh and new, her brown hair was unruffled under her hat, though her face was flushed by the morning's shopping in the close, summer streets. There was a little dust on her 'good' black shoes. She looked at them with disapproval and wondered if she should draw the toes of them up the backs of her black stockings or not.

'But I do like it,' Catherine said suddenly. 'I shouldn't have had Audrey at all if I hadn't liked it.'

Violet winced. She was of the school which didn't admit that one deliberately has children. She preferred to look on children as one of the more dubious acts of God . . . an uncertain blessing, and a very certain charge on time, freedom, and money. She had had two, was ten years older than Catherine, had married younger and more wisely, and looked upon Catherine's marriage as a cheap caricature of everything that marriage ought to be.

'My dear Catherine,' she retorted. 'Do you even begin to understand . . .'

Catherine moved irritably. Her scissors slipped off the bed. They were followed by a cotton reel, rolling noisily, two of William's letters, a sample of baby powder, and *The Queen's Quair*, and *Hetty Wesley*, in sevenpenny editions.

Violet looked at the litter.

'To begin with, you won't be able to sprawl about like that when you've got a house of your own. Who's going to pick up after you, and what sort of house do you think you're going to have?'

'I shall have a lovely home,' Catherine said confidently. 'I shall have huge wood fires, and scones for tea, and wonderful old furniture picked up cheaply. And . . . because I like it . . . I am going to have a long, long family. And I shall have all their friends to stay in the holidays.'

'And wood ash all over the place, mice in the larder, a cook under notice, and William down with a cold. I admire your courage.'

She stood up to go.

'In any case,' she added, 'you won't be able to lie about trimming hats for yourself and reading novels . . . you certainly won't have time to write any.'

Catherine smiled amiably at her. They had a mutual and quite friendly belief in each other's stupidity. Violet had brought Sebastian and Jane up wonderfully, she knew that. They were handsome, healthy, vigorous creatures, with sound teeth and excellent digestions. Jane was competent and Sebastian clever. They fairly shone with polish. Violet had never stopped grooming them from the moment they were born. Her Audrey would never be as highly finished, as up to the minute as Jane. Catherine would never, she felt, become a professional parent. Yet she was sure that she didn't want Audrey to be in the least like Jane. So she smiled.

'Cheer up,' she said. 'None of it can possibly happen for a long time yet . . . worse luck.'

She cleared the rest of her belongings off her bed and on to a chair. Violet no longer irritated her very much. Nothing irritated her now that she had William. Still, she was glad that Violet was going.

Violet looked pityingly at the infant on nurse's knee.

'You won't know how to manage her,' she said.

'No,' said Catherine. She wasn't prepared to argue the point.

She sat up, her elbows on her knees, as the door closed behind Violet, and looked at the rusty sycamore and the hot blue sky outside the window. Soon she would move down into Cornwall, soon William would be home.

William, working hard at a Base Hospital in France, was glad that he had a daughter. He had given a dinner to his friends, and they had had *Langouste Américaine*, which was, apparently, one of those things which one eats in order to be able to talk about it afterwards.

Catherine forgot Violet and began to tell nurse the story of how William had been ordered off to France at short notice. She and William, and her suitcases, and William's valise and haversack and British warm, and her hatbox and her typewriter and the sewing machine which she had bought because she was a married woman, and two cushions covered with pink and green cretonne, and a gaping pilgrim basket, had all come across the ferry from Cornwall in an old Ford car. That car had broken down outside a Baptist chapel in a wilderness of villas beyond Milehouse. They had had to change into a taxi at great speed, in the midst of a departing congregation, all dressed with intolerable neatness, and all registering disapproval of persons in khaki who travelled on Sundays.

Nurse said nothing. She sat with Audrey face downward across her knee, gently spanking her back, and thinking her own thoughts. Catherine knew that she was not the least interested in her, that she looked on her as a careless young woman, whose marriage and whose offspring were the casual by-products of emotion, and in no sense to be reckoned on the same plane as other marriages and offspring. Practically speaking, Catherine wasn't married, unless you counted a marriage by special licence and a couple of months knocking about in rooms, as marriage.

Nurse picked Audrey up and brought her to Catherine. Catherine settled down contentedly to feed her, curling up against the pillows, her own head and shoulders bent forward, so that she might look into the little thing's intent face.

It was wonderful to be able to give anyone else such complete satisfaction. Lying there, with her arm round her baby, Catherine was happy, and she was not often happy. There were limits to what she could give. Usually she wasn't capable or sympathetic enough to give gracefully, but here she could give freely . . . more freely even than she could give to William. The whole business was so natural. She gave, and her daughter took, and no trouble afterwards about gratitude.

Hang gratitude! Why couldn't every other relationship in life be as simple as this one? Suppose that she and William could simply accept their mutual need of one another, without that perpetual sparring for supremacy which seemed to be an inseparable part of even such a marriage as hers and William's . . . which had been for love, if it had been for anything. It had certainly had no financial justification.

Nurse gathered up the books and the cotton and the scissors and the letters and the baby powder. She put them on the dressing-table, out of Catherine's reach. She took the hat and put it on top of them.

'I should like to take this baby away with me,' she said.

She stood over Catherine, looking down severely at her.

'As soon as your husband comes home, you'll forget all about her. You'll go out with him and neglect her.'

Catherine didn't trouble to look up. As though one hadn't room for two kinds of love!

'Oh, no, I shan't. How could I!'

She thought: 'I must look a fluffy-headed idiot! And even if I was one, fancy going out and forgetting a baby, as if it were a pair of gloves, or a latchkey.'

She wondered, lazily, why people always took so much pains to tell her that she couldn't, or wouldn't do things. Quite often she could do them, and did, though she was left with a feeling of humbled gratitude when she sold a story, or made a successful cake, or when William proposed (with great inappropriateness, in the piece, like the inside of a concertina, between two railway carriages).

Anyhow, she had made Audrey.

Though in that business, perhaps, one was rather the instrument than the creator.

Still . . . she had made Audrey.

And liked it.

'You'll never give yourself the trouble of bringing her up properly,' nurse said, pursuing her own line of thought.

CHAPTER TWO

I

Catherine went down into Cornwall. Audrey, from her perambulator at the edge of the cliffs, made herself heard to the village at large.

'Mrs Cohen's compliments, and do the people next door know that their baby is crying?'

Catherine returned a message.

'The people next door present their compliments, and they do indeed know that their baby is crying.'

'As if,' Catherine said, 'anyone could avoid knowing.'

In a few days Audrey gave up crying and resigned herself to the business of eating, sleeping, and growing.

Catherine early discovered that her daughter was no fool.

II

Catherine was unhappy in Cornwall. For her the bare steep hills, the white sands and the weedy rocks had too many voices. The holiday houses were let to strange officers in khaki who came and went abruptly, leaving harassed wives to clear out and shut up the houses behind them. The War had absorbed Catherine's generation like a great sponge. They were all gone, and already many of them had gone for good. The boys who tramped the long, dull miles of Cornish lanes, singing, on their expeditions to the towns along the coast, who had played beach games at low tide, swum, and picnicked and boated, and made life amusing at no great expense of anything except energy . . . all these were gone.

They had loved life, they had been happy, and they had been young.

Catherine remembered how a party of them had climbed, one hot evening, to the hill above the larch woods. They had flung themselves down on the warm turf. All the valley lay below them, though the sea stood like a blue wall at the end. The air smelt of dry grass and wild thyme. Thistledown shed its airy, silvery wheels over the hill. The light was mild, full, and warm.

Oliver had lifted his head from his arms and spoken, out of the heart of their mutual content.

'I don't want to grow old,' he said.

And everyone had agreed with him, though perhaps only Catherine, caught up into that ecstatic moment of evening stillness, had known what he meant.

And now Oliver would never have to grow old. He would never have to change, as those who were left were changing.

Catherine felt that her generation wasn't being ripened. It was being scorched. They were learning too much, too soon. Life . . . just simple breathing, and being, and enjoying, was never again going to be enough.

She thought indignantly:

'It shan't make any difference to Audrey. Everything that we've lost can be made up to her. She shall have a better chance than we had.'

Her generation had been hurt, but there was no need to hand that pain and weariness on to her children.

III

William was disappointed.

He thought that Catherine looked ill, and tired, and shabby. He blamed Audrey for that. Audrey was thriving . . . little devil! Anyone could see that, and hear it, for that matter. Catherine was what he had come home for, what he longed for and needed.

Audrey, pink and clear-eyed in her perambulator, was left to the society of her nursemaid, whom she preferred. William carried Catherine out on to the rocks, at low tide, and sat with her there through the brilliant August mornings.

The cottage woke up, now that William was home. He stamped about the small rooms, singing 'Michigan' and smoking endless cigarettes, telling endless stories. He lectured Catherine about the condition of her hair, her figure, and her clothes. He made lists of the old oak furniture which he had stored up for their future home, and of the furniture which he intended to get, next time they went up to the Midlands. He drew up lists of fruit trees and made neat drawings of the way in which they should be pruned. He made plans of the cottage which he hoped to take. He pointed out that Audrey was costing as much to keep as their combined selves.

'That's another thing,' Catherine said. 'We ought to take out an education policy.'

'Why?'

'You don't want to skimp her education, just because she's a girl. Education costs a tremendous lot. If you start putting down the money now, it won't be so much trouble later.'

William thought they were spending quite enough. He promised to look into it later.

'It's cheaper if you do it before she's a year old,' Catherine insisted.

William said that later on he would write to a man who could put the job through cheaply for him. He'd see about it presently. He threw two or three stones into the sea, and reflected that it was a pity to waste a short leave worrying about Audrey's education. He offered Catherine a cigarette and suggested that they hired the pony trap and drove to Tregantle that afternoon.

Catherine said, 'If you'd only get on with it now we shouldn't be bothered about it later.'

'How could I? I didn't know that we were going to want the pony till this minute.'

'I don't mean the pony. I mean Audrey.'

William produced a cigarette, lit it, scratched his ear with the dead match, and stared out to sea.

'About Audrey . . .' Catherine persisted.

William gave a start. 'Look here. Do you think we want a dozen each of cooking and dessert apples? The dessert apples could be grown on cordons . . . I'm going to goblet train the cooking apples.'

Catherine sighed. She got up, saying that it was time she went in to feed Audrey. William looked round.

'But you do think that six early apples and six late ones will be enough?' he asked seriously. 'There won't be room in that garden for more. We must have some pears . . . and the east wall is for dessert plums. . . .'

Catherine started to scramble away over the rocks. William ran after her and picked her up.

'Naughty!' he said. 'That's bad for you.'

In the garden in front of the cottage they found Audrey lying on her back on Lowe's knee. Lowe was a sturdy, abrupt young woman who whisked Audrey up and banged her down, scrubbed her head, and soaped her face, or scooped her out of her pram as if she thought Audrey indifferent to any physical feelings whatever. And apparently Audrey was. She throve on it, liked it, and loudly resented Catherine's gentler and less confident handling.

Lowe addressed her as 'sossy pusskins,' filliped her nose, pushed her for miles up and down the steep stony hills in her perambulator and seemed to wish for no other company. They understood each other very well.

'Here's your mother, face,' said Lowe. 'Now you'll have to go to her.'

William picked a couple of pink rambler roses off the front of the cottage, and put one into each of Audrey's clutching hands. Audrey lay back, her toes curled up, her eyes bright and intent, looking up past William, past Catherine, at a spray of climbing rose which bobbed between her and the sky. She clutched the flowers which William gave her, working her arms in and out, as if she were swimming.

'She can't see them, of course,' William explained tolerantly. 'She sees everything flat, and she can't distinguish colours. Everything looks grey.'

'Well, she do know how to take hold,' said Lowe, who didn't believe a word that William said.

Both of them smiled at Audrey, superior, yet pleased, as if she were an odd toy, or an ingenious animal. Catherine snatched her up and carried her indoors.

It was the first time she felt that cold rage which visited her so often afterwards when anyone encouraged Audrey to show off. Not because they were fond of her, or even because they wanted to give her pleasure, but simply to amuse themselves. Audrey wasn't William's inferior simply because she was a child. She might well turn out to be his inferior when she grew up. But Catherine was not . . . whatever happened, she was not going to have her children treated as though they were deficient in any way simply because they were young.

It was all there, not even as a plant is all in a seed, but more as a folded piece of fine material is packed in a small box.

So Catherine went off, fuming, and William didn't notice. William, fortunately, very seldom noticed anything.

Catherine sometimes wondered why, if she had been obliged to fall in love, that blazing infliction should have come to her in the person of William, who was half a generation ahead of her, and who had been brought up in such a different tradition that more than half the time neither of them knew what the other was thinking. One was told that love was enough. Catherine began to suspect that it was a much more secondary business than she had been led to imagine.

You didn't, she decided, start marriage hand in hand, as partners, comrades or any other cheering word which her generation was given to using. On the contrary, you started at opposite sides of a dense, dark jungle, full of tangled creepers, tree-stumps, dark water-holes, snaky places, tigerish places, and places of sheer bog through which you had to fight your way to a meeting-place. Or not, as you felt inclined.

Then the thought faded, and she forgot it.

For Catherine loved William.

IV

When he went away again, life seemed to stop, in spite of Audrey. They wrote long letters at cross purposes to each other, letters which, later on, Catherine was to re-read and smile at, ruefully. They were so sure that they knew each other, then.

And Audrey grew. . . .

And Catherine went on writing a long novel in the Wessex manner, full of strong-minded dark women and farms in lonely places and Nature and Destiny, and a great many other things which she knew nothing whatever about. For more than anything else, more than William or Audrey, Catherine loved ink.

To see, and feel, and experience things was not enough. The desire to express . . . to take somebody else by the shoulders and force them to look too, to put into words the beauty which lies on the edge of expression, the rare beauty for which words can hardly be found, this was the strongest impulse Catherine had. It wasn't a quiet feeling. It was a caged beast that padded up and down and banged its head against the walls of its cage and fretted to be let out. The quivering blue silk of the sea, the swimming flame of blue succory in the uncut corn, the sharp gritty sound of wheels in summer dust, the wandering scent of sweet-brier after rain, these things hurt her unless she could express them.

And William was moved from his Base Hospital to a clearing station up the line, at the railhead. Hundreds and hundreds of wounded men flowed through the station, not in a steady tide, but by waves. Sometimes they lay outside the tents in row after row of stretchers, waiting, first for attention, and then for transport. Then the whole staff would work on through the night, through the following day and on into the second night. Presently the tide would ebb and there would be nothing to do but listen to the gunfire, scheme to make the roof of the mess waterproof, or try to wangle supplies of fresh fish, fruit, and coffee.

About the rush hours William preferred not to think. He wrote a little about it to Catherine, but not very much. Telling people wasn't William's business. Also, when he wrote to Catherine he wanted to forget about abdominal wounds, gas gangrene, mud, marauding aeroplanes, and the gummy weariness of overwork.

It was better, when a lull came, and he planned a road and had it put through, a road made of cinders and chalk, which stood firm in spite of the mud of the Somme river valley. He 'attracted' some timber and built a bath-house, to which the station wasn't entitled, and told Catherine all about it, with maps and diagrams.

And the War went on and on, endlessly, and the mud and the wet and the recurrent overwork began to find out all the weak spots in William's constitution. He said nothing about it, because he hoped that at the end of his contract he would be passed to serve again.

V

Audrey left off crying altogether and began to talk.

Lowe made her a couple of very ugly, snuff-coloured crawlers, embroidered with bright blue flowers. She was so proud of them that Catherine hadn't the heart to say what she thought, and Audrey crawled about the floor in them, and pulled herself up by chairs, and stamped the absurd brown button boots which Lowe had insisted were a necessity.

Her hair was curly, her cheeks were red, her wrists were firm and mottled. She sat up straight and bowed her acknowledgments when Lowe dragooned privates home on leave into saluting the Captain's daughter.

'She's extraordinarily like Queen Victoria,' said Catherine. 'Very imposing as long as she sits down, and surprisingly short when she stands up.'

'Ho!' said her nurse. 'She's no queen. She's just a "sossy pusskins."'

She planked Audrey down in her high chair, tied a large

Turkey towelling bib under her chin, and slapped her dinner down before her on an enamel plate.

Audrey looked at it. She wanted milk. Milk in a bottle.

She didn't waste time in crying, she knew better than that. She took the edge of the plate neatly and swiftly between finger and thumb and turned the whole thing over on to the floor.

'There!' she said sweetly, looking down at the wreck.

'Just as well we bought her that enamel plate,' said Lowe.

PART ONE

CHAPTER ONE

I

Catherine stood alone in the square central hall of her house. She felt small and rather frightened. The house was so much too big. It wasn't the cottage of which William had shown her the plans. The house was cheap, William said, and with one child already here and another coming soon they would soon grow out of the cottage. The house had always gone with the practice, they would never get another chance to buy one like it. Money? They could easily raise that on mortgage.

Catherine didn't like the word mortgage. A mortgage was something which impoverished heroes in novels had on their estates, in order that the villain might foreclose in the third chapter. William said that he wasn't an impoverished hero in a novel, but a hard-working doctor in real life, and that mortgages were a good thing.

Catherine liked the outside of her house. It was built of warm yellow ironstone, with white mullions and a roof of stone slates. On two sides the village street and market square came close up to the windows, so that the occupier sat at home, as in a box at a theatre, and beheld the public life of his neighbours. Standing in the central hall Catherine could see out through the drawing-room into the street. The bitter cold of the spring of 1917 filled the house. In the garden on the other side of the hall a tall monkey puzzler clashed its arms with a metallic noise. A gaunt magnolia rattled on the house wall.

'We'll have both those uncanny brutes down,' Catherine thought.

She wandered away upstairs. The large bedrooms were all papered with dark green seaweedy papers, guaranteed to wash. They couldn't afford to replace many of them, but something would have to be done about the few rooms they were actually going to use. The staircase was in dark elm-wood, lit by an old window of yellowish stained glass. There were odd steps and dark cupboards everywhere about the house. The bedrooms had stone mantelpieces which the last owners had whitened with hearthstone. There was a terrific box bath. Catherine looked at it, not foreseeing the day when her children were joyfully to turn its woodwork into a sleigh. It was a mausoleum of a bath. She wandered away from it, downstairs again, through the useless servants' hall, the huge stone-flagged kitchen, the dank wash-house. She looked about across the court at the coalhouse with the fruit-loft over it, the range of stables and lofts, the derelict, unheated glasshouses. It was a complete house of the period of 1880 when country doctors kept three maidservants and a man, when credit was long, and money was money indeed. She felt that the whole thing was grossly in excess of their needs.

She came back into the hall. It had originally been painted Georgian green. Time had changed parts of it to pale blue and weathered other parts to a gentle bronze. She heard William moving about, and found him in the blood-red drawing-room, surveying the mantelpiece.

'I told Dowell,' he said, 'that it was like mottled soap. I told him I was going to paint it white. He nearly had a fit. He said it was English alabaster and was made in the works here. I suppose we'd better leave it.'

Catherine nodded. 'It would be a pity to upset Dowell. He's always right about the old furniture. I expect he knows. I wish you'd measure that kitchen range. Mowsett says if we put a false bottom in, it won't burn so much coal. It looks as it if held about a ton.'

William walked over to the window and looked out into the street. Against a close-packed sky of grey cloud, a sky so heavy that it looked as if it must fall bodily, a church tower stood up like a hill. Square, massive, broad-shouldered, the great bulk of ironstone dominated the cottages round the market-place. It stood under its crown of pinnacles like a king. When he was miles away upon his round William would turn to look at it and feel comforted. Now, under that threatening sky, it seemed the only real thing in the place.

For the village was empty. All the doors and windows were shut. The remains of the last fall of snow lay in thin lines upon the thatch and in the grass at the roadside. It was impossible to believe that inside the cottages there were blazing fires, cats basking on warm hearthrugs, babies crying, and women ironing or setting tables for tea. As William looked at the tower he had a momentary feeling of comfort. Then he shivered and turned away.

'My God!' he said. 'I'm sick of this. We haven't seen the sun since November. Do you really want sixty yards of that cretonne?'

'You measured it yourself. I know it seems fantastic. The settee alone takes twelve yards. We must cover them with something. If we don't they'll get dirty and wear out.'

Catherine came and stood beside him. 'Isn't it always like this here, in the winter?' she asked.

'My God, no!'

On William's face there was a sour distaste for everything. Catherine felt that the War had given her back quite a different person from the one she had married. This William, who had reluctantly been invalided out of the army, was sharper, more irritable. He expected less and wanted more. He felt that he had been done. But what it was that he had been done out of, and what it was that he wanted, Catherine didn't know.

'Besides,' he went on violently, 'it's April . . . look at it! There ought to be warm rain. The daffodils ought to be out. There's nothing planted in the garden. How on earth are we going to catch up? Our seeds ought all to be in. You can't plant when the ground's like iron.'

He broke away from her and went angrily through the empty house to the kitchen. Catherine stood still, running her finger along the dusty window-ledge. All this paint would have to be scrubbed before they came in. She felt tired, small, and insufficient. She knew so little. How was she ever to make a home of this great place? Old, rambling, and unfriendly, it presented the exact opposite to the house of her dreams.

She went wearily through the hall again and opened the door of the little dining-room. She felt happier there. It smelt of fresh paint, the white walls reflected the light. The floor was covered with old, brown linoleum, carefully beeswaxed. A yew hedge ran at right angles to the window, the auricaria stood like a tree of tin, between her and the sky. Catherine shook her fist at it.

'You wait, my friend,' she threatened it. 'I'll get you one day.'

She looked round the room. She had made blue curtains for it, and a rose-pink lampshade. It would look warm and comfortable at night. She had bought a load of peat to burn in the wide hearth, brown bricks the size and shape of books, but much lighter.

She could hear William moving about in the kitchen, and, as always when she heard him coming, she turned in the direction of the sound, her face lightening. For Catherine was completely dependent on William.

II

In May the fruit trees and the crocuses and the daffodils all flowered together. The garden shone with gold and white. Little debased violets bloomed in the roots of the box borders and round the trunks of the pear trees. The old gnarled trees themselves were crowded with masses of white flowers with pink stamens. Blood-red spears of peonies broke the soil. The beds were full of plants that Catherine and William could not recognise. The weeds came up too.

Sow thistle and ground elder, bindweed and chickweed, groundsel and speedwell, squitch and creeping jenny, goose grass and waywind, the garden was starred and pattered with them. Catherine and William were much too busy to deal with them, and nobody in the village had time either, even if there had been any money with which to pay them.

'One year's seeding is seven years' weeding,' said Lowe. 'You'll hear from them weeds later.'

Catherine and William went into the vegetable garden in the long May evenings, and William turned up the ground and cursed, and brought stones to the surface by the million. Catherine fetched tools and seeds and stood over him and read directions out of a gardening book whilst William put the seeds in. Both of them were as pleased as God on the seventh day of creation when rows of carrots and turnips, beans, and peas actually came up and flourished.

William planned a sunken garden, and an orchard, and an alpine garden. He and Catherine talked about them a great deal that summer and made lists of plants in different colours . . . an all-blue garden, or blue and cream, or pink and mauve. But in the end the lists were thrown away and the garden went down to cabbages and potatoes, because both of them were always busy, and because there was no money with which to hire labour.

And Audrey ran and tumbled on the new green grass of the lawn, whilst Lowe put down her sewing and made daisy chains.

The red-faced, sharp-eyed baby had gone. There had developed a little creature like an animated doll, with a quantity of curly, very soft hair, a milk and roses complexion, a small red, determined mouth, and quizzical blue eyes. Audrey's eyes missed nothing. She looked on with a bright contempt at Catherine's attempts to control her.

'She'll give you somewhat when she's older,' said Lowe admiringly, as she dumped the recalcitrant Audrey (her mouth screwed up to a button) into her pushchair, and strapped her firmly in. 'She's a madam. That's what she is.'

'Little beast!' said William, and watched Audrey, nose in air, being pushed away by the indifferent Lowe.

Catherine understood William. Audrey wasn't demonstrative. She never clung. Her hard little hands pushed against the chest of anyone who picked her up, she turned her cheek to those who wanted to kiss her.

'Perhaps it's a good thing,' Catherine said. 'She can't really love us yet. She doesn't even know us.'

She didn't want Audrey to love her if Audrey wasn't ready to love. She wasn't bound to, just because she and William had begotten her. Love had to grow, like everything else. She would have to obey, and at once, without argument, life was so sudden and dangerous for the very young. But love? She loved Audrey, that was enough for the present.

She went back, through the house, into the garden with William.

'But don't you think she's a little beast?' William insisted.

Catherine kissed him.

The white stars of the clematis hung thick all over the back of the house.

'They look all right,' said Catherine. 'But they die at once if you put them in water.'

'Filth,' said William. 'It's clawing down all the guttering. It wants cutting back . . . hard. Come and look at those pear trees. Every one of them will have to come out. They're past praying for. I think we can get three new ones in on that wall.'

They went out and looked at the doomed pear trees. They planned to plant two pink may trees, a prunus, and an acacia along by the north wall. Some day they would build a summer-house in the corner, a summer-house big enough to sleep in on hot summer nights.

Through it all Catherine thought of Audrey, sitting bolt upright in her pram with her nose in the air. Her heart laughed that she should have had such a self-contained daughter, when she herself had been far too ready to give love to those who didn't need it, and simply asked her to take it away again. It was so much better to be a self-contained snail than a defenceless and unhappy slug.

'We'll get the summer-house thatched,' said William. 'I can get it done on the contra account.'

'What's that?'

'There are always one or two patients who had rather pay us in kind . . . in goods of some sort, or in labour. It doesn't work very well, but it's been the custom here for years, and so we let them keep on with it. There's a small bill outstanding against one of the thatchers now. He can take it out on the summer-house.'

They stood side by side on the neglected grass, looking at the angle of the old brick wall where the summer-house was to be. From under their feet the daisies ran out in constellations . . . a heaven of shining silver flowers. The crocuses blazed furiously along the wall. Bees hung over them. Warmth filled the garden. Catherine came a little closer to William, she was happier in the garden, it didn't look as hopeless as the house. She didn't touch William because she knew by now when he wanted to be touched and when he didn't. When he didn't want to be touched he was liable to go off like a large size in popping balsams, scattering imprecations, and making the air vibrate with his disproportionate irritation.

So Catherine simply stood, letting her happiness soak into her. She was glad because her house was clean and airy, and was beginning to show that one day it would look charming. It had a scrambling, spacious homeliness. They hadn't half the things that they ought to have, their china was makeshift, and their table appointments a joke, but their new curtains had brought colour into the rooms, and their old furniture was beginning to show a dark gloss. The house smelt of flowers and beeswax, with a faint undertone of damp earth and a whiff of drugs from the surgery . . . the smell which Adam, years later, was to register and remember as the home smell.

At moments like this, the dark cloud of the War, the continual thought that somewhere out of sight hundreds and hundreds of people were killing each other for other people's ideals, would lift from Catherine's mind. Something serene and peaceful, a light from over the edge of the world, shone into it, lighting up every corner, and driving out her worries as a sudden current of air drives out dust. She felt that if only she could hold that mood a little longer she would never again be angry, or impatient, or depressed.

It was as well that she couldn't see into William's mind. He was wondering, doggedly, how they were going to manage, though he didn't mean to fail. William was not one of those who sit down when the road begins to go uphill. But they were going . . . confound it! . . . to have a child they couldn't afford. They were bitterly poor already, and he would have to work like a demon if they were going to keep out of debt. So would Catherine. He was sure of himself, but he wondered how she would stand the racket. She ran at things, and then stood still, aggrieved, because there were difficulties. The one child . . . self-sufficient little beast! . . . would have been enough. He loved Catherine, but he was damned if he could love Audrey.

So they stood, side by side on the violently green grass in the midst of that unusual spring, each thinking their own thoughts. Catherine, who saw rather more of everything than could possibly be there, and William, who, on the whole, saw rather less than actually existed.

CHAPTER TWO

I

The strange spring ran out into a cold and disappointing summer.

'It's queer about those seeds,' William said. 'They went in about two months late and look at them! Those broad beans are nearly ready to pick.'

'Don't forget that they were going to be blighted because we put them in on a Sunday.'

Catherine sat on a stool in the vegetable garden, with one of William's socks over her hand, her needle poised, her eyes wrinkled against the glare of a grey and threatening day. In the corner of the garden which they had contrived to scratch up, rows of carrots, and turnips, and beans were thick in their differing shades of green. William paced up and down the path, measuring distances.

'We'll be thinking of putting those trees in in a couple of months,' he said. 'They won't bear for a year or two, but when they do . . . ! You won't know where to put the fruit.'

'Hadn't we better buy some blackcurrants for jam this year?' asked Catherine. 'I've saved up some sugar.'

William didn't answer. That was like Catherine. She wouldn't look ahead. She always wanted things now. She wanted everything on the spot, at once, and before you had time to turn round.

William liked to talk for months about anything he was going to have or do. He liked to draw maps and diagrams and consider it from every angle. At last, if it was a piece of work, he would begin on it, do two days' work and then drop it for a week or two, prowling round it with a pipe in his mouth now and then, when he had an odd moment to spare. Eventually, when he was tired of it, and wanted to begin on something else, he would work furiously at it, cursing bitterly, and turn his back on it as soon as the last nail or the last brick were in position.

'The blackcurrants are in now,' Catherine suggested. 'They won't get any cheaper.'

She wished she needn't remind him. But they were plentiful and he would be sure to want blackcurrant jam in the winter. He always did. In another moment she would find herself asking for the money to pay for them. However hard she tried, any conversation always worked round to that point, and . . . 'How much can you do with?' and 'What do you want it for?' William would ask. Catherine hated those two questions, and the worried, harried look that went with them. She bit her lip and went on with her darning.

'All right,' William agreed suddenly. 'We've got to have them, of course. I'll get them on the round. They'll be cheaper.'

'Then you'd better put it on your visiting list.'

William prowled up and down the cinder track.

'When we've finished putting in the fruit trees we must get something to make a shun.'

'What's a shun?'

'Something to keep the place private. We don't want everybody peering into the garden.'

'But they're only bedroom windows,' Catherine objected.

William laughed. He knew the devouring curiosity of village people, to whom the affairs of their neighbours were more interesting than scandal about celebrities, newspapers, or even rumours about other villages. Their own folk were 'hot news' all the time, and every house was a glass one.

'But do they really want to know about us?' Catherine was incredulous. 'I don't care what happens to them. I hate gossip.'

William nodded approval. It was right that a doctor's wife should avoid gossip. A still tongue and a long memory were essentials for a woman in her position. But at the back of his mind he was uneasy. Surely she ought to care a little more about her neighbours' affairs, even if she didn't talk about them? Such detachment was uncanny. Sometimes he thought that she felt the same about him. She only cared for him where his life touched hers . . . she wasn't interested in his practice or in his garden. He didn't think very clearly about this, but it worried him, and it wasn't only professional caution which kept him from talking to Catherine about his cases. He was beginning to find out that Catherine was too deeply engrossed in her present problems to be able to help him with his.

'That's all right. Much better keep out of it,' he said easily, and began to sing:

> Love must in short,
>> Prove kind and true,
> Through good report,
>> And evil too.

William's courage and humour were coming back with the summer. He had a garden to work in, an unmade virgin garden, all his own, and a house so large and rambling that he could tinker for evermore at its alteration and repair.

'Tom ought to be here soon.'

'Who's Tom?'

'He's a character. There isn't a thing he doesn't know about fruit trees. You ought to see him take the roots in his hand and spread them out when he's planting them. He takes all the little fibrous roots and spreads them out in a fan. He doesn't dump them all in in a tangle and leave them to sort themselves. He takes his time over it, mind you. Oh! He takes his time. But if Old Tom plants a tree it *grows*.'

William stuffed his pipe and lit it. He began to turn over the pile of loose stone beside Catherine, out of which he proposed, some time that autumn, to build a dry wall.

'But you aren't going to plant those trees for quite a long time,' Catherine objected.

'No. But I want Old Tom to look over the ground. He knows more about it than I do. He'll know exactly where the trees'll do best. You mustn't mind if you find him strolling about in here. He'll take his time, looking over the ground.

A tree's like a house. It's got to stay a long time, once you've planted it. You've got to be sure of the soil, and the sun, and the wind.'

'They didn't think of the sun when they built this house,' Catherine said. 'Half the windows face north. And old Mowsett says that it's built slap down on the clay without any kind of foundation. I wonder that it's stood up for three hundred years.'

'It probably wouldn't if the walls weren't so blooming thick.' William tugged out a lump of ironstone, streaked with rusty ore and speckled with white fossils. It rolled down on to the path with a thump.

'This stuff wants grading,' he went on. 'A whole lot of this is too big for a dry wall. And look! Here's the top of a lancet window! That must have come out of the castle ruins.'

Catherine touched it. Everything was so old here. The very stones in the house had been used over and over again since they were first worked. The stones themselves were studded with the fossils of dead creatures. And here she was, bearing yet another living creature in the long succession. Life seemed to have no end and no purpose. Trees and houses were more lasting than men and women.

'The carving is quite sharp still,' she said.

'It's never been weathered. The castle must have been burnt down about fifty years after that window was put in. Since then everyone who's used that bit of stone has turned the worked surface inwards, so that they could use the flat.'

William went on sorting.

'I wonder what you'll think of Old Tom. He used to

work for a hunting parson, over in the Bicester country . . .
something between stable lad and gardener's boy. The old
fellow where he worked used to breed terriers . . . sporting
terriers. He trained them on cats. Tom used to turn a cat out
of a bag in the stable yard. If the pup didn't nail the cat before
it got to the wall – goodbye to the pup. The old man hadn't
any more use for it.'

Catherine darned steadily. Her sympathies were with the
cat.

'Tom used to go round the villages at night with a sack. He
got on famously at first, but presently there was a general
rumour that cats were disappearing. Someone kept a watch
and Tom was caught, complete with cat, and brought up
before the magistrates. They fined him half a crown. "Thank
you kindly, sir," says Tom. "It bean't a farthing apiece for the
cats I've had."'

William chuckled softly to himself. 'It bean't a farthing
apiece for the cats I've had,' he repeated. He failed to see that
Catherine wasn't amused.

The gate at the bottom of the garden opened, and an old
man in white corduroys and a dusty 'rat-catcher' cap came up
over the broken soil. He didn't look at Catherine and William;
they didn't, apparently, interest him. He stopped, and looked
up and down the garden with a shrewd curiosity. Then he
moved slowly on over the broken earth. Once he stopped and
kicked a clod, scattering it. He bent stiffly and picked up a
lump about the size of a nut, and brought it over in his open
hand. He greeted them with a finger on the peak of his cap,
and a jerk back of his head.

'Look at that now!' he began. 'That's a nasty streak of clay, that be. That bean't no good to nobody, that bean't.'

William took a grey, slimy lump out of Tom's hand.

'Clay it is, by gum!' He looked as serious as Tom.

Catherine looked at the old man's dry, lined face. It was creased by the weather into a network of deep wrinkles, every one of which went to express the old man's character, his shrewdness, and deep knowledge. One of his eyes was a cold grey, the other lid was drawn over an empty socket. An apple tree, he told Catherine, later on, had put it out when he was a boy. The solitary eye seemed to spin and twinkle as he looked at her.

Old Tom liked William. He'd seen him grow up. He was glad that he'd the sense to have his garden set out properly. It was a pity he'd married a woman picked up no one knew where, and whose family none of them knew anything about. Now she'd have it all to learn from the beginning. Not that he thought much to these young women nowadays, any of them. Thinking themselves ill-used by the War. They ought to have kept house in the 'forties. That would have taught them somewhat. He and his brothers had been glad of a bit of sour bread in their bellies . . . many a time he'd been glad to pinch a turnip when he was out scaring crows. And now these young women set up a squeal if they hadn't white sugar for their tea. Called it a shortage! He could have told them.

'But will the clay make any difference?' Catherine asked at last.

'Ah!' Old Tom turned creakily and looked at her. 'Us can't do nothing with clay. That bean't no good of, that bean't.'

'Then we can't plant anything that end of the garden?'

'Not in that clay you can't.'

'You can't expect anything to grow in clay,' William broke in.

'Then is that piece all to go to waste?'

They both looked at her as if she was utterly devoid of sense.

'Waste a good bit of ground! Not likely,' said William.

'But if nothing will grow in it . . .'

'Us'll have to dig it out,' Old Tom explained.

'It's just a narrow streak,' William elaborated. 'You get it about here, like that.'

Then they weren't worrying about the clay. Only about the extra work involved in getting it out. Of course . . . Tom and William both knew far more about the job than they were able to tell her.

She watched them move away together up the garden. To her it was just so much ground. The old man saw more in it than he, or any written book, could express. Some of it was instinct, some of it was slowly gained experience. She began to understand William's hesitations and delays when he was starting a job. When you were dealing with 'things' you felt your way, watched your weather or your soil, tested your material. A long-standing result needed a lengthy preparation.

She remembered that afternoon later, when, in the autumn, Old Tom planted the trees. They went in slowly, a few at a time, their roots spread out in a circle as their boughs spread in a circle to catch the sun, the earth rammed and stamped hard about them.

'And don't you let none on'm go digging and poking round about my trees,' he said fiercely to Catherine. 'That don't do a tree no good, that don't. You can see how far the roots goes for yourself.'

The naked, silvery boughs of the trees filled all that end of the garden with a network of faint pattern. They looked dead, insubstantial. But next spring the buds turned woolly, and presently that end of the garden was a mass of flower.

All that next summer Old Tom visited his trees. He would come in and out, dragging pails of water to those which were flagging, and picking off the too abundant green fruit.

'A little apple he takes just so much out of a tree as a big one do,' he told Catherine. 'You take 'em off of 'em. They bean't no good to the tree, they bean't.'

II

It was a new thing to Catherine, this craftsman's love of his material and of the craft at which he worked. She liked to see Dowell, silent and melancholy, fingering one of the 'cripple' chairs which she and William had picked up. His fingers would run over it, feeling the wood; he would walk away from it and look at it, still silent. Then abruptly:

'All right, sir. I daresay I can make a job of it. You leave it to me.'

And silent, melancholy, he would walk slowly away with the chair. Many weeks later – for he could not be hurried – he would return with it, cunningly mended and smelling heartily of linseed oil.

He showed Catherine how to take a little polish on a piece of flannel and sit and rub, with a circular movement, hour after hour, till the starved wood took up the beeswax and turpentine, till the glow came back and the pattern of the grain showed up as its maker had intended it to do. Time meant no more to Dowell than it did to Old Tom. He hung suspended, in the fourth dimension, when he was at work. If Tom had the mind of a tree, there were moments when Catherine was sure that Dowell was thinking like a two hundred year-old chair.

Rarely he would talk, and once started would flow on in a monotonous stream, standing still with an oily rag in his hand. He never spoke of people. He told Catherine where every piece of furniture had stood in their house in the old days – which was really old and had a story attached to it, which had been made in the local workshops, and which had been 'made-up' pieces. Dowell's scorn for the 'made-up' piece was beyond bounds. He would go over a suspect piece of furniture, tapping it with his pencil and pointing out pieces of wood which were new, or of different workmanship, his moustache curving lower and lower with disapproval.

He lived alone, doing everything for himself. He had one other passion. Bell-ringing. Perhaps their loud voices were a relief to one naturally so silent.

CHAPTER THREE

I

Catherine saw very little of the village which lay all about her. She was busy, she was worried, she was too self-centred to be much interested in anyone who didn't directly concern her. Her passionate interest in her husband and children blinded her to everything else.

The village was absorbed too. It was exasperated and browbeaten by the War. The best of the men had gone, and the pick of the girls were in munitions. The remainder had to 'worry through' two people's work. There was more money to be had, but there was less comfort. The strained, overtired stale feeling of the War made itself felt, even here. The village worked on doggedly, looking askance at the queer strangers who settled amongst them.

A Belgian family had come first. They were dumped into an empty cottage and immediately began to thrive on wages which the average labourer looked at with disdain. They were hard-working, thrifty, acquisitive. They kept themselves to themselves.

Catherine would see the dark, broad-shouldered girls going stockily off to work in the fields, their eyes on the road, their black hair straggling across their expressionless faces. Sometimes she wondered if she ought to try to speak to them in French, but she reflected that they probably used an unintelligible patois. They didn't look as if they wished to be spoken to. They went their way so steadily and quietly.

The Portuguese who were working on the new aerodrome and who were billeted here and there all over the countryside, attracted far more attention. They gave the streets a touch of brightness and colour when they came home at night. They sat on doorsteps and twanged on stringed instruments. They danced shuffling dances and sang interminable high-pitched songs. Sometimes they fought, rolling over and over in the dust, whilst their friends screamed encouragement. On wet days they went to bed, tied red handkerchiefs over their heads and sent over to William for certificates that they were too ill to work.

The villagers stared at them with amazement. They looked on them as scarcely human.

Later still a farmer applied for a batch of German prisoners for land-work. The children of the village went down to meet the train with beanpoles and rotten turnips, and were bitterly disappointed that no demonstration was allowed and that the prisoners never afterwards appeared in the village. As an excitement they were a failure. They lived in the farm outbuildings and worked steadily, if without enthusiasm, in the fields.

Catherine went her own way. She too was a stranger, and had not yet learned to understand and like the countryside in which she had come to live.

II

Adam the unfortunate was born on the only really hot day that summer. The long, thin, pale baby took the most languid interest in life. From the first Catherine felt herself to be unjust to Adam. He was at once so demanding and so inert. He needed, Catherine felt, all one person's time and patience. Catherine had very little time, and less patience.

For Lowe had left to go into munitions, and Catherine replaced her with an untrained country girl, not old enough to do more than clean the floors and push the perambulator. The days were too short for all that there was to do. Life was crowded, uncomfortable, and unsatisfactory, everyone was worried, underfed, and under strain.

In the towns conditions were much worse, and Violet's letters began to show a thread of irritability.

There was no butter. She had had to stand in a queue in the rain to get meat, and then the quantity was small, and the quality poor. Sebastian was growing very fast and it was difficult to get enough food for him. Edward was away, doing office work on Salisbury Plain, having been declared unfit for active service. There was a difficulty in getting maids.

Above all Sebastian and Jane were, in some undefined way, unsatisfactory. Again and again she complained of them that Sebastian was secretive and Jane headstrong.

Catherine remembered Sebastian as an absorbed, shock-headed youth, always tinkering with some home-made gadget or fiddling with his motor-bicycle. Secretive? She supposed that his interests never had been Violet's interests, and never would be. And Jane was eighteen . . . an awkward age . . . an unhappy age.

Perhaps it was all part of the general worry. No one seemed to be getting on particularly well with anyone else, at the moment. It was in the air.

They were all so tired. She had been enthusiastic about Audrey, but she looked at Adam with dismay. He was so different and so difficult. He ate away so many hours out of an overfilled day. She tried to keep Adam, his needs, and his perpetual crying, away from William.

CHAPTER FOUR

I

The winter of 1917 shut down heavily and inauspiciously on Catherine and William.

William spent his days toiling round twenty-seven villages and putting up endless bottles of medicine when he came home at night. He was often wet, nearly always cold, and incessantly hungry.

That winter there was very little fat or sugar and very little meat. Catherine did her best to fill the want with cocoa and suet puddings, lentil soup, and vegetable curries. There was always food of a sort, but it wasn't very satisfying. Their old-fashioned range and their half-trained maid between them turned out some amazingly bad meals. Catherine and William ate them because there was nothing else.

William never grumbled. Heavy or tough, burnt or curdled, he ate the food uncomplainingly. Catherine could have cried. He needed the best she could do for him, and her best was often very bad indeed.

Prices rose, but their income stayed still. They were caught, like so many others, in the trap of a budget which could not be calculated in advance. Catherine had to admit that she was beaten.

'How can I keep the books down?' she pleaded. 'There are some things we simply must have, and I never know what they are going to charge for them from one week to the next.'

Slowly, fighting every inch of the way, they were driven into debt.

William worried and worked harder, Catherine worried and ate less. Neither of them were ever anything but tired, and their tempers were ragged and uncertain. William would break out into bursts of irritability over the merest trifles, and Catherine would go to bed at night and weep helplessly with nervous exhaustion.

The terrific business of keeping her house warm and clean and her household fed and clothed took up all the foreground of her mind. There was no time to love Audrey and Adam. By the time she had provided for their bodily needs she had little energy left for their affections. She didn't want to love anybody or to be loved. She wanted to sit down, and not even to think.

Audrey came to meals with Catherine and William. Their meals were punctuated with:

'Oh, Audrey! Not so much. Audrey! Put half that down. Audrey! You must not drink with your mouth full.'

Audrey stared. She wasn't noisy, she knew better than to protest, but she went on cramming her mouth. William endured her with difficulty.

Catherine thought: 'How badly I manage! I ought to feed her first. But then there's Adam . . . he won't feed unless I hold him, and he takes such an age. . . .'

Spilt milk, scattered crumbs, continual reproofs, these things marred their meals and made them unrestful.

When she was alone with William, Catherine was comparatively happy, or when she was alone with Audrey and Adam.

Catherine had always supposed that a family was a united whole from the beginning. Life wasn't as easy as that. A family of adults and young persons was a loose collection of human beings, each living in a different world and travelling in different directions. Catherine wore herself out trying to travel with all of them.

Slowly the cold of the first winter crept into the heart of the house. Painted walls ran with condensation moisture. Wallpapers bulged and smelt of sour paste. Stone floors went patchy with damp. The little oil lamps made ineffectual spots of light in the gross darkness of stairs and passages. Doors whistled and rattled, the auricaria rattled its tin leaves in the garden. The house, in spite of all the people in it, felt unused and empty.

Catherine and William looked forward all day to the evenings. They piled up the peat fire and sat close to it, reading again books that they knew by heart. Then, with the curtains drawn and the lamp lit, they could forget the soddened country outside and the long and difficult day that was coming tomorrow.

They felt then that life wasn't altogether hostile. They took stock of the position and were thankful that Audrey and Adam throve in spite of the discomfort. The long, thin baby grew red-faced and began to rummage round and round his cot. He was tired of being there, and didn't know what else he wanted.

Their fruit trees were planted, their dry wall was built, earthed mounds of potatoes and roots stood about all over the garden.

II

Catherine taught Audrey to say her prayers.

'Why don't you leave her alone?' William protested. 'She can't understand anything yet. She's nothing but a little animal.'

Catherine didn't argue the point. She still thought that Audrey was no more and no less of an animal than she ever would be. Catherine had no great opinion of organised worship, either public or private. Her consciousness of God, like William's, was a continual blessing, like sunlight or fresh air. She would have been stifled and frozen without it. But she wasn't sure whether Audrey would arrive at that conclusion by herself, or whether by some means or other she wouldn't have to be brought to it. And there were other considerations.

'If I don't teach her,' she explained, 'someone else will. You know what people are. They won't leave other people's minds alone. I've found Ellen teaching her about hell and the devil already. She was shocked because I hadn't told her. To her it's one of the things you automatically teach a child . . . like washing behind its ears or cleaning its teeth.'

'Tell Ellen to stop it and leave it at that.'

'I have told her. But don't you see, Ellen isn't the only one. We can't stand over her all our lives, screaming, like a couple of robins over their own patch of territory. She'll have to leave us some day.'

'Then teach her "four angels" and leave it at that. That can't hurt her.'

So Audrey learnt . . .

> Four angels round my bed,
>   Four angels round my head,
> Matthew, Mark, Luke and John,
>   Bless the bed that I lie on.

Only, because she spoke the folk tongue of her own county, she said:

'Fower aingels round moi bed . . .'

With the rise of the voice towards the end of the sentence and the slur on the last word which gives the Oxfordshire dialect its peculiar cadence.

Four angels. It was an exciting thought. Four angels, all as tall as bedposts, and all devoted to Audrey.

William left Audrey's spiritual education at that. He had said what he thought. The children were Catherine's business, and, after all, Audrey had a fairly tough mind.

So Catherine had her own way and taught Audrey all those rolling phrases out of the Bible which had delighted her own childhood. She learnt . . . 'Ye mountains of Gilboa, let there be no dew upon you, neither fields of offerings,' and 'Remember now thy Creator in the days of thy youth,' and 'I will lift up mine eyes unto the hills.'

Audrey learnt obediently, like an interested parrot. She had a wonderful memory, she could record anything, down to the very trick of the voice in which it had been spoken to her. But it was Adam the unfortunate who, years later, was to astound Catherine by bursting out, in the middle of a dull, necessary walk, with:

'Ye daughters of Judah, weep over Saul, who put ornaments of gold upon you, with gorgeous apparel.'

He gave her the whole passage with great fervour and feeling and then shut up, like one bitterly ashamed of himself.

But Audrey was a natural metaphysician. She loved, as she grew older, the facts which Catherine had taught her, simply for the sake of argument, deduction, and speculation. Also, the people in the Bible were human exceedingly, beyond anything in the world of history or literature. That they did, they did nakedly and without shame. They were greedy, they were ambitious, they lost their tempers and were rude to each other and the Almighty. Heroes did mean things, gross things, betrayed their friends and their women and yet came again and did gloriously. They were irascible, covetous and fanatically cruel. Yet behind it all Audrey could trace the trickle of a steady purpose . . . the conviction that life was not enough. They were even comic, some of them, but always the conviction was there.

III

As the spring came back Catherine longed for the West Country. She missed the soft air, the crying of the gulls, and the steep banks spattered with primroses. Whenever she climbed a hill she looked over the distance for the gleam of the sea and felt empty because it wasn't there. In this tame, open, and pedestrian country there were few birds and fewer flowers. All was cultivated, orderly, rational. There were no ragged coppices or banks of furze. The slow streams flowed inaudibly under the lopped and tidy willows.

Later, much later, when Catherine went fishing with Adam, she learnt to love the quiet beauty of the still, olive water banded with silver, the small leaning leaves of the willows, and the yellow Cherwell buttercups floating amongst the tangles of arrowhead. Later, she found a place, far from roads, amongst the fields, where Audrey, with one of her rare elfin flashes of her under-self, exclaimed:

'It's enchanted! I love this hollow place. It's enchanted.'

Audrey's under-self was Catherine's consolation. Suddenly, astoundingly, the greedy, self-contained child would flash out with one completely rounded sentence of another speech.

'Oh, look!' she cried, as the first warm day opened on them after that dark winter. 'Oh, look! Sun-marks on the happy grass!'

She ran in and out of the streaked shadows, throwing up her little woollen cap and catching it again, the ends of hair bobbing against her absurd, round face.

And a week later. 'Come! Do come! Fleets of daisies.'

Or later still, as she and Catherine threaded their way along a path through a field of green oats, coming into ear:

'What a silver sound!'

Catherine caught these stray sentences which shot up, bird-like, out of the depths of Audrey's mind, like larks out of a cornfield. She never dared encourage them, lest they should vanish altogether. She held her breath and waited, breathless, for the next.

IV

If angels, why not fairies?

No one had ever suggested to Catherine and William that it was immoral to teach children about fairies. Both of them kept, at the back of their minds, a half-belief in the pretty legend. Catherine cherished, untold, the certainty that she had once seen a pixie, at dusk, just beyond Cadover bridge, on a snowy day. A little fat man about as big as a rabbit and much the same colour. It wasn't a rabbit. No one ever saw a rabbit without a white scut. He had dashed into a gorse bush, and when Catherine had peered and felt under it there had been nothing there, not even a rabbit hole. She never told William about that experience, she was certainly not going to tell Audrey and Adam.

Audrey and Adam hardly needed to be told about fairies, for four or five years the house and garden was full of the unseen stirring of the little people.

Audrey the indifferent loved them as she had never loved Catherine or William, with a love warm and maternal. Particular trees in the neighbourhood got themselves named for them. She used to leave berries, flowers, and acorn cups under them. She and Adam had their own tales of the fairies which they never told anyone but each other. A sun spark on the wall, the twisting shadow of a leaf, the rustle of a bird in a hedge . . . she and Adam saw a fairy and ran.

They had no playmates. Distances were long, there was no spare petrol. It was impossible to drive small children four, five, or seven miles out in a pony trap, and back again in the raw winter nights. They were an isolated family, for the countryside had been emptied out by the War, and those who were left were working hard. Their social world began and ended with themselves.

June came in with fields of white clover, and Catherine spent long mornings in the open, reading to Audrey whilst Adam slept and the sunny countryside slept too, mile after undistinguished mile, all about them. Swifts swung overhead, blue church spires pricked the distance, the scent of clover was solid on the windless air.

It was Catherine's first summer in the forgotten world of little things. Clover blossoms sucked for honey, four-leaved clovers found for luck, fortunes told on the long, tinker-tailor grasses, bracelets made of red and green rose thorns, she remembered, and used them all again. The gold dust of the buttercup pollen was on their skirts and shoes, the larks let down their song as though it was a thin chain which bound them to earth.

Then Catherine loved both of them with a whole heart. She went back with them into the child's knee-high world, a world so small, bright and momentary that trouble had no longer place in it than the passing shadow of a bird's wing. Sometimes she felt that she had been born again with them and that all her life had been lived only that she might understand what Audrey and Adam were feeling.

She would come back to the dark, cool-smelling house,

to the rattle of dishes and the smell of cooking. She would trail upstairs with the half-awakened Adam in her arms and feel that her mind, as well as her eyes, had been dazzled by the sun. She would sit down and attend to him, slowly awakened by some reminder of the many things she would have to do. Fruit to pick, weeds to hoe, a button to sew on William's coat when he came in at lunch. The grass edges needed clipping, there were muslin blinds back from the wash that needed tapes, and there was that place on the dining-room table where Audrey had upset the milk at breakfast.

Fruit first, whilst the table was being cleared. Then the mark on the table, before she forgot it again. Then the grass edges. The lawn looked like a Skye terrier. Then ... no, it would be tea-time by then, and Audrey would come down ... then there would be their baths. The blinds must be done after supper. The week's mending wasn't finished yet.

So Catherine sat and thought, slowly feeling her way towards method, which she hadn't got and sorely needed.

Life was less bitter in the summer. There were strawberries in the garden, roses on the old bushes which they hadn't troubled to replace. Little things mattered so much. It made so great a difference that they were not cold, that the sun was shining, and that William had time to work again in the garden.

His new apple trees were breaking in all the right places, his vegetable garden was nearly all planted. Next year he would put in an asparagus bed. He bought six mongrel hens and hoped that they might be able to have eggs at last. For eggs went to sixpence each in the winter and even at that price they were not easy to get.

In the summer evening, when the last can of water had been tipped over the parched borders, he and Catherine would take chairs out on to the lawn and watch the stars come out, one by one, above the band of unearthly green behind the church tower. As the stars came out, the swifts, flying higher and higher, vanished as though they had been picked out of the sky. The notes of the church clock would fall into the stillness like a stone into a pool, so that it seemed as though the air rippled with it.

The peace would lie on their minds like the cool air on their faces. They would forget the hundred and one things they ought to be doing or worrying about. They would remember each other, for during the day they were too busy, and at night they were too tired. They didn't talk . . . talk turned at once to their problems and their troubles. When they were not speaking they could think kindly of each other, glad to be together, much as two horses will stand together out of harness, under a tree.

CHAPTER FIVE

I

They went down, all of them, into the black winter of 1918. It was a winter which Catherine could never clearly remember, a blurred nightmare of fatigue and overwork.

Peace came at the beginning of a spell of bitter weather, when the country cowered, terrified, under the influenza epidemic.

'It's swine fever,' William's patients assured him. 'It comes from putting the pigs' vittles into the bread. It's swine fever. Don't they turn black when they die, same as the pigs?'

Nothing he could say would shake them out of that belief.

The village was very quiet the day the Armistice was declared. Catherine wrapped her children up and took them out. A few people stood at their doorways, talking in low voices, and with no joy in their faces. On the church tower half a dozen flags had been stuck, but the wind had knocked them crooked and wound the bunting round the poles, so that they looked like drunken umbrellas. Outside the Golden Lion a man with a copper shovel was tossing hot pennies to the children. His face glowed, he shouted with laughter as the children shrieked, dropped the pennies and sucked their fingers, and then scrambled for them again.

Farther on, down the main street, voices in the Horse and Groom were raised thinly in an old song about 'Tommy lad'.

The wind blew shrewdly, sending whirls of dust down the street. Adam sat up, solemn and wide-eyed. Audrey ran from tree to tree, touching each in turn, lifting her feet high and bringing them down with a smack. The sound echoed in the empty street.

Presently the children from the market square trailed past them with a couple of flags, small boys beating tin cans and tea trays, a girl or two dragging shamefacedly at the rear.

'Why! There's my Vi'let!' said a woman in a doorway. 'I won't half give her somewhat when she comes home. Making a fool of herself like that.'

At twelve o'clock, when the men came in from work, the bells in the church tower clashed all together – a jarring, jangled sound. Churches at a distance sent back an echo. Stridently above the listless villages, tower called to tower. Everything else was dead still. A few flakes of snow came down grudgingly, in the bitter cold.

II

The influenza epidemic went on. William worked twice as hard, visiting patients, scolding scared relations and neighbours into nursing them, keeping on the road from nine in the morning till nine at night and making up medicine and giving advice for two and three hours afterwards.

'It's a queer business,' he said. 'It takes the strong, middle-aged people. The old people and the children are hardly touched. I've never seen anything like it before.'

In the end he took it himself.

'I know where I got it,' he said wrathfully, furious with himself for being unable to hold out. 'Damned fools. There they were . . . the whole family . . . sitting round the kitchen fire in a fug you could cut with a knife. Wouldn't go to bed, preferred to sit there like stewed owls. Idiots.'

Catherine took his temperature. It was 104.

'You never ought to have gone out today!'

'Could I help it? Who's to do the work now, I don't know. Patterson's got his hands as full as I have.'

Catherine put him to bed and telephoned for help. The promised locum announced his arrival six weeks later when they had forgotten all about him, the nurse didn't come for a week.

'You'll catch it!' William fretted. 'Don't stay in the room.'

Catherine saw that there was nothing else to be done, then she went out and sat on the stairs, within call. She felt helpless. She knew very little about nursing, and was fairly certain that William would do nothing that she asked him to do. She was glad when the doctor from the neighbouring practice arrived, vetted William, left a bottle of influenza mixture, and took his visiting list. He departed to cope with patients by the household, scattered throughout twenty-seven villages.

Catherine came back to William. 'You'll catch it!' he said.

'I shan't. I've too much sense,' Catherine snapped.

She made up the fire, opened the window as he told her, and fetched him hot milk. Then she put her bed in the spare room and set the alarm-clock to wake her an hour after she got into bed.

For three days and nights she went on, mechanically filling William with alternate doses of hot milk and influenza mixture.

'I'm saturated with the damn stuff,' William complained, and refused to have anything more to do with it. He turned his shoulder on Catherine and went doggedly off to sleep. The doctor from the next practice, running over his chest the next morning, found a resolving pneumonia and congratulated William.

Catherine, heavy in the head, and gummy about the eyes, went off, shakily, to feed William's rabbits.

At the top of the stairs to the stable loft a noise of running and stamping made her stand still. The young bucks in the long hutch by the wall were running round and round in a great hurry and commotion. Catherine went closer and looked in.

One of the bucks was lying on its side in the corner, the others were running over it, striking back with their hind legs at its ribs as they passed. The buck lay huddled, not attempting to resist or run away.

Catherine fetched a shovel. She hadn't the courage to put her hand in amongst the stamping rabbits. There was something beastly and terrifying about the whole business. She shovelled the buck out and laid it on a pile of sawdust. Its head rolled over, it stretched out and its eyes glazed.

Eb, their jobbing gardener, came up and found her looking at it.

'They've stamped it to death!' Catherine said. 'They were all jumping on it.'

'Maybe there was somewhat the matter with it,' Eb said, picking the rabbit up. 'They'll do that if one of 'em's sickening. I'll open him up and see.'

Catherine sat down on the top of the stairs and cried uncontrollably. She hardly knew whether she was crying with relief because William was better, or merely because rabbits were so horrible.

She went down to find a friend from four miles off waiting to help her with William.

'But you've had a far worse time than I have,' she said. 'You've been nursing it for weeks. Aren't you worn out?'

'I had to come and look after William,' the friend said firmly. 'Where all the rest of us would have been without him I don't know. It's time you had a rest.'

She sent Catherine out for supplies. Catherine managed to get a tin of beef essence and, with great difficulty, a small supply of cream. She also contrived to get a bottle of champagne, the bill for which infuriated William so much that he refused to pay it for over three years. He liked to take it out and look at it, work himself up into a rage over it, and put it away again.

'He must be fed now,' the friend said. 'Look here . . .'

She wrote recipes and planned diet sheets.

'All right,' Catherine agreed wearily. 'But for heaven's sake show them to him yourself or he'll wear me out about the expense. He'll take it lying down, from you.'

Her friend sent her away, sat up all night with William and returned by day to deal with her own parish, to come back, still fresh, in the evening.

The doctor from the next practice took aspirin and carried on, visiting innumerable patients in twenty-seven villages.

Patients banged at William's own front door all day. He was indispensable, it appeared, to some of them.

'Ah! Dear now! Not up yet? Just run up and tell him I'm here, he'll see me for certain.'

Or:

'Still in bed? Ah now! We've never had anybody else but him or his father. Just run up and take him my name.'

'One gathers,' Catherine said irritably to William, 'that doctors are never really ill. One thing is perfectly plain. As soon as you can stand on your feet you go away – even if it's only for a week.'

'I can't possibly go,' William objected. 'Don't you see that I must get back to the round? The other chap can't hold up for ever.'

The nurse came at last and Catherine retired to bed with a streaming cold, a temperature, and a large towel – she and William between them having used up every handkerchief in the house. In twenty-four hours she was perfectly well, and a day or two later nurse – who agreed with Catherine – took William, protesting to the last, away to his people.

Catherine, by contrast, was happier than she had been for years. Adam and Audrey were well and there was time to remember that, at least, the War was over. Slowly, the relief of that knowledge seeped into her. She remembered how in

1914 the nights had been broken by the sound of feet passing, passing down the road under her window from the barracks to the docks. Feet, and voices singing (Tipperary) and the rumble of baggage waggons. Feet of men who would never come back. That sound had been in her memory, at the back of her mind, all these years. Now it had stopped, and the guns had stopped. It was all over.

She no longer believed that a new heaven and a new earth would come with the peace. It was too late. They were all too tired, too spoiled and broken.

> *Les lauriers sont coupés,*
> *Nous n'irons plus aux bois.*

There were no laurels for Catherine and her generation. Cut. All cut.

Something dark, bitter and fatiguing had been worked and kneaded and ground into the very stuff of their natures.

So Catherine only knew in a numb way that she was relieved. She lived on black coffee and bread and dripping and onion soup and sat over the fire in the evenings, discovering an unknown author, one Shakespeare, the Elizabethan dramatist, who had nothing to do with the Shakespeare of the schools. She found his world a lustier and a more cheerful one than her own.

At the end of the week William came back, very hollow under the eyes, and greyish yellow in colour. They found a man to drive the car and Catherine abandoned her children and went out with William, a brandy bottle in her pocket. William could just manage to walk from the car to the cottage doors and back again. Somehow he struggled round the countryside, stuck at it, and mended.

The winter dragged on. Prices soared up and up. Butter went to four shillings a pound, and sewing cotton to tenpence ha'penny the reel. Shoes were two or three pounds a pair. Nothing that anyone ate or wore or used was made of quite what it ought to have been.

The War was over, but the nightmare went on.

III

What did Audrey and Adam do in the nursery when they were left alone with Ellen? Catherine never knew. The toy cupboard was a mess of torn picture books, odd bricks, cups out of tea services, naked dolls with one leg missing, bits of material, ninepins, flattened tin toys and pulverised chalks.

Wet afternoon after wet afternoon she set them all to tidy it. But it never stayed tidy, and none of the toys were ever put to their proper uses.

'They've far too many toys,' William declared.

'But they don't play with any of them,' Catherine objected. 'I could understand it if they preferred one and left the others alone. I wouldn't mind their breaking them if they did something constructive with them first. But they simply haul them all out into a heap on the floor and walk on them.'

'They've too many toys,' William repeated.

Audrey preferred following Catherine round the house to playing in the nursery. It never occurred to Catherine that

Audrey did this for anything else but company until she found her lying flat on her stomach one morning, peering under the grandfather clock.

'Gwendoline never dusts under there,' she said, in a hard, accusing, mistress-of-the-house voice that Catherine would have given worlds to be able to put on.

It didn't occur to Catherine to give her a duster and let her make the clock her special care, nor did she encourage her to come into the kitchen. Perhaps she felt that Gwendoline, who was an undoubted learner in the art of cooking, had nothing to teach her. She did, however, try to teach her to sew. She bought her a whole series of aimless little cards with pinholes ready marked for outlining in coloured cottons such pleasing natural objects as pigs, eggs in egg cups, and kittens playing with woollen balls.

Audrey sewed badly, and with distaste. The cards were no use, when you had done them. They were not even pleasing to the eye. So she hung about the fringes of the grown-up world, picking up what she could and storing it at the back of her retentive mind.

She knew what Catherine was likely to order for dinner on any given day, she knew where the jam was kept and how to tie it down. She knew that bread was kept in an earthenware pan, smelling rather like a flower-pot, in the larder, cake in a tin in the cupboard. She knew that salt and eggs both made silver go a queer colour, that pastry was made with your hands and cake with a wooden spoon. She liked the hot smell of the oven, part grease, part warm metal, when the door was opened to put the pastry in. She loved the smell of rising bread, and of bread hot out of the oven, the queer, ether smell of steaming potatoes and the flat, washday smell of boiled pudding.

When she and Adam were alone in the nursery they made what use they could of the toys they both despised. They turned bricks into trains and shunted them from one side of the floor to the other. They scribbled in corners and on the linoleum with coloured chalk, and built books up into piles for the pleasure of knocking them down with a crash. They pulled pieces of paper off the walls and chewed them into fascinating novel shapes . . . or simply flattened their noses against the wet window and stared at the market-place outside.

IV

Audrey was spanked.

Catherine and William lived in a world in which psychoanalysis had yet to become popular and which had not yet heard of 'complexes'. The spate of 'little books' on child management had hardly begun. Both of them tried to deal with their children by the only methods which they knew . . . William by the simple and fairly just code in which he had been brought up, Catherine by trying to think back into her own childhood, its fears, its pleasures, its wrongs and disillusionments.

She couldn't remember that spanking had done her much harm. On the contrary, though she had early been brought into contact with the wooden side of a hairbrush, the punishment had always struck her as necessary, natural, and conclusive. It closed the score and didn't lay one open to public ridicule like the 'moral force' applied in her school-days.

Still, in the beginning, she left Audrey alone. Her daughter having a different nature, might see things in a different light.

One day she had her up to her bedroom after the major crime of biting Adam, who had taken a favourite mantelpiece ornament (two white kittens coming out of a blue boot) and broken it.

'Animals bite,' Catherine explained patiently. 'You're a little girl. You mustn't bite Adam. He's smaller than you, and he didn't mean to break your kittens. Besides, he's your brother.'

Audrey stood listening, clear-eyed, serene, and pink-faced, the front of her overall sticking out from her tubby little body, her feet wide apart, her hands behind her.

'So you must simply bring things to me if Adam drops them,' Catherine went on. 'I'll mend them for you. It's not Adam's fault. Now, promise you won't bite him again.'

Audrey waited a moment to be quite sure that Catherine had finished, then she stepped back a little, her chin in the air.

'Wow wow wow,' she said, imitating Catherine's tone. 'Wow wow, wow, wow, wow.'

Catherine gasped, bit her lip on a laugh at the aptness of the imitation, then pulled her up over her knee and spanked her soundly.

'Now,' she said, setting her back on her feet. 'You hurt Adam, he's smaller than you . . . I hurt you, you're smaller than me. Have you got that?'

Audrey clenched her hands.

'Nasty mother, nasty mother, nasty old mother,' she scolded.

'Very well,' Catherine retorted. 'If I'm nasty when I hurt you you're nasty when you hurt Adam. Now you know how it feels. If it's nasty for me to hurt you, then it's nasty for you to hurt other people. And because it *is* nasty you'll be spanked every time you bite Adam or push him down – whatever he's done.'

Audrey's lips stuck out, quivering, but she didn't cry. Years later when, in the nick of time, she pulled Bill the aggressive's finger out of the lawnmower, and he bit her in his turn, she kept her temper, and waited whilst Catherine removed him, hacking stoutly at her shins, to justice.

Catherine hated administering corporal punishment. It was her share, for William was never on the spot, and they both felt it to be unfair that he should punish a crime which he had neither witnessed nor detected. She was aware that she often punished, in fatigue or irritation, offences which she had let slip before without comment. None the less, there seemed with Adam, who, as he grew older, would cheerfully forgo anything, from chocolate to a party, rather than give up the crime of the moment, with Adam for whom 'diversion' was simply an idle pretence, there seemed to be no other means of driving a point home.

For Adam, unlike Audrey, didn't go his own way. He insisted on going no way at all unless he was very firmly and constantly pushed. Progressively he would not feed, he would not walk, he would not talk. He remained as mute as a fish for nearly three years, then one morning he sat up in his cot, looked accusingly at Catherine and William and said:

'Time I got up now.' He was then mute for another fortnight and produced another perfect and grammatical sentence.

He would stand outside a door for half an hour, bawling lustily, rather than try to open it. He would walk all over the house, weeping, till he found someone to lace his boots for him, and when made to lace them himself he wept anew at the trouble of tying them. Catherine discovered Ellen and Audrey lacing up a boot apiece one morning and told them to stop.

'Leave them alone,' said Adam. 'They like it.'

The next morning he wept bitterly because he wasn't a Scot. The Scots, he explained, wear kilts, and kilts have no buttons.

He would not read, he would not write, he wept anew over any game which demanded a moment's concentration. Two things he would do. He would scribble on any blank surface that presented itself, and he could count and multiply with an ease which annoyed and disconcerted Audrey.

He was a handsome child, with a mass of curls and the expression of a serious angel. Kind-hearted strangers thought he was religious, but Catherine, who knew how adroitly he would thieve anything he wanted, how ingeniously he would portmanteau his prayers in the hope that nobody would notice that two-thirds of them had been left out, and how loudly he would bawl if he didn't get what he wanted at the moment he first thought of wanting it, was not at all impressed. She found it increasingly difficult to be just to Adam.

CHAPTER SIX

Catherine and William had one common liking which kept them together through the difficult days, and made their lives bearable. They were both fond of books.

Catherine read because she had to read or starve, William read for diversion. His practice, however much he reviled it, was his chief interest, and next to it in importance came his garden.

Catherine read every book in the house: Plutarch's *Lives*, John Stuart Mill *On Liberty*, *Grettis Saga*, *The Arabian Nights*, Jocelyn de Brakelond and George Crabbe, the books of William's boyhood, dog-eared and covered with ink, the agony column and the house advertisements in the newspapers, the Parish Magazine and the advertisements which came through the post. Anything would do . . . anything which gave her mind a change of air and fresh material to work on.

The same rage for reading was to take Audrey in the 'difficult' schoolroom days. Catherine had seen nothing wrong in it whilst she had it herself, in Audrey she realised its dangers. By that time she knew that life was better than books.

Sometimes that spring, as the days lengthened and William got stronger, they found time to go as far as Oxford.

They would start off with a list of things which had, somehow, to be bought. Boots for Audrey, wool to work up for Adam, breakages to replace, underclothes for William. They would wander from shop to shop, taking notes and comparing prices, for the value of money still changed from one week to the next. When they had succeeded in finding the thing they wanted for the price which they could afford to pay they would feel triumphant and hastily recalculate the money which was left, to see whether some necessary thing or other, not on the list, couldn't be bought after all. Sometimes it could, and William, who loved a bargain, would feel that the day had been well spent.

Afterwards they would walk from bookshop to bookshop, and they knew them all, considering the books which, one day, they were going to buy. The very look and smell of them was fascinating, their clean wrappers, the exciting reds, the sombre blues and rich browns. There was a bookshop smell, too – a smell of old settled dust, watered down in layers, printer's ink, and a taint of glue. They would stand close together, looking in through the window.

'We'll have that some day . . . and that . . .'

'We must get it in a really good edition,' William would add. 'I like a book that opens decently and has good clear print. I never feel the same about a book I've read in a cheap edition.'

'I'd sooner have a cheap edition than no edition at all,' Catherine would argue.

They would drift on, turn over second-hand books and reduced library editions, stare into print-shops.

There was a dark Japanese shop in Ship Street where

William bought a print of a crow upon a branch of cherry blossom against a sky of faint green. It cost eighteenpence, smelt of grapefruit, and gave them both pleasure for many years. They were fond of that shop. Nobody minded if you looked at things you couldn't afford to buy. There Catherine bought a fat plaster dog with gilt ears on either side of a round head and a Union Jack plastered across its rump. She kept the absurdity in a drawer, and years later it was the first love of Bill the aggressive.

At the end of the afternoon they would have coffee and scones at a window in a tea shop in the Broad where you could still see hansoms plying up and down in the spring dusk. Then the lights would come out, the wonderful orange lights of a town, as exciting to country people as the first spring day in the woods to those who live in a town.

Sitting opposite to her in the train, William would look at Catherine, whom he loved.

She was woefully shabby. Her hair was tucked up, anyhow, under the dreadful velvet hats she made for herself. Her cheap tweed skirts sagged, her shoes looked old and hid the shape of her feet. William knew that Catherine had nice feet, he hated to see her in those shoes.

Catherine was naturally indifferent to what she wore, and she was a careless worker. She would remember a neglected duty, and dash at it hotfoot. She got earth and soot, flour and candlegrease on to her clothes with a fine impartiality. She would work manfully to repair the damage, but her few clothes had a draggled, worried look. Her stockings wrinkled and she bought cheap gloves.

William hated to see Catherine careless of her hair and her hands. It hurt both his own proper pride and his love of her. She was a different person from the woman he had married. He missed her freshness, that freshness that he now only saw in her at night when, in her white nightdress, with her hair tied back with blue ribbons, she became once more the young girl whom he had left at the beginning of the War.

It irritated him that she kept the children better than herself. There was always time, there was always an odd shilling or two to spare for a frock for Audrey. Audrey loved clothes, clothes for their own sake. She would run to the glass, pirouette, run away looking over her shoulder, and come back.

'Oh, nice Audrey! Oh, dear little me!'

'Nice frock, not very nice Audrey,' Catherine would say firmly.

'Nice frock on nice Audrey,' her daughter retorted.

William would shrug his shoulders and turn his back on her. He hated Audrey to have what Catherine had not.

Looking at her, as they sat amongst their parcels in the train, the dark country passing like smoke outside the window, he would wish that he had more to give her. He worked so hard, and there seemed so little beyond the work's self, to show for it. They lived, and that was all.

That spring he bought her a length of pale pink material, utterly charming.

'You can't go about looking like that,' he said, whilst Catherine fingered it, and thought wistfully of Audrey. 'It's bad for the practice. It's bad for me, too. Go and have it made up decently.'

'I could make it up myself.'

'No . . . you . . . won't! For God's sake go and get it made decently.'

Catherine got it made. When she put it on she could see how her colour had faded and the light gone from her hair. But she liked to take it out of the cupboard and look at it; she began to brush her hair longer at night, and to manicure her fingernails again.

PART TWO

CHAPTER ONE

I

Catherine dated their return to normal life from the discovery of Irene, and for Irene she felt that she had to thank Eb.

Eb was William's Providence. He could do everything in the garden for which William had neither the time nor the inclination. Cabbages and potatoes flourished under his hurried and apparently casual treatment. He dug and stoned the poor soil, weeded it, built bonfires and burned them down for ash, traded potato peelings for soot with the sweep (who kept pigs), traded spare cabbage plants and seed potatoes for manure and 'road grit', made paths of stone brash and cinders. He was a good all-round worker, tied to no particular job. He liked William, and to put in odd days on William's garden gave him pleasure. William was a worker, he rose early, as he himself rose, he worked hard and late, gave his best and defrauded nobody.

When he wasn't gardening Eb would turn his hand to haymaking, harvest, or threshing in their seasons. He could splash a hedge, clear a ditch, make a hay rope, thatch a rick, do any of the hundred and one jobs that a handy labourer learns young. But his passion was onions. Year after year he sifted, rolled and sooted one corner of the garden, hoping that in the end he would raise a crop of Rousham Park that would be a crop of real onions and not a gap-toothed row of failures.

But for women Eb had a deep and bitter scorn. They were no good of. They were lazy . . . especially the girls. They didn't get up at five and work all day . . . not them. Women cumbered the earth. There were a few . . . like his own wife . . . who were worth their keep . . . but them girls!

A guerilla war raged between the kitchen and the vegetable garden and burnt up to its fiercest round the coalhouse and the wood pile.

The kitchen complained that Eb sent the sticks in damp on purpose, and that there was too much slack in the coal.

'Think I'm going to dry her sticks for her? Naow! She can take and dry them herself, overnight,' Eb retorted to William. 'Nor she ain't going to leave all the small coal to the last neither. And look at the great lumps she sends out in the cinders! She can burn what she's got. She won't get no more till tomorrow.'

Catherine sighed. The stove smoked and the cook gave notice. Not that she was a cook of any particular value. Catherine had had great trouble in finding maids. They thought her too particular. She was always worrying them to keep milk covered, scald out milk jugs, burn out dustbins, boil drinking water and scour sinks and slop pails. Things that nobody ever saw! What was the good of cleaning the like of that? She made an endless fuss about these things and cared nothing about the condition of her front hall, which anybody might see at any moment.

It was commonly full of children's mackintoshes, shopping baskets, clothes waiting to be brushed or to go to the cleaners, old umbrellas, cricket bats with the binding half off them, newspapers, seedy hats, and stray numbers of the *British Medical Journal*.

Catherine was violently untidy, and knew it, but she was also passionately clean. The maid who took advantage of her untidiness to be slovenly received in good, terse, Elizabethan English the full impact of Catherine's wrath. So they sulked and left her.

But, because she fed them well and let them do their work in their own way, there had always been some kind of a maid in the huge, inconvenient house with its dark cellars, stone-flagged kitchens, and endless passages.

William sent Catherine in search of Irene.

'I can't recommend her. I know nothing about her. She's only just left school. You might be able to do something with her. The mother's a good worker.'

'Is there anything against her?' Catherine was not yet used to William's habit of faint praise.

'Nothing – that I know of. Her father's Costard's shepherd. He's been there ever since I can remember. Uncanny, the way he has with sheep. Last spring Costard had a field of green clover penned out. They fed it off, and then the rain came. The clover came as thick as ever. Oh! a beautiful crop. "I've a good mind to put the sheep back on it," says Costard. "You do and you'll lose them," says the old man. "Have you ever seen it done before?" asks Costard. "No, not that I mind on. But you see. Put them back, and you'll lose them." Costard put them back. Sure enough they came down sick and he lost half the flock before he'd time to move them. Now, how did the old man know when Costard didn't?'

Catherine didn't know, and she wasn't interested. She was thinking that she must do something at once about the new maid.

'Where's the cottage?' she asked.

'Up the jitty. Third house to the left. She's expecting you.'

Catherine thanked him, dubiously, and went to get her hat. She found the cottage with difficulty. It was up a narrow alley between houses and across a drying-yard full of flapping sheets and odorous with pigs. The walls of the row of cottages were splashed with damp, the windows were small and forbidding, the paintwork old and blistered.

The door was opened by a small, broad-shouldered woman whose face was a network of wrinkles. Her eyes, of a washed-out blue, had a peculiar expression. Catherine had seen it in the eyes of suffering animals. She had seen it in William's eyes when he was dealing with a difficult case. A look between anxiety and pain, but without fear. Her lips were tightly pressed together. They were thin lips, rather pale, but their expression was neither severe nor bitter. The hand upon the door was knotted, the thumb broad, the fingernails worn down, the wrist-bones prominent from much scrubbing. The wedding-ring, worn to a thread, was deeply imbedded.

'Come in, will ye?' she said, in a non-committal voice. Catherine came in, doubtfully. They sat down on opposite sides of a deal table. She saw, with surprise, that the room was clean. It hadn't been hurriedly tidied up for her coming, it was clean with the deep cleanliness which comes from long habit. Catherine counted the doors . . . front door, back door, staircase door, parlour door, cupboard door . . . there wasn't much wall-space left. When the table and four or five chairs and herself and Irene's mother were there, there wasn't much floor-space either.

The room was pleasant enough. The clock ticked, the fire rustled, the brass door knobs gleamed. Half a pig hung against the wall beside the fire, herbs hung from the beams, a saucepan on the fire hissed and bubbled. Evidently this was a job at which, if you didn't go under into squalor, you became superlatively good.

Catherine looked across at the other woman. She had a distinct feeling that she was under examination.

She stated her requirements.

'She's a good girl,' Irene's mother said when she had finished. 'She won't give you no trouble. I'll say that for her. But she don't know nothing.'

'I don't expect very much . . . as long as she's able to scrub and clean . . . and to prepare vegetables . . .'

'Oh! She's not simple! But if you was to want any fancy cooking . . .'

Catherine smiled. 'I don't think we're likely to want that. What Irene doesn't know we can puzzle out between us.'

Irene's mother rubbed the side of her nose with her finger.

'I see. You all work in and out together like.'

She scrutinised Catherine afresh.

'Mind. She's got to be told. She may be a bit rough like for you. You'll have to tell her.'

Catherine nodded. She saw what Irene's mother wanted. The girl had been taught all that was possible at home. Catherine was to be her first 'little' place on the way to good service.

The keen, pale-blue eyes looked her all over from head to foot.

'You'd like to see her, I expect?'

'We hadn't settled the wages . . .' Catherine hesitated.

'I'll leave that to you. You see what you think she's worth.'

She called Irene, who came in, giggling, and hanging back in the door. Catherine wasn't impressed. She thought how much rather she would have had the mother. Irene had frizzed her hair and looked overdone about the head as she stood rubbing one foot against the other. Doubtfully, she agreed to take her for a month on trial and to fix her wages at the end of it.

As she stood up to go she looked out at the stretch of garden behind the cottage. The newly turned earth was studded with green plants, against the spring sky a plum tree stood up, hoary with blossom. Irene's mother looked at the tree and her blue eyes took on a deeper colour.

'It's a wonder, isn't it?' she said. 'When I go up the garden to shake it, so as the blossom shall set, I could fair worship it.'

II

Irene suited Catherine extremely well, though she often wondered if she was doing anything to turn her into the sort of maid whom anybody else would wish to employ.

Like Catherine, Irene was virulently untidy . . . but clean. She never learnt method. She would drop her work in the middle of a crowded morning to mend a bicycle tyre for Ellen, disentangle Adam's fishing line or execute minor repairs on the stove or kitchen furniture. She would then work at double pressure till late at night to make up the lost time.

She could cook anything for which any sort of recipe existed. She learnt to make superlative bread, pastry, and omelettes. Her doughnuts, warm, oily, and succulent, were among the highlights of Audrey and Adam's childhood. A natural extravagance pervaded her excellent cooking and was by dint of tears and deprivations curbed without killing that cooking's excellence.

Her kitchen, to the end, looked as if a bomb had burst in it and was always encumbered by invalid bicycles, rag animals in process of construction, and the novels of Bulwer Lytton and Mrs Henry Wood.

The children adored her, for she taught them all in turn to ride bicycles and then disappeared with them into the valley where they learnt to catch roach and perch. Audrey, also, she taught to cook, backing up her teaching with the clinching argument of 'our mother says'.

Catherine learnt to respect 'our mother'. Thrifty, self-respecting, and full of hard common sense, she had contrived, through all the vicissitudes of the agricultural wage, to bring up a large family and place them out well. As witness to her philosophy there was Irene . . . a good sort, a tireless worker, a willing improver, a girl who did without, improvised, made substitutes on the spur of the moment, and was a mine of information at all times.

A good girl. Irene's mother was right.

CHAPTER TWO

Catherine began to appreciate the flavour and character of her own village.

It was a village that had no squire, no settled family. The land belonged either to the church or to one or other of the colleges. Much of it had long been common land, and there were squatters' cottages strung out along the roadside, without gardens at the back. The village had a local reputation for independence and self-sufficiency, and had been stigmatised in the past as backward and drunken, a reproach no longer deserved. William, in his boyhood, had once counted fifteen public-houses.

Catherine found the people likeable, once you knew them. They were loyal to their families, thrifty, and swift to repay a kindness. A gift to any of the cottages always provoked a gift in return, even if it were only a boiling of spring greens or a few sticks of rhubarb. They were clever with their hands, and the village had a long tradition of craftsmanship, had once been the centre of several small manufacturing concerns. The people had a hard, sardonic humour, apt to find the one word which would bite most deeply into the memory, a sane humour, natural to the rational, slow-moving temper of the village. Even their vices and their failings were consistent and could be understood and taken into account.

Children abounded. Children with straw-coloured hair, children with hair like coir matting, children with heads redder than copper. The air of the place seemed to breed them. On Saturdays the market-place was rowdy with shrill voices and tackety boots.

Nobody took very much notice of them. Babies were another matter. Babies were little kings and queens, dressed in the best the family could afford. Suddenly the baby was a baby no more. He became a rowdy urchin whose home, when he was not eating, sleeping, or in the street, was in school. It was no wonder. There was hardly room for a woman to work in some of the cramped old cottages. Something had to go.

The children drifted about in gangs. They had their own games. There was a special season for peg-tops – dreaded by motorists. One week the street and square would be full of rapt performers forgetful of anything but the spinning top, the next the season of hopscotch would have come, and a little later that of marbles. The games were always played in the same order and never at the same time. Juvenile cricket occupied the square outside Catherine's house in the summer. In the winter they made slides down the northerly road in front of the police station, or went tobogganing on home-made sleds.

Occasionally they went 'leasing' in the harvest fields with their parents or blackberrying on warm Saturdays along the field roads. Sometimes in spring they searched the ditches for violets, but unless there was something definite to be got out of the countryside they rarely left the streets. The fields, when they grew older, might be their workshop, but the streets of the village were their home.

Catherine was astonished to find that Irene, who knew so much about so many things, would have been hard put to it to tell one bird from another, and did not recognise any but the simplest kinds of wild flowers. Eb had the same ignorance. A new field, a new flower were as surprising to him as a new country would have been to Catherine. It is natural for people to go along the lines laid down for them by their neighbours, but Catherine had never realised how very narrow and deep those lines could be, and how many people travelled along them without even wishing to get out on one side or the other, and felt lonely, naked, and ridiculous if they were doing something that they had never done before.

The ties which bound the people to the village were very close. The children never left it till they were fourteen or older. The greater proportion did not leave it then. There was no break in the home relationship, no change of viewpoint. Many of them grew up and had been out in service a year or two before they even went as far as the market town. The railway was some distance off and travelling was expensive. Yet this limitation did not prevent them from growing up shrewd, handy, and alive to life. They had none of the heavy indifference of the lonely villages out towards the wolds.

William knew village from village extremely well. There were bad villages, places which seemed to attract the shiftless families and the rogues of the neighbourhood. Frowsy out-at-elbow villages where you saw torn paper and cabbage leaves on the roadside grass, and ill-kept children on the roads. There were firmly managed villages with well-repaired cottages, and pipes for water, and large new village halls. There were congenial gossiping villages where there was never any difficulty in finding a neighbour to look after a lonely patient, and there were independent villages of smallholders with poultry runs, fruit gardens, and wayside goats. Villages where every cottage had its weekly shirt on a horse. Clean villages always short of water, dirty villages with plenty. Villages that had fallen out with their neighbours a mile away, and had no intercourse with them from one generation to another, and villages that always did things by couples. William knew them all so well that he couldn't have told anyone else how much he knew about them. It would never have occurred to him that there was anything to tell; he had absorbed his knowledge of the countryside as Eb had absorbed his knowledge of onions and Irene of the ways of pike. It was something he couldn't pass on.

Catherine would never have it, though perhaps some day Audrey and Adam would – and most certainly Bill. To the stranger it was all very hard to understand. The infinite and unchangeable series of grades and castes which made up the countryside gave Catherine a headache.

There they were – shaken a little, a very little, by the War, but still laid down like layers of geological strata, calcified with age. There they were, through all the shades of *Debrett's*, *Who's Who*, and the *Landed Gentry*, down to parsons, doctors, solicitors, large and small farmers, tradespeople, craftsmen and master workmen, carters and shepherds and cowmen, field labourers and ironstone workers, each with a different position, which Catherine was expected, subtly, to understand and recognise.

She made all the mistakes of the townswoman fresh to the country. She ran up to the post without a hat, she sat on the wayside grass beside her children, in full view of passing motor-cars, she assumed that the wrong people were on friendly terms with each other, she carried home her own parcels. She went to church at eight o'clock in the morning, and was seen working in the garden with her husband at eleven, or strolling carelessly through the church-goers in an old tweed coat.

There were other and more subtle mistakes.

One blazing morning when she was sitting outside a patient's house in the car, the remote and dignified lady of the village approached her to inquire for the carter's wife, who was ill.

Catherine replied that she knew nothing about the case, but that her husband would be out in a few minutes.

'Then I'll walk up and down and wait.'

Catherine looked up and down the blazing, empty fields, parched and treeless.

'Won't you sit in the car? It's so hot in the sun.'

The little lady bit her lip. 'Oh, no . . . thank you . . . That would be just a little too remarkable, wouldn't it?'

She moved away down the road, small, and very erect in her severe black clothes.

Catherine looked at her back, aware for the first time that a woman who moves from one town to another may be changing her air and her water, but the woman who moves from the town to the country had indeed left her own country and her father's house.

CHAPTER THREE

Catherine wondered how Audrey and Adam would behave when she took them to their first party. She need not have wondered. She soon realised that her problem had been the problem of every other woman in the countryside. They were not the only ones who were making, for the first time, contact with children of their own age. Quietly, without any fuss, the guests decided to ignore each other.

Each child selected a toy and went off with it to a separate part of the wide lawn, whilst the occasion of the party rolled happily down a bank, climbed it, and rolled down it again. The bank was more important to her than her company, she hardly saw that they were there. The garden was dotted with absorbed individualists.

Catherine stood and talked with other mothers. They admired each other's children and exchanged recipes for eggless cakes and meatless suppers. They talked at length about Flemish rabbits and Anglo-Toggenburg goats, kohlrabi and perpetual spinach. And about bobbed hair, which was coming in, but not very violently, and triple-ninon silk night-dresses, which none of them could afford and all of them longed to possess.

Catherine caught scraps of conversation – conversation out of a Victorian novel . . .

'My dear, what else could I do? She wasn't in at eleven o'clock so I sent Tom out on his bicycle to look for her. He found her walking back with that boy of Dyer's. So he took her *straight* back to her people at once. We couldn't possibly have her back with the other maids.'

'Oh, yes. We've called on them. She was one of the Tollingates. The Shropshire Tollingates. My brother was with her husband in Kashmir in nineteen-sixteen.'

'My dear . . . who *are* all these people?'

'And as I said to Tony, he's a perfectly sound horse if you don't cross your whip . . .'

'A sawdust litter, with straw on top . . .'

Catherine realised that the woman next to her was talking, and forced herself to show attention.

'. . . and so of course we sent her away. We found out that she *never* undressed. She simply took off her cap and apron and rolled into bed, stockings and all. Simply revolting. And her nurseries! And then she had to tell me that when she was with the Micmacsons (the margarine people) she never had to put up with any interference . . . So she's gone and I can't hear of a soul. And it is so important to have a really good girl for little children. . . .'

Audrey was sitting on a large wooden horse. She was patting its mane and singing shrilly. A small boy with a wheelbarrow passed within a yard of her. Neither of them noticed the other.

'Aren't they odd?' said Catherine wistfully. 'Each of them might be the only person in the world.'

'They might indeed,' her companion streamed on. 'Forty pounds a year, and uniform and all found. And they won't attempt to fit in with the rest of the household. Oh, no! Everyone's to consider them. And as to lending a hand when one of the others is out . . .'

'Oh, no, never,' Catherine agreed absently, though as a matter of fact hers always did.

The sun was making silver-gilt of Audrey's hair. How pretty the little creatures all were – so clean and tended, so much better dressed than the tired, shabby, haggard-looking women who stood about and watched them. For they were shabby. Clothes were still a dreadful price, no one, as yet, had any money to spend. Suddenly Catherine admired the woman who had spoken of the Shropshire Tollingates. What a country! To have the sheer stupid pluck to keep that sort of thing going after all that they had gone through!

'. . . and nothing like it in their own homes. They come to us and expect absolutely everything. . . .'

Audrey and the small boy with the wheelbarrow were walking round and round each other, stiff-legged, like strange dogs. Catherine almost expected to hear them growl. All at once Audrey abandoned the boy as dull and made a dart for the wheelbarrow.

It was blue, lined with bright red. A solid, home-made toy. Audrey patted it all over, as she had patted the horse. The boy hovered round her, doubtful, longing to attack.

Catherine stepped forward.

'Audrey . . . dear . . .'

Audrey turned a dulled eye upon her, and went back to the wheelbarrow.

'Audrey! The little boy had it first. Come away.'

Audrey hunched her shoulders, she didn't turn round.

'Oh, no!' a pleasant, shrill voice intervened. 'He must learn to give up. Mustn't you, Robin? He must learn, you know. You must give it up, Robin.'

Catherine hesitated. She didn't want Robin to use Audrey as material to learn on, but she knew better than to push the matter, publicly, with Audrey. Audrey would give way stoically when they were alone, confronted with an audience she held out to the last gasp.

A cabbage butterfly drifted down into the group like a scrap of paper. Audrey wheeled round, and ran after it, beating the air with her sun-bonnet. The boy turned his back on the barrow. He strolled over to the wooden horse, looked critically at it, and stood it on its head. Then he set the wheels spinning. An absorbing job. First one, then the other – you had to work hard to keep them all going at once. He panted gently, his tongue hanging out, like a terrier on a lead.

The two mothers smiled at each other.

'Well!' said Catherine.

'You don't know what they're thinking, do you?' said Robin's mother. 'I often wonder what goes on in Robin's head. Of course, living in the country is too perfect . . . but it doesn't teach them to get on with other children.'

'It's difficult,' Catherine agreed. 'We never see anybody else. Where do you live?'

'Right out the other side – beyond Hook Norton. I've often heard of you. But we've only the pony. How do you manage?'

'My husband takes me . . . when he can.'

'Oh, well . . . perhaps some day . . .'

She smiled enchantingly at Catherine. She had pretty pale hair which looked strange under a straw hat which was too old for her and too heavily trimmed. Her eyes were beautiful – blue, 'put in with sooty fingers.' She had slim shoulders, she talked with them, and with her eyes and hands.

'Some day,' Catherine said hopefully, and smiled back.

'How do you manage your girl?' Robin's mother went on. 'I feel sure it's right to bring the children up on a system. I do think it's wonderful to bring your children up on a system. We started Robin with Froebel, but I think Froebel's rather inadequate, don't you? It's no help later on. I've been trying Montessori. It teaches them to do such a lot for themselves.'

Catherine murmured confusedly that she had never heard of either of them.

'Oh, but you should! Think of the aimless way in which we were all brought up. It is so important to be consistent. It's difficult to choose, of course . . . there's the Parents' Union . . . and those terribly interesting American books on Child Psychology . . .'

They followed the others in a drift across the lawn towards tea. The long, dim room was full of a green light from the garden. An old house, Catherine thought, never looks mean and shabby. This room with its white, shallow panelling, blurred with age, its shining floor and its bowls of roses, was like something in a book or in a dream. Catherine looked anxiously down the long table for Audrey. She was sitting quietly, staring down the room, hand in hand with Robin. They were not talking, they were not looking at each other, but the two remote creatures seemed to have come to an understanding.

'I'll lend you some of my books . . .'

Her new friend broke off, and darted away to hand round cups of milk.

Catherine, suddenly shy amongst so many strangers, sat down in the nearest chair. She was stupid in company, after being so long alone. She wished she had gone to help with the children, but it was too late now. She wondered if her hat was straight and whether, after all, she had remembered to bring the handkerchief out of her coat pocket. If she had forgotten, Audrey would be sure to want it in the middle of tea.

'And *her* mother, of course, was a Lydiatt . . .'

'And I said to Tom, of course, the relatives of the people who gave the old hangings . . .'

'Only three shillings for making . . . and she looks a picture in it . . .'

The voices went on around Catherine, and over her head. Someone slipped into the chair beside her.

The newcomer addressed her, brusquely, unexpectedly.

'This is something like a tea!' She took a piece of chocolate cake and admired it lovingly before she put it on her plate. 'This is the first piece of iced cake I've seen for three years. I'm going to enjoy myself.'

She beamed at Catherine.

'How long have you been here?'

Catherine reckoned up. 'Just over three years.'

'We came in 'fifteen, so I shall have to call on you. We've got a car at last.'

She looked down the table.

'Those are my two urchins . . . Hilary and Edward . . . down there in holland tunics. How many have you got here?'

'Audrey and Adam.' Catherine pointed them out.

The newcomer stared at them for one critical moment, decided that she liked Audrey as much as she liked her mother, and let the lines of her face relax into their accustomed humour.

'She looks a nice person. You must bring her to play with Hilary and Edward.'

'It would be splendid,' Catherine muttered.

'Try some of this cake. You mustn't miss it. Don't you find that nowadays you're a perfect pig about sugar? I am. I do think it's the thing that hurt me most.'

Catherine found herself talking. It was a relief to be with others, after all, to learn that they had had very much her own experiences and her own troubles. And really . . . she might take her eye off Audrey . . .

CHAPTER FOUR

'I can't think how you stand it,' Violet said. 'You look up the street, and you look down the street, and all you see is an old man wheeling a wheelbarrow.'

'Things don't happen in the street here,' Catherine answered.

They were sitting in the garden. The acacia, after dying back twice, had recovered and was full of milky flowers. The borders had thrown up blue and white spikes of lupin, white foxgloves and bell flowers. Catherine was shelling peas. She put one into her mouth. It was sweet, like a drop of sugar.

'But what on earth do you and William do with yourselves?' Violet persisted.

'We work.' Catherine thought it was no use telling Violet that they had made the garden and built the summer-house (somehow, and without spending any money on it); Violet wasn't interested in any work but needlework.

'We all do that,' Violet said acidly, driving her needle through the linen with a click. She looked much older. There was a dusty look about her brown hair, though it wasn't grey yet. The colour in her face had set in patches. Its pleasant lines had turned peevish and disappointed.

'And when you've done it all,' she went on, 'nobody thanks you for it. They don't take the least bit of notice. I've slaved for them all these years and now – they just go off.'

Catherine went on shelling. She knew by heart what was coming next.

'They're not grateful. They just walk off and leave us. As if we didn't count. I told Jane in my time she wouldn't have been allowed to go off and teach eurythmics when there was plenty for her to do at home. I don't mind Se's going. I always expected that, though it is disappointing that he couldn't go into the office with Edward . . . But we have to look to the future, and things aren't what they were. The whole thing was let down while he was away. It's simply sickening the way those who didn't go pushed and grabbed and took things away from those that did. I told Jane that her leaving us was just the last straw.'

'What did she say?' The peas bounced out of a full pod into the bowl.

'She said, "Why, mother, I've got to look after myself, now, haven't I?" As if we hadn't always looked after her!'

'But you'd be pretty hard up if anything happened to Edward,' Catherine said mildly.

'There'll be time enough to think about that when it happens. I wanted her at home. I'd looked forward to it so. We could have run the house together, and gone shopping in the morning, and paying calls in the afternoon. We could have done everything together. And when I said that to her she said, "My God!" and went out of the room without even shutting the door.'

Catherine sighed. She agreed with Jane but didn't like her. She was a hard young woman and a prig. She flung her notions at you as if they were bricks.

'She said she wanted a good time,' Violet burst out. 'Good time. That's all they think about. Running about all over the place and coming in at all hours. It makes my head ache.'

Catherine smiled reminiscently. 'I had a good time.'

Violet snorted. 'D'you think so? You start to tell Jane about your good times and see what she thinks. She'll simply stare at you and grin. She told me I had an awful time when I was a girl . . . said I was repressed and that my upbringing was immoral and my inhibitions were simply ghastly and a lot of other rubbish out of these books they all read now. Frankly indecent I call it. . . . Oh, yes! And a lot of stuff about being free.'

'It sounds fine,' said Catherine, 'and frightfully important. It all boils down to the fact that Jane ought to teach somebody something. She'd pine away and die if she didn't. She's one of that sort. Has Se said anything about it?'

'Not to me. That's another thing. The aggravating way in which they hang together. They get together and talk . . . and if I speak to them they turn round and look at each other and laugh. You wait till yours do that.'

Violet paused to thread her needle and bite off the thread. 'Then, when I ask them what they're giggling about, they say, "Isn't she priceless!" or "What's the use of trying to explain to you, mother . . . you'd never see it." Surely we never behaved like that!'

Catherine put down the full bowl and stretched her bare arms. She tried to remember. She thought on the whole that she and Violet had had more compunction. Tact and consideration were 'out' for the moment. A disillusioned and disappointed generation were not using them.

'Our parents were such noisy thinkers,' she said at last. 'Supposing we had talked like that . . . they'd have kept us under a perpetual shower-bath of their feelings and emotions . . . they'd never have let us forget it. Besides, by the time we were that age we'd surely got used to the fact that we could think for ourselves. Jane's awfully raw.'

'Raw! You've never heard her being what she calls downright. The things she says! Everything we never mentioned, they make a point of bringing into conversation. I didn't even *know* things like that when I was a girl.'

'Oh, yes, you did!' Catherine thought. She watched Violet's face. It looked less tired. Catherine understood that to talk about her grievances was a pleasure to Violet. It was like rubbing a gnat-bite. It brought up the swelling, but it relieved the irritation.

It was, she reflected, one of the delightful things about William that he didn't mind what Jane said. William was a decent soul, but he had no reserves. He never pretended to himself or Catherine that anything didn't exist. He had told her from the beginning stories, true and otherwise, that would have reduced Violet to pained tears. Catherine didn't mind them. The gross humours and animal impulses of life had to be accepted along with everything else. William liked Jane. He liked her hard young mind and her lust for argument. He liked to wrangle with her and draw her out. She was better educated than the women he had known when he was a boy, there were no closed subjects on which you could not talk to her.

Catherine didn't think that Jane was clever. She was efficient and had made the most of her training, but she was incapable of seeing more than one point of view. Once she had read or assimilated a subject her mind was closed to any further opinion on it. Catherine thought that she was very like Violet – she ate like her, walked like her, and kept herself and her clothes with the same uninspired cleanliness. Catherine treated Jane as an equal and was polite to her, Jane treated Catherine as a manifest inferior and an uninteresting person.

It was difficult to live with your family again after such a long break . . . more difficult still to have them in your own house. When she had left Violet, Catherine had been little more than a girl. She had had no home of her own. Now she was settled into her own house and her own ways.

Violet would say: 'I don't like the way you've got that Chesterfield. It doesn't show off the cushions.' She would pull it round, making one end of the room look stripped and ugly. Or, 'Having all that silver out! How you can! Sheer waste of time cleaning it. . . . And all those mantelpiece ornaments, collecting dust!'

Or: 'Why do you let that girl Ellen talk to you like that? Chatting away to you! You ought to keep her in her place.'

Or: 'I can't think why you wanted to put Audrey into colours so early. It's so common-looking. I kept Jane in white till she was nearly four years old . . .'

Suggestions, complaints, and advice came from her at all hours. 'Why do you put up with it?' William would ask wrathfully. 'I like the way she talks! Answer her back!'

But Catherine didn't answer back. Violet would soon be gone. She wanted to make her comfortable while she was here. Secretly she felt that Violet was a little jealous of the old house and big garden. She found Jane far more trying. She didn't like the way in which she got up and went out of the room when the children came in, twitched her skirts out of Audrey's fingers and put her belongings out of her reach. She didn't like the way in which she sat about to be waited on, and never seemed to realise that two extra people in an under-staffed house make a great deal more work. She hated the way in which, when Violet tried to lead her into the conversation, she shut her up or turned to some other subject. Violet was dreadfully aggravating, but she was pathetic too. Jane ought to have sense enough to see that.

Violet folded her work up and sat looking down at her neat black shoes. She had changed her way of dressing very little in the past few years. She was one of those women who set early in a definite mould. Catherine felt as though it was in the very air of the garden how obstinate Violet was. She might grumble and worry about Jane and her ideas but they would not influence her in the least. She would go on living in her small house with the same furniture which she had bought when she had married, she would have her meals – economical and well-cooked – always at the same time, would go out shopping at the same time, call on the same people. Jane and Sebastian might wound her, but they could not shake her. She would go no part of the way to meet them.

She's never been friends with them, thought Catherine.

Ellen came in with Audrey and Adam. She left Audrey and took Adam to wash him for dinner.

Audrey pushed a bunch of daisies into her mother's hand. They were wilted and fading. 'I picked them for you,' she said sweetly.

Catherine took them and turned the withered petals up in her hand. Over Audrey's head she could see Ellen looking back at Audrey from the end of the garden – maternal, watchful, and derisive. Catherine understood. Audrey had picked the flowers, grown tired of them and tried to throw them away. It was Ellen who had forced her to bring them to her. She said:

'They're lovely. And I'd like them even better if you got a saucer from Ellen and put them in water for me.' Being a mother was troublesome, you were never off your guard, you could never pretend. She had wanted to take the flowers and kiss Audrey, pretend to believe wholeheartedly in the gift. Audrey looked squarely at her. The lines of her face dropped.

All that trouble to pay for a moment's pleasure in picking them. First the flowers to carry home, long after her hand was hot and her fingers ached, and now the trouble of putting them in water. It wasn't worth it. They were only fit to throw away now. She had enjoyed picking them, they had been so fresh with their pink edges and their golden eyes. But what a lot of trouble it had given her! She dumped the flowers in Catherine's lap and went off to fetch the saucer, trailing her feet.

'You aren't very loving to your children,' Violet said.

'She didn't bring them home for me. Don't you see . . . I mustn't let her get away with a pretence like that. It's dishonest.'

'Oh! You never believe anybody! It's just that sort of thing makes life worthwhile.'

Audrey squatted down on the grass at Catherine's feet, her fat pinkish brown thighs pressed firmly down amongst the green blades, her fingers picking the flowers neatly up and dropping them into the water. Catherine looked at the back of her neck. Audrey's neck was lovely, white, firm, and of a beautiful shape. A solid, warm white under the flaxen tangle of her curls. She put the palm of her hand against the warm flesh of her daughter's neck. Sometimes she was filled with a purely physical love for the sturdy healthy body she and William had made. She loved Audrey's plump wrists, dimpled knuckles, and sturdy muscular legs. She loved the springy feel of her flesh under her hand and the cool slippery feel of her hair. Audrey leaned back against the pressure of her hand and looked up.

'Fairies poached eggs!' she said, pointing to the floating daisies.

Catherine laughed, her face close to Audrey's. She kissed her.

Audrey rose, deliberately, holding the saucer in her out-stretched hand. She went slowly away with it down the lawn, her eyes on the floating flowers.

'You don't encourage her for doing something for you,' Violet said, 'but you kiss her when she talks nonsense. As if she was always going to be a baby!'

Catherine said nothing. She thought her daughter had

really done something more deserving of kisses than the dumping of discarded flowers. She stood up, the bowl of shelled peas in the crook of her arm, and reached for the basket of pea shucks with her other hand.

As they went down the path they met William and Jane coming in.

Jane was clean, she was cool, her coat and skirt were suitable and uncreased. Her face was alight with interest for what she and William had been saying. William was quoting and laying down the law – emphatically – because he wasn't quite sure of his ground.

Catherine remembered that she was wearing an overall, that her hair was ruffled and her sleeves rolled up. She looked quickly at William to see if he minded.

William looked at the bowl of green peas in the crook of her arm.

'Green peas!' he said. 'That's the stuff.'

He kissed her.

Catherine felt as they walked into the house that William loved her for all the things for which she didn't want to be loved.

He praised her if she made a successful boiling of jam or a good cake or if she spent a morning polishing a piece of furniture. He would say to her when they came away from a party:

'I thought you were the best-looking and the best-dressed woman in the room.'

Or: 'By gad, Madam! You don't look a day older than when I married you!'

Catherine felt that she ought to be pleased with these tributes, they would have pleased most women. She wanted him to say that she was a help and a trier and that she was doing her best for the children. William said none of these things, it never entered his head that Catherine wanted them said. Neither did he argue with her as he had argued with his niece, and it seemed to him only natural that she should rarely write now. A woman usually gave up that sort of nonsense when she got married.

Catherine rarely talked about her writing. She had finished and sent out the novel in the Wessex manner, though she was not as sure as she had been that it was a great and original piece of work.

She discovered that it made hard reading. But she felt that a book which had been written with such difficulty, and which had taken such trouble to produce, must surely be worth publishing.

She looked anxiously at her lunch table. To Violet's critical eye her housekeeping would appear hopeless in any case. Everything was clean and in order. She breathed a prayer of thanks that the meat was cold and that the fruit tart was as good as fruit tart possibly could be. It was a nervy job preparing meals for a woman to whom the whole business of buying and cooking meals was a sacred ritual. There only remained a series of conversational pitfalls to be avoided.

1. To head William off politics, topical novels and careers for women, on all of which Violet and Jane disagreed.

2. To prevent Audrey from talking about food – this upset Violet, who thought it wasn't nice.

3. To keep Violet off the servant question when the maid was in the room.

4. To keep Jane so busy talking to William that she had not any time to notice what Violet was saying.

She sighed. Ordinary people didn't need all this overwhelming display of tact and good generalship. Or did they? And did she only notice her relations because they thought they had a right to say what they thought?

She slipped into her place as the others came in and watched William carving beef. He did it very well. The helpings looked tidy and sufficient, the joint looked decent afterwards, it hadn't that haggard look – as if it had seen too much of life – that it had when Catherine carved it. And everybody got enough although they were actually eating less. Ellen, with the 'shut' expression which she reserved for visitors of whom she did not approve, planked down a dish of steaming potatoes and a plate of lettuce in front of Catherine.

Violet beamed at Audrey, who was watching Jane talking to William with a bright eye for Jane's individual peculiarities.

'Did you have a nice walk, darling?' she said.

Audrey sat up with a jerk. 'Yes. What do you think we saw?' She began to bounce up and down on her chair.

'Sit down, Audrey!' Catherine wondered why it was so difficult to get mashed potato out of a spoon onto plates. 'What did you see?'

'Squash duck! Up the Birmingham road!'

Violet's face contracted into a knot of disapproval. Jane stared. William stopped talking and laughed.

Audrey bounced again.

'Squash duck!' she repeated, with unction. 'All bloody!'

There was a silence. She looked round at their faces.

'It was a squash duck,' she insisted obstinately.

'That'll do,' Catherine said firmly, and put her dinner in front of her.

Audrey filled her mouth with beef. Grown-up people were hard to satisfy. You told them something really interesting and then they looked down their noses. Sometimes she wondered if they were worth worrying about.

CHAPTER FIVE

Catherine's novel came back. Catherine took it away upstairs before anyone else could see it, and looked at her manuscript.

It was in a most astonishing mess. The pages were grimy, the edges were torn and tattered; the whole thing would have to be re-typed before it could go out again.

But how . . . and when?

Other women had managed to write novels and bring up families. Catherine wondered if they had all washed behind their children's ears and pushed them about in perambulators and swept under their beds and weeded the garden and picked the fruit and made their children's clothes and done the hundred and one odd jobs that fell to her share, because William was always out and odd labour was ruinously dear. Perhaps they were so successful that they managed to pay for decorators and carpenters and sewing-maids and expensive, reliable nannies.

She shut the manuscript into her drawer amongst her clean frocks and shut the drawer with a bang. That was that!

She stood up. The house was quiet. Irene and the children had gone out into the fields with their lunch. Ellen was out. William wouldn't be in for two or three hours. She ought to be picking strawberries. Pounds and pounds of them were sweltering under their nets in the sun. She stood still and looked at the auricaria. Its boughs looked like a tin design copied from a skein of darning wool.

'I believe Eb could cut that down,' she thought. 'He seems able to do most things.'

The backs of her eyes were smarting with tears. She thought:

'I must get over it before anyone comes in.'

She took her hat and went out into the glaring market-square. She crossed it into the main street, went over the jitty and through a gap between the houses into the fields. She could be alone here almost at once.

She went straight ahead through the wheat, drawing her hand over the green ears as she walked. The sound was cool as running water, the heads swung and rebounded in curves on each side of her as she pushed her way along the narrow path. It made a pattern as broken water does round a boat. But it was wider than that. More like the pattern round a swimming dog. The dry earth smelt warm and pungent, larks shrilled, poppies burned like steady flames deep in the wheat.

Catherine went straight on. She was not far enough away. She knew these fields too well.

She would have to give it up. What was the use? No one could do two things at the same time and do both equally well. It was silly to feel tragic about it. She would never be happy about Audrey and Adam if she left them to anyone else. She loved them too much for that – she wanted too much for them. If she had not had the writing always at the back of her mind perhaps she would have managed her house better in these early years. Your whole mind . . . yes, that was what pushed things through. Nothing else would do.

She walked on.

Other women found their houses and their husbands and children enough, why couldn't she be like them? Suppose she poured out all her energy, all her imagination upon them? She would be doing no more than she ought to do. She would have nothing to grumble at.

She thought:

'Lord, look away from me that I may accomplish as an hireling my day.'

If only He would. If only He would free her of the continual need to 'tell' . . . to show . . . to create. If only she could shut her eyes to the sweetness and wonder of the world – to the queerness and complexities of people and to the odd accidents of life. If only she could so blunt herself as to forget it all.

Short grass now. The old, fine grass of the common which had not been opened for hundreds of years. Here were harebells, yellow-bedstraw and clumps of gorse. Horses and sheep were feeding. The sparrow-hawks, whose home was in the bird-cherry at the foot of the field, hung whistling. Rabbits fled, stamping.

This was a field they all loved. She had spent long days here with Audrey and Adam. She walked on. She wanted to be away, for this one hour, from all of them.

She crossed a field of roots, gaudy with weeds, went on across a field of barley, flat as the sea, on along a farm road which ran over a ridge. Wooded hills, new to her, lay off on her right hand. She passed through the farmyard where a dog barked hollowly in the empty house, climbed a gate and went on down the hill.

She found a clump of gorse bushes and lay down in its shade. She took off her hat and stretched herself close against the earth. The warmth of the earth struck upwards through her clothing, through her flesh, right down to her bones. It was a friendly warmth; she felt as though the body of the field were alive. She rolled over and buried her face in a clump of wild thyme. She stopped thinking. Everything stopped. Her mind went slack, her muscles relaxed.

Bees were booming, the gorse buds crackled in the sun. All about her she could feel the July day ripening towards evening, as though the whole day were one single perfect fruit of time. She could feel the springy, even pressure of the turf and the deep underlying strength of the land. It was good to be like this. It was good to take off everything – your life, your hopes, your fears, your worries – simply to be part of things. Words flashed into her mind . . .

'Out beyond desire, beyond hope, beyond having . . .'

Having! That was the trouble.

She felt that the world would go on; it didn't matter, she didn't need to care. There was no reason to be hurt. Thought came back to her.

'Oh, God!' she thought. 'Help it not to hurt me. It's foolish to be bitter. Teach me to put *that* into everything I do. Even into the things I hate doing . . .

'Why should I want to *show*? Other people can't even *see*.

'And if I could . . . could I ever create anything . . . show anything as good as Audrey and Adam?

'I don't think I could . . . even if they turn out quite ordinary people.'

She sat up and looked into the sky. How deep it was! If you looked long enough you felt as though you were falling downwards through it.

She stood up. She felt rested all over, clean and new. She felt as if she had been a very long way away . . . not in space or in time, but into some unknown dimension of the spirit.

She thought:

'I must do this again, some day. One's mind needs taking down and cleaning sometimes, like a watch.'

She went back across the fields. When the church clock came in sight she was astonished to find that she hadn't been out for an hour.

CHAPTER SIX

I

It had been snowing, then in the early afternoon a fine rain had set in which later had changed once more to heavy, damp flakes of snow. They clung to the windscreen in a fleece, slipping reluctantly. The car banged and rattled from one pothole to another on the unmended road, the side-curtains flapped in the wind.

William put his foot on the brake.

'Damn! It's market day! The place will be packed out. Must we go on?'

Catherine clenched her hands in the pockets of her overcoat.

'William, there isn't another day left before Christmas on which you can get in. I won't be a minute longer than I can help. You needn't come with me.'

William accelerated suddenly and the car skidded sideways down the hill through the slush. Catherine bit her lip and pushed her feet hard against the floorboards. She reminded herself that William couldn't help it. It wasn't his fault that he was like that.

'How much are you going to spend?' William asked.

'Not more than I can help. I only want something for Audrey and Adam . . . and the maids.'

'Slovenly brutes.'

William felt that people in their position shouldn't have to give presents. He didn't see why they should be forced, simply because it was the custom, to give other people things which they couldn't afford themselves.

Besides, they could afford to give so little. He hated the covert smile with which Catherine's gifts were received.

Catherine went on looking ahead at the black trees and bleached grass. Well . . . it *was* Christmas, the first Christmas without war or gross trouble in the house. Audrey and Adam should have something to remember this year, something bright, something magic. A Christmas that hung like a bright red lamp in the dark heart of winter.

> The holly bears a berry,
> As red as any blood.

Over the market town the smoke hung like the steam over a saucepan. In the splashy streets scared and dirty cattle with tickets on their rumps barged and slithered amongst women with string-bags, women with perambulators, women with pink silk stockings and cheap fur coats, boys on bicycles, farmers in Ford cars and numberless carrier's carts whose black tilts bulged with every need of humanity, from dead pigs and stove-pipes to Christmas trees and sewing machines. An old man in a greasy red flannel gown and hood with a white woollen beard tied round his chin, and a sandwich board on his chest, trudged through the mud, looking thoroughly ashamed of himself. Outside the Blue Boar, the Dewdrop, and the Friendly Hand, a crowd of men in bowler hats, cutaway coats, and drab breeches and splashed gaiters stood and talked, blocking up the pavement and half the road.

William turned the car into the sheep-market and stopped beside the empty pens.

'There doesn't seem to be anyone hanging about to fine us ten bob,' he said, as he clambered out. 'I suppose we're safe here.'

He beat his hands together and stamped his feet. He grinned at Catherine as they started to dodge in and out of the crowd. She was happy, her feet danced. She liked the crowd, the many colours of things in shop windows and the bustle and universal good-humour. Then she saw that William was liking it, after all. He dropped back and took her elbow.

'Look here, you want stockings. Pink ones.'

Catherine laughed. 'No, I don't. I want a horse for Adam . . . a wooden horse.'

William looked down at her. 'Jove! That's an idea. If only we had a paddock Adam could have a pony.'

'But we haven't, and Adam's too little. He'd rather have a wooden one.'

Outside the toyshop in the narrow street the horses hung in a grove, a forest of bushy manes and tails. Their harnesses were red and blue, their barrels were of white beechwood, their legs were straight as broomsticks. Their blue eyes were square and staring, their manes were grey. Catherine stood and smiled at them.

'Those!' she said happily.

'Those cheap things?' William looked doubtfully at them.

'It would have to be cheap . . . and they are strong.'

William followed her into the shop. It was nearly dark. A gas jet popped and squealed over the counter, lighting that end of the shop like a stage. The assistant fetched a pole and hooked down half a dozen wooden horses. They stood on the bare floor grinning amiably at Catherine and William.

William laughed.

'Gosh! What a queer-looking crowd!'

The girl laughed with him. 'They're not much to look at, and that's a fact. But we sell a lot of them. Old-fashioned . . . aren't they? They make them in the New Forest.'

William was interested. The queer beasts were English, then, traditional. He picked one up.

A wooden horse for Adam.

'Right, then. Which shall you have?'

Catherine picked out one, not too high for Adam to get on and off alone. Her eyes shone. He would be sure to like it. Boys always liked horses.

'Now a doll for Audrey,' William said firmly.

Catherine looked doubtful. Audrey didn't mother her dolls. They lay about in a legless condition, without clothes, and bald.

'Well . . . what on earth else would you give her?'

Catherine hardly knew. None of Audrey's toys seemed to give her any real pleasure.

The assistant went away to collect dolls. There weren't very many. A few cheap composition dolls with eyes like boot

122

buttons and crimson cheeks. A few rag dolls with stiffened muslin faces, and some cheap little china dolls with pointed heads and goggling eyes.

William picked up a leering china infant with an aniline shamrock stamped on its fondant-pink chest.

'Now, how on earth,' he asked, 'can you expect a child to love a thing like that?'

Catherine said nothing, she knew Audrey too well to expect her to love any doll, even if it was as beautiful as the morning.

'Look!' said William.

Under the gaslight, across the shop, another assistant was holding up a beautifully-modelled doll, dressed in fluffy pink silk. Its yellow spun silk hair gleamed softly, the buckles gleamed on its white kid shoes.

In front of the doll stood a very tipsy young farmer, smiling hazily and rocking to and fro on his heels. His face was red, his bowler hat had slipped back, his hands were in his pockets. A haggard young woman with untidy hair and a depressed-looking hat hovered near him. Her red, work-roughened hands fluttered with eagerness. She was too anxious to speak, but she smiled ingratiatingly. Catherine read her thoughts.

Had he enough money left? Was he too tipsy to be persuaded? She watched, as anxious as the woman herself. She drew a deep breath of relief when the man pulled his hand out of his pocket and showed a handful of silver. The woman, pouncing, took what the assistant had asked. Her cheeks were flushed, her eyes were wide and shining.

'Pity,' William said. 'Have you got another like that?'

'N-no. Not like that I haven't. There's this one. Perhaps you might care for that.'

This one was an adorable, fat, stockinette baby. Its hair, its eyes, its features were darning-wool, it wore a short white shift and a tight bonnet. It was stolid, observant, human.

Catherine cuddled it under her arm.

'Yes,' William said, 'yes . . . that's distinctly good.' He prodded it as though he expected it to smile. 'All right, we'll take that.'

Either side the crowded dirty street the lights were coming out in the shop windows. Snow fingered their faces like cold feathers. They went gay. They bought red, green, yellow, and solferino candles in a box for a shilling at an ironmonger's, they bought a red and gold cake frill for sixpence at a cash drug stores, and two boxes of fancy notepaper and two pairs of gloves at a draper's. They bought oranges, and chocolate mice, and soap babies, and penny whistles for the stockings of Audrey and Adam. They piled them all into the car and drove off through the snowy, steamy dark. They felt warm and happy because for the first time they had got everything they had meant to get and still had a little money in hand. Ahead of them and behind them tipsy, happy Fords were wallowing home through the slush.

Catherine leaned against William and thought of the woman in the toyshop whose husband had bought the pink doll.

Her poor, worried, silly face! Her poor hands, all red with scrubbing! She must have been pretty once and in love and proud of her husband. Life wasn't kind . . . not to a woman.

'Damn!' said William. 'I never bought your stockings. I say, old thing . . . what a shame. You haven't got a Christmas present.'

Catherine rubbed her cheek against his coat-sleeve. 'Neither have you. D'you mind?'

She sang under her breath.

'A wooden horse for Adam.

'And Audrey has a doll.'

It fitted the carol tune quite nicely. She was happy. Out in the greenhouse at home there was a little spindling thuya in a pot. She would make a Christmas tree of it . . . a little shining tree with paper butterflies and bright candles. But William wasn't to be consoled.

'I wanted to buy you a pair of pink stockings. A pair of pink silk stockings.'

II

Catherine awoke at midnight on Christmas Eve. The air was full of iron voices, metallic inhuman voices from the sky. Voices that clamoured like hounds hunting down the frosty dark. In the nursery she could hear Adam raising scream after angry scream, to match the bells.

Half awake, she fell to her feet and lit a candle. The grasping cold took hold of her body like a hand. She flung her dressing gown over her shoulders and stumbled down to the nursery. She lifted the hysterical Adam out of his cot. Nurse and Audrey stared sulkily, sullen with sleep. Catherine held the writhing Adam against her shoulder.

'Silly! Stop! It's only the bells.'

Adam roared. 'Ah! Ah! Aaaaah!' The bells clashed. Her voice cracked as she tried to raise it above the double din. Audrey looked wisely at her, turned and burrowed into her pillow. Adam buried his face against her shoulder and clung, his tears blubbering her nightdress. He stopped screaming.

'Don't they ring beautifully?' said Ellen, her face shining with pride. 'Our father, he always gets up to ring the bells. Our father and Mr Mowsett and Mr Dowell, they always rung the bells ever since they were boy chaps.'

Catherine went to the window. Great stars snapped in a blue sky, the church tower was like black velvet. Impossible to connect its quiet bulk with that pagan racket.

Pagan? Christ was born and the heathen night was being awakened to hear it. A cock crowed against the pealing.

'All right,' Catherine said, 'I'll take him into bed with us. It's quieter there.' Then she smiled at Ellen. 'It must be cold, hard work up there in the tower.'

'Our father, he don't make nothing of it.'

Catherine went back. William flung an arm over Adam.

'Poor little devil, come here.'

Adam snuggled down, snuffling. He felt safe here between two large, protecting people. The awful voices couldn't hurt him here. He tucked his head into William's armpit, sighed, stretched himself out and slept. The bells rang on, striding wider and wider through the dark. Catherine lay flat, jarred and beaten by the sound. Her feet were numb, her knees ached with cold. She stretched out straight, she would soon be warm again. She thought of the village turning in its beds to hear the first Christmas bells for five years . . . and of the women who would turn to find no husband beside them, and of the eldest sons who would hear no more Christmas bells.

She thought. 'They need not . . . they need not . . . why can't they let them sleep . . . ?'

Then she thought of the children wakening to scream at the righteous pursuing voices. Christ was born . . . hunt down evil across the dark . . . Christ was born . . . hunt down war and falsehood . . . Christ was born . . . awake thou that sleepest . . . Christ was born again in Audrey and Adam on the black midnight.

She thought of Ellen's 'our father' and old Mowsett and the taciturn Dowell, and the 'boy chaps' in corduroys and overcoats and mufflers in the cold tower. The hurricane lamp would send the shadows streaking the wrong way up the wall over the card with the changes on it, stuck where the boys could see it. They would be standing there, their hands stiff and knuckly with cold, stiff in the back with pride because they were ringers . . . because they were the ringers who gave a voice to the great tower and let loose the iron voices. . . . Presently they would go home to pipes and grog and lie late in bed because it was Christmas morning . . . the other team would call the village up at six o'clock . . . at six o'clock.

Catherine turned on her side and slept, carried away on a wave of sound.

III

She woke in candlelight. William was sitting on the side of the bed putting on his socks. The air smelt cold and raw. She sat up and began to pull her vest on, huddling the blankets over her shoulders. Her eyes were heavy with sleep.

William kissed her.

That was the surprising, the lovely thing about William. He was just as fond of her when she was tousled and untidy. She kissed the back of his neck and slid to her feet in her petticoat. She pulled an old stuff frock over her head. Thank goodness she had had a bath last night! She ran to the bathroom and splashed her hands and face hurriedly in the ice-cold water. Already the bells were at it. She ran to the day nursery and put a match to the fire, hammered at the nursery door to wake Ellen and Audrey, back along the passage to wake Irene. The house awoke in rustlings, bangings and cracklings of the fire. She twisted her hair up, pulled a velvet cap over her head, shrugged herself thankfully into her greatcoat. William was brushing his hair, William was finding a clean handkerchief, William was cleaning his fingernails. They ran about the room, colliding with one another in the candlelight.

'Hullo,' said William, 'that's the five-minutes bell.'

Adam slept deeply, flat on his back with his arms stretched out, his lips pursed, his cheeks bright red.

Catherine and William ran downstairs and out into the grey frosty morning. The streets were hard as metal, the grass along the side of the road was withered, there were no birds.

The church was immense, shadowy, bare. It smelt strongly of gas and old hassocks. A few gaslights hissed and roared in the vast nave. On the altar the lonely candles burnt pale and stiff. Catherine and William, and two others, knelt in the dusty pitch-pine pews.

The old priest came in, fumbled at the gate of the altar rails, passed into the sanctuary. Then his voice, deep and clear as one of the tower bells, rose surprisingly in the stillness.

'Our father . . .'

Catherine pressed her forehead against the shiny wood of the pew. She thought of her little nursemaid sleepy and proud in her pink flannel nightdress.

Our father.

A simple business. A pity the church forgot that. It was so easy to say 'Our Father'. She knelt, satisfied, for the deep voice was creating for her that country of peace in which, wherever she was, she was at home. It didn't belong only to the big bare church; at any time it would rise round her, its spirit and its beauty would inform the world in which she lived.

The grey morning hesitated at the window-panes, the gas roared, the great ironstone church was hollow as a cave, but the service went on. Catherine and William missed nothing, needed nothing. The church had always been like that, they were used to it, but their God was all about them, and they were happier in their worship than even in their closest moments they were with each other.

Outside the grey sky was wearing thin as though the mist had been stretched too tightly against the blue. The houses they passed exuded a secret and intense smell of frying bacon.

Catherine and William hurried down the road, not arm in arm, because that wouldn't have done, but so close to each other that they were touching, and their sleeves rubbed together.

'I wonder who's going to jerk me out today!' said William.

'You won't have to take a boy with a spade in the back of the car this Christmas – or even a party of people coming back from church to push you up the hill!'

They laughed together as they remembered the deplorable accidents of their snatched and uncertain Christmases.

Catherine ran upstairs. Audrey was dancing about the nursery in her vest, blowing a penny whistle. The air was full of steam from Adam's bath, red with firelight. The mantelpiece was decorated with chocolate mice and soap babies, Adam stood before the fender having his braces buttoned and staring up adoringly.

'Audrey! Your clothes!' Catherine snatched up a pair of knickers and a petticoat. Audrey ran to her, caught her about the knees and rubbed her face against her skirt.

'Stand still, darling,' said Catherine.

She pulled Audrey's blue jersey over her short kilt. Her fat little arms were like sausages. Audrey concentrated seriously upon buttoning her jersey. Catherine flung up the window, took Adam on her knee, and sat down by the fire. She heard William put the tin back in the corn-bin out in the stable yard and run upstairs to wash his hands.

She wondered if they would be as happy if they were rich and important, if they hadn't both of them to work every minute of the day and snatch every chance of saving. It would be peaceful to sit down even for a little while and feel that there was nothing she need hurry to do. But though she and William quarrelled so furiously and suffered so much both from life and from each other, they had had no chance to settle down to the sulky indifference and well-fed boredom of other married couples. Life was a drudgery, life was a grind. The pair of them were, she supposed, pretty small beer, but life had its moments for all that. No one would ever make a song about her love for William, she would never now have time to make it for herself. For Catherine who was sometimes inept and always unequal was on the road to becoming thorough. She was Audrey's, she was Adam's, she was William's . . . a pair of hands and a contriving brain. There was nothing else that mattered any more.

She stood up with Adam in her arms and went down to breakfast.

IV

Audrey and Adam had bought two pink sugar mice with white worsted tails for Christmas presents and a sugar cage with a cardboard bird in it. Neither Catherine nor William had seen anything of the sort since they were children spending hand-warmed pennies at little sweet-stuff shops on a Saturday morning. They looked at each other and laughed.

'Hold yours up by its tail and see if its eyes drop out!'

'It's not a guinea-pig, it's a mouse!'

Audrey stared at them. It had cost her agonies of self-control not to eat even a little bit of the mice, and now they were being treated as something to play with – they might at least have offered her a bit.

They sat down to breakfast. No more presents yet, there wasn't time to sit down and enjoy them. Breakfast, Catherine said, had to be a meal and not a welter of brown paper and string. Catherine spooned porridge into Adam, her mind already running on ahead.

If William's sister Dora and William's brother-in-law John were coming in to tea – as Gregory and Millicent from Hillditch certainly would if the day stayed fine – and if his cousin Grace came as she said she might – if all these people, who, being her husband's people, always left you in doubt to the last minute as to whether they would come or not – if all of them came (her mind envisaged them severally and together, the chairs they would prefer to sit on and the people they would prefer not to sit next to) . . . if they all came, should she give them tea in the drawing-room? Or let them have a fine comfortable human froust in the dining-room, and then escape to the drawing-room where there was room for everybody to spread out and choose their neighbours? They could only have the big oil-lamp to light the dining-room, and the Christmas tree would light the drawing-room for quite a long while . . . till after Irene had cleared out the tea. Yes, it would be the best way.

William's family, collectively, made her feel small and strange. William and the children seemed, when they were all together, to belong to them . . . but the children *were* hers. She had put something into them which the practical, normal, family William came from would never have – a pinch of ginger, a little extra sand. When they were grown-up they would be hers and William's . . . a new combination, a different family.

Audrey went on eating bread and butter and marmalade. It was exciting to eat. It had three tastes. The bitter jelly taste with the candied peel in it, the smooth taste of the butter, and the woolly taste of the bread. Food was wonderful. There was frost on the yew hedge. It was grey and rough, it looked like an old man's head. Adam's bib had two black cats on it . . . like wicked, slinking Tibby, the kitchen cat, who had a private life and didn't want to be loved. Mother's hair was coming down on one side. It had several colours in it . . . some of the hairs were yellow and some were brown, and some were copper like the bowl on the mantelpiece. There was holly in the bowl and the mantelpiece was crowded with cards like a shop window.

Soon she would put on her white coat with the fur collar and her fur cap. That coat and cap made her feel a different and better child. They were so beautiful. She loved to touch them. No one else she knew had a coat and cap half as nice as that. She drummed her heels against the chair in an ecstasy as she thought of it.

'Don't do that, Audrey.'

'Don't what?'

'Don't drum.'

'Why?' Audrey stared at her father.

'Because I tell you not.'

'Because it's a hideous din,' Catherine amended.

Audrey thought about that. Drumming your heels was a hideous din. Din was a new word. Was it a new and special crime? Hideous meant uglier than ugly. She drummed again as she tried to think it out.

'Audrey!'

Audrey stared.

'You have been told once.'

'What is a din?'

'That is.'

'What is?'

'Drumming with your heels.'

'Why is it a din?'

'Because it makes a hideous noise, and disturbs everyone else.'

'Oh.' Audrey wasn't impressed. It didn't disturb her. It made her feel warm and happy.

'Nobody,' Catherine said doggedly, 'nobody has any right at all to upset other people.'

'Oh,' said Audrey.

She watched her mother wiping the crumbs from Adam's mouth. Catherine held him firmly by the back of his neck, and got well down into the corners of his mouth and the creases of his chin, despite his wriggles and protesting whines. When Audrey had children, she meant to hold them by the back of the neck and clean their faces in just that way, however much they wriggled.

V

Catherine and Audrey stood side by side in church. Catherine wondered why Audrey liked to go. Perhaps it was a natural taste for a 'gathering', so few social occasions came Audrey's way. It was not even as amusing as the church of Catherine's day, when the pews were packed tight with ladies in wasp-waisted frocks and flower-garden hats, with old gentlemen in frock-coats and with scrubbed, frizzed, starched little girls in high button boots and white silk gloves, an upholstered, stuffy, and faintly exciting affair, unlike the vacant and drowsy atmosphere of the great stone church in which Audrey stood upon her hassock as lonely as a thrush upon a lawn.

For Catherine matins was a deep pit of fathomless tedium, relieved by moments when some beauty of rhythm or feeling made itself felt through the drab stuff of the service.

But Audrey loved people. She saw people in church who never appeared in the streets during the week. People not in the least like Catherine or William. Old Mr Dudgeon, the solicitor, who carried in front of him a hat which started as a bowler, then changed its mind and went flat on top. Immediately behind the hat came a round swell of waistcoat decorated with two loops of golden chain, behind that his coat curved back like a bird's wings. The hair on the sides of his face was like birds' wings, too, and his deep-set little eyes looked as if they had never missed anything. Then came old Colonel Fraser in tight-fitting grey trousers and a short over-coat, who walked as if he were wearing spurs and sat down as though he thought he had to leave room for his sword. It looked odd to see him without his terriers. There came Mrs Dust in a blue coat which fitted her so closely that you could see the line of her stays across the back. She had so much hair, coiled round and round at the back of her head, that her hat wouldn't go down on to it but had to be held in place by a piece of brown elastic under the coils of hair. Everyone was hurrying, for the bell was slowing down, and the man who pumped the organ was pushing the long wooden bar up and down with all his might, so that Miss Custance might play the choir into their stalls.

The music broke loose, suddenly, the echoes went ringing down the hollow church.

'O coom all ye fy-ithful.'

The choir were singing their way in. Audrey looked about her, around the church, at the congregation which Catherine had once described as looking like a few tall camels in the wilderness.

Jumbo Smalls was singing very loudly and out of time, just to show everybody that he had as good a voice as the rest of the choir, even if he had been turned out for 'shouting' his top notes. He pressed his chin down between the points of his collar and went red in the face and showed the rims of his eyes. Nobody paid the least attention to him.

Dingo Warner had made a pile of three hassocks and was standing on top of them so that the pew only came to the top of his socks. Everyone could see that he hadn't washed the backs of his knees. Mrs Warner was too busy singing to notice him. Her gentle, tired face was turned away from Dingo towards the chrysanthemums on the screen. Audrey wanted to laugh at Dingo, then suddenly she wanted to rush across the aisle to pinch him and make him get down. People were looking at Mrs Warner and grinning. It wasn't her fault Dingo hadn't washed the backs of his knees. Audrey wished

Dingo would look round so that she could put her tongue out to show how she despised him.

The service went on, a monotonous sleepy noise to which Audrey paid very little attention . . . quite a lot of feathers came out of Mrs Oliphant's cushion every time she sat down. She had a special small red cushion to herself, in case the pew gave her lumbago. It got thinner every Sunday because no one ever mended the hole in the corner.

Behind the chrysanthemums and holly the choirboys were sucking cough-drops and whispering whilst Mr Bunny read the lessons. A man in the back row leaned over and hit one of them a loud 'blip' on the head with a Prayer Book. Neither the boy nor Mr Bunny took any notice, and Miss Custance at the organ was quietly setting up the music, but Audrey saw the man looking ruefully at the cover of the book.

Mr Bunny read the lessons in a big, booming voice which hit a pillar and came back, like a second person muttering the lesson after him. His mouth made a hole in his white beard. He had a trick of working his hands up inside the arms of his surplice as he read. Audrey watched him. Suppose he got them stuck up there? Would anyone be allowed to help him get them out, or would the service have to stop?

All at once she sat up, straight and stiff, listening.

Mr Bunny had said 'Bethlehem'.

Mother had said that, and Ellen . . . she pulled at Catherine's skirt, but Catherine's face had a far-off look. Perhaps she was going over her week's accounts in her head, like Mrs Power.

Bethlehem. Then that was a true story. Not a home story. . . . Then the little baby who came from a heaven of gold to lie in a cold stable . . . the baby for whom the bells were rung last night . . . then that baby, and Bethlehem, had something to do with church, and Mr Bunny.

Audrey sat, disturbed and critical. Long afterwards, when the fairy baby had become a human child in a great human story, she was still perplexed and critical. For the child who was born in a stable, preached by the wayside, and died upon a hill, seemed, as she grew older, to have less and less to do with the inside of a church.

Outside the church, Audrey danced on the frosty stones, running round and round Catherine, eager for an explanation.

'Mother. Mr Bunny said Bethlehem. I heard him. He said Bethlehem.'

'Audrey! You mustn't call Mr Brere, Mr Bunny.'

'Daddy does.'

The light of argument lit in Audrey's eyes. She forgot Bethlehem.

VI

Catherine threw a log on the drawing-room fire. It was one of the old pear trees, and gave out a faint, sweet smell.

She swept the hearth, rearranged the chairs and counted them.

Two people on the sofa, two easy chairs, one from the dining-room, one from her bedroom. That made six obviously easy chairs. No one would be left out, sitting on a straight chair and looking as if the iron had entered into their soul. She spread the deerskin rug from the dining-room in the middle of the floor, shook up the cushions and fetched the tree in, ready dressed, from the cupboard under the stairs. In the frosty light the colours looked rich and brilliant. The candles were translucent. She straightened them carefully and put Adam's horse on the table on one side and Audrey's doll on the other. Then she piled up the parcels that had come by post and put beside them the pencil and paper to note down from whom they had come. Sometimes you were left to puzzle them out by the postmark.

In the hall she looked up at the mistletoe. It was good this year, with plenty of berries. She had made it more imposing by tying it with a bunch of red paper ribbon. Nobody ever kissed under it and nobody, Catherine thought sadly, ever would. She put her hand up and touched the yellow leaves. The golden bough! They had peace this year, at least. Perhaps in time goodwill would come too, though in print people were still snarling at each other and nations were 'calling names'.

Ordinary goodwill was so common that nobody noticed it. Three days ago the tyre had come off the wheel of Audrey's pram, so that it limped and wobbled, whilst Adam shrieked and clung to the sides, sure that he would be tipped out. A labourer, cycling home to his dinner, had stopped. He had replaced the tyre, covering his hands with the mixture of grease, grit, and mud which tyres pick up off the road, had barked his knuckle, muddied his coat and received

139

Catherine's thanks with a grin and the – quite genuine – remark that he was only too glad to be of any help.

People were like that.

Catherine fetched a dry mop and cleaned over the hall and the dining-room floors. She polished the dining-room table and set out the best tea-set, the lump sugar (William's sister), the dark fruit cake (William), the fish-paste sandwiches (Gregory), the rye bread (Gregory's wife) and the mixed biscuits (Audrey and Adam).

Her hand hovered over the plate. There was only one pink biscuit. In theory Audrey, the eldest, ought to give way to Adam, actually she always took advantage of a good public to argue the point that the 'eldust' should be served first. Friction in front of the massed forces of William's family? No, not on any account. Catherine removed the biscuit and took it out to Irene, who was cutting bread and butter. Irene looked at it, and put it carefully on the corner of the mantelpiece.

'I'll take it home to our Maggie,' she said.

Catherine knew our Maggie, a heavy lump of a child with a chronic sniff. She realised, afresh, the solidarity of the Oxfordshire family. Any small treat that came Irene's way went to Maggie by right.

Catherine went upstairs and laid out the children's white clothes and fresh socks. She loved to have an excuse to dress them daintily. A fresh blue ribbon for Audrey, a brooch with a blue stone. How wise and right feast days were, and how cleverly Christmas broke up the winter . . . just when the weight of the cold and darkness were beginning to make themselves felt.

She ran down to make up the fire. William was asleep, his hands crossed over a book on his chest. He needed it, he was never still when he was awake. Between the practice and the garden and the chickens, the oil engine for the pump, and the odd jobs of carpentering and repair, he had enough work to keep him going fourteen hours a day and sixteen on Sundays.

They lived as hard as they could, worked like beavers, and were always in debt.

Not that anyone ever pressed them for money. The countryside understood their position and treated them more than fairly. But they both loathed it, and it gave Catherine a nagging sense of dishonesty.

She ran upstairs and washed, splashing the water over her arms and rubbing them vigorously with a rough towel.

Her pink silk dress had been dyed black. It had a white lace collar; Catherine fastened it with an old paste brooch, and put a piece of black velvet ribbon in her hair. But she didn't look either matronly or respectable. She had a gipsy look. She had seen faces like hers, only harder and more weather-beaten, under the naphtha flares at St Giles's Fair.

She looked at her own face, without much affection, and wondered when she had better tell William that she thought that she was going to have another child. She was still doubtful, but on the edge of certainty. She hunted out a clean handkerchief. Not yet, she thought, not till after the January bills have been paid. She didn't really care very much, things were so dreadfully difficult already that a little more or less wasn't going to make very much odds.

She shivered. The room, with its four open windows, was cold. She must remember to shut all the windows before tea. William's people liked the air to be of one dense, even texture from one end of the room to another, like an invisible felt. It made Catherine and Adam stream at the eyes and nose all night afterwards, but the greatest good of the greatest number had to be considered.

She took the presents from the top drawer and looked at them, ruefully. Money didn't go far. It was a pity she was such a poor needlewoman. Books, pipes, and pocket handkerchiefs didn't make very large parcels. Still, the things were the best she could buy, none of them were bargains. From the bottom of her soul Catherine hated a bargain. There was always a catch in it, somewhere.

She ran downstairs. In so large a house she had got out of the habit of walking from one place to another. The fires were burning brightly. The big bunches of holly and ivy out of the garden gleamed darkly over the gilded picture frames. She looked up at the old brown picture of the mill, she had realised how often her eyes came to rest on it; she didn't notice how often Adam looked at it, too.

She thought the room looked warm, clean, and welcoming. She straightened the candles on the Christmas tree and William, stretching, stood up and kissed the back of her neck. His lips felt warm after the cold air upstairs, and slack with sleep.

'I must have just dropped off! What a rotten waste of an afternoon!'

VII

Audrey stood and looked at the Christmas tree. She had had a good tea, though not as good as she would have liked, or could have managed. Now there was this new and shining thing. The little spindling thuya which she had seen, dusty and lonely, in its pot, stood translated. Its spiky boughs stood out stiffly, bright with red, yellow, and pink butterflies, hot and shimmering with candles.

The points of the flames strained upwards, there was a smell of warm wax. She was too happy to shout or sing. She was so happy that she had a hollow feeling in the pit of her stomach. It hurt, yet she wished that this minute could go on for ever. The wonderful tree was true. It was much truer than walks, and tooth-brushing and being put to bed, and all the things that happened every day. . . . Someone threw on a log and with a crash the fire reddened and a shower of sparks flew up, like goldfinches disturbed in wayside thistles.

Catherine pushed parcels into her hand to give round. Audrey stood glumly, looking down at them. She wanted to go on looking at the tree. Ungraciously, quickly, she pushed them into the hands of the family, sitting round on chairs. Then she stood looking. Two things to watch at once . . . the opening of the parcel and the surprised and pleased face of the person who was opening it.

Catherine rolled up string and folded brown paper, rescued useful cardboard boxes and labels. Audrey and Adam were hurrying through their own parcels now, quickly, skimpily, with one eye on the tree.

It was going well. It was going to be all right. They all looked comfortable, settled. The critical chill of the beginning had thawed out. The candles had long black wicks, and there was a smell of hot pine needles. Spatters of wax were falling on the floor, flames shot and towered. William began to blow candles out, puffing his cheeks and making a great fuss. Everyone laughed. Audrey ran round the tree crying out: 'Look! Come! Here's another!'

Somebody was blowing up a balloon. Adam was winding up a mechanical engine and letting it run down again, wheels in air. Everyone was eating chocolates.

Catherine gave Adam his toy horse and Audrey her doll. Adam patted the horse all over, slowly, his face grave and puzzled. Almost he seemed afraid of it. Audrey turned her doll up and looked at its cotton drawers, pulled its frock down over its fat pink stockinette thighs, prodded its eyes, and dropped it face downwards on the floor.

A thin wailing pierced the noise in the room.

I saw three ships coom sai-iling in.

William hunted in his pockets.

'Poor little devils! Fancy having nothing better than that to do on Christmas night!'

The voices swelled as Irene opened the front door.

And 'oo d'you think was in them then,
      in them then, in them then,
Joseph and hi'is young lydy!

'Sheer blasphemy,' Mrs Gregory said, nearly choking over a chocolate. 'Don't give them a penny. Not one penny.'

144

William dumped the coppers into Audrey's hands.

'Run out, kiddy. That'll stop 'em.'

Catherine took the hall lamp and went out with Audrey. A row of children's faces swam up suddenly out of the darkness outside.

Now Christmas is 'ere,

they chanted:

We wish you good che-er,
We wish you a merry Christmas and a
     Happy New Year.

Round eyes, blinking in the lamplight, round red noses, open mouths, bright-coloured mufflers crossed on their chests. They looked like young birds waiting to be fed. Audrey dumped all the coppers into the nearest hand.

'Now then . . . g'way!' she said firmly.

She didn't want them to go. She thought 'Three Ships' was beautiful. Even better than 'Abey my Boy' or 'Who's your lady friend?' and the other things that those lucky creatures, the children who were allowed out after dark, sang in the streets.

The children grabbed the money and ran, their boots clattering up the frosty street.

'Poor little beggars,' said Catherine.

'Young varmints,' said Irene, slamming the door. 'I'd learn them to beg. My mother she warmed our Maggie to rights, the only time she went out carolling.'

Adam had got Audrey's doll. He was hugging it, mutely, but protectively. The creature's pink arm hung down over his

145

wrist, he stroked its head, crooning softly. Catherine drew an unhappy breath, awaiting outcry and violence from Audrey.

Audrey walked straight across the room to the wooden horse and ran round with it, banging the wheels and shouting. Her curls bobbed, her eyes were bright. Catherine looked at the pair of them. Well! You never knew!

She sat down on the floor at William's feet and rested her head against him. Two balloons were being tossed about. Gregory's wife and Edward's wife were talking frocks, nobody noticed the noise that Audrey was making.

William put his hand on her shoulder. He was glad that his family had chosen his house to meet in. It wasn't really central, but they had all come. He was proud of Catherine and of Audrey and Adam, and of the pair of home-grown cockerels they'd had for lunch. He'd never bought a pair of birds like that anywhere else, so large and yet so tender. That was a good cake Catherine had made, too. Dark and close, and full of bits of peel. This sort of thing was what he worked for, wasn't it?

He liked the black ribbon in Catherine's hair. She was a nice-looking wench, when she wasn't overtired or untidy. A messy worker . . . but a trier. He pressed his hand a little harder on her shoulder, and wished that life allowed them more of such evenings.

PART THREE

CHAPTER ONE

I

Slowly, laboriously, the years swung through the cycle of the seasons, crawling up to April, tumbling over into the glory of May, waning, falling away like a dead leaf, and leaving behind them as little impression as is made by a leaf's fall. Catherine wondered that so much trouble should have so little result.

The same tomorrow, and the day after that, the same next spring, next autumn, next year, the year after next.

'Audrey! Blow your nose. Don't sniff.'

'Adam. Lift your feet up. Don't shuffle.'

'Bill! Bill! Drop that. It's not yours.'

'Oh, Irene! It's no good. We simply can't afford to burn coal at that rate.'

'All right, William. . . . Coming!'

Round and round, with a steady swing from Monday to Saturday, without pause, without break, without any apparent progress. Yet there were changes, for William seemed to get further away, the children's needs seemed to become every day more insistent, more diverse.

Sometimes she would look up to see that the country round her was changing too.

The country of William's boyhood had gone. The white roads, cambered for horse traffic, and worn into wheel tracks at each side, had vanished altogether. The wide, black, tyre-polished roads, filmed with oil, were changing the face of the country. Trees Catherine and William had grown to love and look for were cut down. They missed the familiar print of their boughs upon the sky in winter, and the blocks of shade upon the wayside grass in June. It seemed to be nobody's business to replant, although in the open country the loss of a tree was as remarkable as the loss of a house or a hill.

Houses came slowly, the neighbourhood was not one which tempted the bungalow builder, but cars came through all day long, and all of them left something, more or less unsavoury, on the wayside grass. Torn newspaper, greasy cotton waste, orange and banana skins, cigarette cartons, broken bottles, egg shells, old motor tyres . . . anything the motorist couldn't be bothered to take home with him.

The people looked at the roadside, and turned sourly to watch the swarming cars. Town people were a shiftless set at best. It looked as if some of them had too much money into the bargain.

One by one the woods to which Catherine had taken her children were scattered with litter, sprouted notice-boards, and went out of bounds. The streams, below the bridges on the main road, were fouled with tins and torn paper. The kingfisher, who had always lived below the first of them, moved his quarters.

The world in which Bill crawled and stamped, and finally tramped sturdily about, was one which had already changed its tempo.

Catherine considered these things as she pushed the pram along the road which ran straight as a canal along the ridge of the hill. It shone like water. The elm trees were crimson with catkins, the hedges a tangle of new reds and browns. She and Audrey and Adam knew the look of the road so well that every tree, the position of every gate, stack and barn was printed on their minds for ever. They knew how far it was in paces, in chains, furlongs, and miles. They had raced it, told stories over it, shut their eyes and been led over it, sung it to 'Marching through Georgia', 'Loch Lomond' and 'We want a wet canteen said the privates' till the very sight of it was a weariness. But every wet afternoon they were forced to turn up it, away from the roaring, overtaking, uncivil traffic on the high road. It was increasingly difficult to keep Audrey and Adam interested, to find new material for their minds to work on. But today they were busy. They leaned across Catherine, shouting at each other across her skirts and against the spring wind.

'I shall swim in the sea, and then I shall go up to the prairie and catch my prairie horse and race you up to the top of my snow mountain . . .'

'It's not my snow mountain. I'm not going up the snow mountain. I shall go back to my palace, and have tea, and dance.'

'We'll dance this evening. We're going up the snow mountain. Up . . . and up . . .'

'Silly. You've forgotten the fight. You can't go up the mountain if we're going to have a fight . . . I've made them dig pits on the beach with spikes in the bottom. And then when the enemy land and come rushing up the beach they'll all fall in and lie in a mix at the bottom . . .'

'Or let loose tigers . . . a regiment of wild tigers.'

'Wild elephants.'

'I said tigers first. Didn't I, Mother . . . Mother, I did say tigers.'

'Yes,' said Catherine absently. 'Bright yellow tigers.'

'Elephants and tigers,' Audrey insisted.

'Won't they just run back to the ships when they see the elephants and tigers coming. Hoo! Silly old enemy!'

Their voices rose shriller and shriller, they took long, hopping steps in their flopping gum-boots.

One wet day they had drawn the island in chalks on the floor of an empty attic. A green island with brown, caterpillar mountains and a blue rim of sea. It was Adam who had made it come alive, who had covered it with fir trees and green mossy glades with lakes of still water. Its few inhabitants lived in log huts and devoted the endless leisure of their days to fresh-water fishing. Sometimes they 'went gay' and wandered about by droves at night, singing. Adam, the ruler of the place, put this down sternly. But Audrey, with her wider range of needs, had annexed, altered, and improved the island. It was a gayer place now, but Catherine and Adam loved it less.

They were still wrangling over it when Catherine stopped at a gate to draw breath.

In a raw field of stubborn earth a man was driving a two-horse plough. The heavy clay clogged the horses' feet, their fetlocks were ropy with it, their flanks were dark and streaky with sweat. Heads down, manes flying, they strained forward against a background of far blue hills and trees. Man and horses were alone upon an empty countryside. Catherine stopped, taken, as always, by the beauty of the difficult movement, by the solid furrows, shining blue on one side and dark brown upon the other, and by the satisfying pattern of their converging lines. The children climbed up the gate and leaned their elbows on the top bar.

Bill, who had been sitting upright in his pram with the oily complacency of a soapstone Buddha, leaned forward, watching happily. He loved horses. He loved all animals, but horses above all. They were large, gentle and hairy. He loved their sad, kind eyes and their warm, dusty smell. He would follow a horse with his eyes as far as he could see it.

Catherine watched his face. Bill was so easy, although he had such a dreadful temper. He found his own interests. He was always busy. Audrey and Adam had to have their interests induced for them . . . and now there was this queer business of the island, which had been Adam's and was now Audrey's . . .

But they had stopped talking of the island. They raced ahead singing:

B with an I, I with an N, N with a G . . .

It was a pity they lived in such a lone village. There were plenty of Christmas parties, birthday parties and hay parties, but there was no one to come in and out every day and rub their corners off. She sometimes thought they were getting very cornery indeed.

Audrey and Adam weren't sociable. Their shadowy wrangle over the island was more real to them than any other child could be. Sometimes Catherine worried because they hated to go out.

'But why should I if I don't want to?' Audrey would protest. 'I could stay at home in the garden.'

'You've been hanging about the garden all the morning worrying me about what you're to do.'

'I shan't know what to say to them.'

'Don't say anything. You've only got to do what the others are doing. You'll soon find plenty to say.'

Audrey would give up, sullenly. She couldn't explain to Catherine that she hated strangers. People were different when you knew them, but it added to her difficulties that her manners, from sheer nervousness, became bad.

She knew that she talked too much and too loudly, that she grabbed at the food, hung back when a game was started and played boisterously at the end. All the time she was on edge, and all the time Catherine, anxious too, was watching her.

Catherine was distressed that Audrey made so little response to the friendliness of her neighbours. For they were friendly. There were endless small occasions, picnics, garden teas, treasure hunts, planned for the children alone.

It was pitiful that Audrey should be shy of Robin's mother, working valiantly round her huge vicarage and bringing up Robin on a new system every half year, or of shy, slow, engaging Robin, with his snub nose, his freckles, and his wide smile. Or of Hilary's mother, breaking in ponies, growing early garden stuff, and eking out the pension of a lieutenant's widow as best she could . . . or of her bluff, noisy, and gorgeously stupid sons. There were so many friendly and gracious people who filled their houses with children from twenty miles round in an all-embracing hospitality. There was a quality about these parties which made them memorable, a simplicity and warm friendliness, a real desire to give pleasure.

The wet day, the children's intimate hostility over the island, their loneliness, all these things hung about Catherine like a cloud as she tramped steadily on up the wet road. She felt on edge, at the end of her patience with them and with herself.

II

The road dipped steeply downhill. Audrey and Adam ran back to her.

'The brook . . . the brook . . . go down to the brook.'

'All right. But you must help me pull Bill back again.' Audrey and Adam tore down the hill. Catherine frowned, straining back to keep the perambulator from running away from her. Suppose they fell? Adam made a shattering noise if he fell, even if he wasn't hurt, and their clothes wouldn't stand many more of the savage brushings they had had to have that winter.

They ran safely, flung themselves on their stomachs on the low parapet.

It wasn't safe. Catherine bit her lip. It would be worse to
call them back and frighten them, for both were naturally
timid. She hurried down, her eyes on their waving heels.

The river was yellow, thick as milk, gorged with snow water,
streaked and flecked with patches of foam. The dumb brook
had found a voice, full, deep, and hurrying. Bits of stick and
straws whirled and danced.

Audrey and Adam threw twigs in on one side and raced
across to see them come out on the other.

Upstream half a dozen youths out of work were walking
aimlessly across the fields with a wire-haired terrier. At the
brook's edge they, too, stopped and began throwing sticks.
The terrier, yelping, flung itself into the stream.

The current took the little brute and swung it round,
its draggled head and black muzzle just above the water. It
pawed helplessly, was carried backwards, choking, and sucked
down under the bridge.

Adam screamed.

'Oh! Save it! Save it!'

Audrey dashed to the parapet and hung over, whilst
Catherine held her skirts.

The dog shot out from under the bridge, still struggling.

'It's all right. It hasn't knocked its head. Look . . . the
current's bringing it in.'

The river swirled it into a backwater, where it found its feet
and scrambled up the bank. It stood, its sides heaving, its
head hanging down, dripping with yellow water.

A youth ran down the bank, grinned, touched his cap to
Catherine, seized the dog by the scruff of the neck and ran

back down the field. He regained his friends, shouted something, laughed, and threw the puppy in again.

Catherine gasped. Adam began to cry. Audrey ran to the other parapet, shaking both fists in the air, stamping, breathless with rage.

Back into Catherine's mind flashed the picture of a farm boy on the Cornish sands, flogging a horse which was struggling to 'break out' a heavy cartload of seaweed. She had run to tell him to prop the wheel or lighten the load. He had stared at her, angry at her interference in a piece of work she couldn't have done herself. Two minutes later, from the top of the cliff, she had seen him lashing the horse, more fiercely than before, because she had shamed him.

She put her hand on Audrey's shoulder. 'Don't! Come away. No, Adam. They won't let it drown. . . . It's horrid . . . but they don't understand . . . they think it's a joke.'

'Why?' Audrey asked.

'Want of imagination.'

Audrey looked at her, and filed the long word for reference.

Catherine set them to pull the pram from the front, by the curved springs. Laughing and pulling, they forgot the terrier, but not, Catherine knew, for long.

She wished they hadn't to see things like that. A few days ago a calf, with its head in a sack, had escaped from the slaughterhouse and run blindly into the street, chased by the butcher. Adam had wept helplessly. 'It can't see! Oh! It can't see!' and they had hurried away out of sight.

Last spring they had found a bird's nest in the grass at the side of a farm road. They had watched it till the eggs hatched

157

out and the nest was full of shapeless naked birds with gaping beaks. Then, one morning, they had gone to look, and there was nothing left but a hoof-mark and a mess of trodden flesh and moss and sticks. A horse, going back to pasture, had put its hoof down and wiped the nest out.

Catherine was town-bred. Life in a town was more decently covered, better managed. She wondered if it was as good an upbringing. Cruelty, ugliness, blind misfortune, they were everywhere. In the country, children came to know about them early. Audrey and Adam wouldn't expect as much of life as she had done. But it was difficult to teach them to believe in a merciful God when a horse could, in ignorance, put its foot upon a nest of singing birds, and a calf had to die, in panic, in the dark.

Catherine, pondering, remembered how difficult it was to remember physical pain, or even ugliness. Yet, every time she encountered them they shocked, not her eyes, but some more sensitive inner self.

Yet still more strangely, the episode of the dog had broken up the heavy strain of the morning, the tension within herself and between the children had snapped. Audrey and Adam ran ahead, singing. She felt lighter, almost happy.

She thought, what a beast I am to be made happy by a little excitement. But no, she thought. It wasn't that.

For a moment they had all felt together, in sympathy, and strongly, about the same thing. It was the first time that it had happened.

III

At the cross-roads they stopped to let a string of hunters, out for exercise, go through. Sleek, shining, supple, the beautiful creatures picked their way over the greasy tarmac. Bill watched them. He loved the play of the long, interlacing muscles under the cropped coat on their withers, the high gloss on their haunches, their quivering, smartly-docked tails. He wished he was a stable boy, sitting, grave and responsible, perched up in the saddle. He leaned forward, his eyes shining.

'When will there be another meet?' asked Audrey.

'Another meet!' clamoured Adam.

'Not till next winter.'

Next winter. A century. A lifetime. Their feet dragged as they crossed the road.

They stopped. There was confusion at the crossroads. A car was ramming on squealing brakes. There were shouts of: 'Hi!'

Catherine spun round. She saw a youth running, slipping, recovering himself, all in a flash, in front of a big touring car. The car skidded sideways, came to rest. The youth saved himself by a hair's breadth, slipped again in the mud and lurched onto the grass. Catherine saw that a draggled puppy, yellow with water, hung by the collar from one hand.

He stood the puppy on its feet and, quite unconscious of angry shouts from the car, felt its legs over carefully, whilst the little brute licked his hands, wriggling and squirming. The youth looked up as the car moved off.

'If so be as you'd run over him I'd have . . . well, pushed your . . . face in!' he shouted.

CHAPTER TWO

Catherine shot the lesson books into a drawer and slammed it shut.

She felt limp and discouraged. Audrey watched her, sullenly. Adam, who had been crying steadily for ten minutes, dropped off his chair, perfectly cheerful, snatched a mouth-organ from the dresser, and ran up the garden. Audrey followed him with a supercilious stare. She wished she could cry as easily as he could. But Adam was a fool. There he was, sticking at 'at et it ot ut' whilst she was reading *Tales of Troy and Greece*.

Catherine flung up the window and leaned out into the garden. The very air of the room seemed charged with irritation and with Adam's facile emotion.

Parents, she thought, ought not to teach their own children.

They cared too much, expected too much of them. Because they cared so much they were impatient, they exacted, drove, baffled the child, and then punished it for stupidity.

But, as always, there was no money. There was no one else to teach them.

Catherine knew that her teaching was faulty. She was too much afraid of failure. So much depended on the children's doing well at school. William could only afford to keep them there the shortest possible time. They must find work at once when they left.

It was fortunate that Audrey learnt easily and intelligently, that she wrote fluently, and that her memory was remarkable. But figures had no meaning for her, and no beauty.

'But figures are dead easy,' William would argue. 'You can always be sure of them once you've grasped a few simple rules.'

Leaning against the window, Catherine remembered how William had taught her the simple recurring pattern of the tables, and how for her, too, figures had neither meaning nor beauty.

Table by table, rule by rule, she had driven simple arithmetic into Audrey, whilst Adam, like William, looked on and marvelled that anyone could hesitate over a thing so simple.

Catherine had had to work Audrey's sums out overnight, and prove them with beans before the eyes of the sceptical Audrey. William, discovering her paraphernalia, had laughed at her and loved her. She sighed, feeling that in a better world it would be unnecessary to teach anything so difficult.

It was more serious that Adam could not read. A girl could get on well enough without much arithmetic. But reading! Letters meant nothing to Adam, conveyed no mental picture. And he was tone deaf. He learnt each word separately, like an ideograph.

Adam got to the pitch of nervous exasperation where he simply blubbered at the sight of a book. A week ago Catherine, in despair, had turned him over to Ellen.

'He's an awful child,' Ellen confessed, at the end of four lessons. 'I can't do nothing with him neither. He won't heed.'

Catherine wondered if it wasn't good for Adam not to heed. Adam's mind, like his delicate body, was developing slowly. He was finding it difficult to grow, he wasn't ready to learn. A wiser world would have left him to his scribbling paper, his sums, and his mapping pen, and would have grasped that what he had been told, or had seen pictured, was his at once, and for ever. But life was getting more difficult for the boy who broke step. There was no common entrance, no public school for the backward youngster, and behind the common entrance lengthened the shadow of matriculation.

They had already had the list of subjects required by Adam's preparatory school.

Reading and writing, simple arithmetic as far as vulgar fractions, a general outline of English history and the geography of the world. A little French, and most certainly the beginnings of Latin. It was a good deal to cram into the head of a boy who had no intention of learning anything at all.

Catherine knew that William was hiding his disappointment from her. He had always wanted Adam to go to his own school, had looked forward, unreasonably, to the day when Adam would take a scholarship. He had never had any difficulty in passing examinations, he had expected his boy to have the same mind. The mind, in the game of cross purposes known as inheritance, had gone to Audrey.

Adam was quite happy so long as he was allowed to do sums, or to lie on the hearthrug drawing pictures of the Danes, in fat, black, greasy lines, demanding money from

Ethelred, in thin and wobbly ones, or of Hector being dragged round the walls of Troy, and he would cover pages with meaningless interlacing lines which Catherine presently discovered to make quite a clever pattern.

Adam was a terrible problem. He ran through her fingers like water, his mind simply eluded control. He would learn exactly what he wanted to learn, in his own way and at his own pace; beyond that he would learn nothing at all.

Catherine stood up. Life, which seemed in detail so slow, so horribly tedious, was really a race. A race to catch up on their debts, a race to develop efficiency, both in themselves and in their children. She heard William come into the hall.

He looked across the width of the room at her.

'Well?'

She shook her head. 'William, it's no good. I'm not doing them any good.'

William flung his hat on a chair.

'You teach them jolly well.'

'I lose patience with them. Adam gets on so slowly.'

'Little devil. I'll talk to him!'

'Oh . . . better leave him alone. But he's not really dull. If he was it wouldn't matter.'

'He's bone idle.'

'If somebody else were teaching him . . . if he were being taught a different way . . .'

'Who else is going to teach him? Can you tell me that?'

'I'm afraid of hurting them . . .'

'I'd hurt them. You give me half a chance. Besides, what the devil are you worrying about? They're only kids.'

'Even kids have to know a lot when they go to school. Adam can't read anything at all yet.'

'Couldn't Ellen teach him?'

'No. He simply yelled. I had to take him back.'

'Well, who on earth is going to teach him? I ask you! Can we afford to pay a governess?'

'No.'

'Well. They've got to put up with it, and so have you.'

'It isn't putting up with it. . . . It matters so much.'

'What on earth can I do?'

William stared at her, uncomprehendingly. Why did she make such a fuss? Such a ridiculous fuss. No child wanted to learn anything. It never did. If only she wouldn't be so earnest. He was tired already by the long morning, and the day wasn't half over.

Catherine blinked, her eyes full of tears. She was full of the rage of a person who is being forced to do something he knows that he doesn't do well, full of rage with William because he wouldn't understand her point of view. It gave her a caged, desperate sensation. She wanted to shake William, to hit him, to beat understanding into him.

'I suppose you can't do anything,' she said bitterly. 'But if you'd only try to understand. If you'd only think. I can't see a way out.'

'What can I do? By the Lord, Catherine, I do enough already.'

'You might try to do something about it . . . if it's only what I'm doing wrong. They're yours as much as mine. You ought to help me.'

'Oh! Ought I! I work, don't I? What else can I do? Can you tell me that? You tell me what it is that you want me to do and I'll do it.'

William went out and slammed the door. Catherine looked at the panels. The stupid tears smarted in her eyes.

She was a fool, to expect William to understand. Why should he? It was her job. Yet, unreasonably, she hated him. She wiped her eyes. She would go on. She had always meant to go on. But if only William could have understood her feeling of defeat.

She opened the hall door. Audrey and Adam, chattering lustily and already very grubby, were being dragged in from the garden by Ellen to get ready for lunch.

CHAPTER THREE

Catherine still had letters from Violet every week. Sometimes Catherine wondered why she wrote. Perhaps Violet really had an affection for her which never showed itself when they met. Perhaps the weekly letter was simply one of the things that Violet did.

For Violet, in a changing world, remained unchanged. She still wore her neat coats and skirts and smart hats, still knew the same set of people, bought her food in the same shops, went to town in a tram and walked out in the afternoon to call on her friends. She gave the effect of being more than ten years older than Catherine. Her mind, her opinions, her habits and even her mode of dressing had scarcely changed in twenty years.

Then, one day in early summer, came a letter over which Catherine knitted her forehead. She put the letter in her pocket. It would have to stand over till she and William were alone.

In the afternoon she took it up the garden to him. William looked over his shoulder from amongst the apple trees.

'Read it to me.'

Catherine sat down on the edge of the wheelbarrow.

'Edward's broken down . . . or retired. I don't know which.'

'What! Edward?'

'So Violet says. Listen. "Edward says he isn't going back to the office any more. He says he's going to sell this house and go and live in the country. He won't listen to what I say. He says the office is more than he can bear. What we are to live on I don't know. Nothing I say makes the least difference. I can't get Se to come down. Edward says he won't talk to him if he does. He says he never could stand either him or Jane, and he doesn't care if they know it. He won't reason it out with me. He just has to have his own way at once and I'm not to be considered at all."'

'Well!' William paused in his pruning. 'Who ever would have thought that Edward would quit?'

Catherine felt puzzled. No one had ever thought of Edward. No one ever reckoned Edward in. He had gone his way so quietly, had always been so satisfactory, kind, and obliging. She tried to remember his face. Now she thought of it, it had always had a patient, worried look.

'"And what's the use if he wants to come back later?"' she read on. '"If he sells out we shan't be able to come back. Everybody's talking about it and sympathising with me . . . Everyone knows. They would! And Edward just says, 'I've had enough of it and I'm going to give up, and I don't care what you say. Will you go out of this room and keep quiet?' I wish William would write to him."'

'No,' William objected. 'Poor old horse. I'm blowed if I do.'

'It's awful for Violet,' Catherine explained. 'She simply can't see his point of view. All she can see is the upset, and the bother of the thing.'

She turned a page of the letter.

"'Jane's no use to me at all. She isn't even coming home. She won't be there to help me with the move, and you know how much help Edward is likely to be. She's going to the Dolomites with some friends she's made in Town. People I've never heard of. She says Edward has a perfect right to do exactly as he likes, and if it doesn't suit me I can break away and make a life of my own. Me! I told Edward he ought to go for a sea voyage and take three months for it. I told him not to mind me, I wouldn't be left alone in any other circumstances, but I'd understand it if he wanted a holiday. He wouldn't listen.'"

'He wouldn't go,' William said.

He and Catherine looked at each other.

'It's no good telling Violet what I think,' Catherine concluded wearily. 'She ought simply to give in to him and go with him . . . but she'll have to go right away from her own life. She'll have to live in a place where she gets her shoes muddy when she goes out, and walk along country roads alone, which she hates. And she'll have to make do with a day girl and only see a hat shop once a month . . . and then she won't be able to afford a hat. I suppose Edward's been dreaming of this all his life, and never even told her.'

'Do her good.'

William wondered about Edward, that reliable, earnest soul who had always appeared to be so contented. Had he been simmering, unhappily, all the time, or was his breakdown just some freak of age and ill health?

He stopped pruning and looked through the branches at Catherine.

'Old girl . . . if you think I'm going to do that . . . scold me . . . pull me up sharp.'

'I shouldn't want to scold you. Would it do any good?'

'Yes. It would.'

Catherine put the letter away. 'You know, I'm sorry for Edward. Of course, he isn't considering Violet. He simply wants to get out . . . now . . . at once. If he wasn't a reasonable soul he would simply have walked out and left everything in a mess. I do so understand how he feels.'

William stopped pruning. 'Why? Do you want to get away from me?'

'Not from you in particular. Just from the mess and bother of things. From always being tied down and kept in.'

'Do you feel tied down and kept in?'

'Sometimes. Don't be silly. You know you feel like it, too.'

'There's too much work sometimes, and not enough money. I want to do a great many things I can't do. And never shall. But get away? No.'

Catherine rubbed her forehead with the back of her hand. She thought that a great many people would have understood what she meant. Not young people like Jane whose restlessness was part youth and part fashion, but staid, surprising people like Edward.

William was on the other side of an apple tree. The shears

clicked and a long twig, straight and clean, innocent of fruit buds, fell into Catherine's lap.

'It's not only me. People are so restless.'

'You mean that you always knew what a steady old horse like Edward was going to do? He's always run in harness. Well, now the harness has worn out, for one thing.'

'You mean . . .'

'People used to know exactly where they were. They were kept in place by a set of ideas and a social position. Now the ideas are exploded and the social position hardly counts. . . .'

'Are we to be left at the mercy of noisy people like Jane? People who let someone else do their thinking for them?'

'Who did the thinking for Edward and Violet . . . or for you for that matter?'

'It wasn't done for me.'

'Wasn't it! I bet you read Kipling and H G Wells and wore one of those silly tight skirts and talked through your hat about the right of every woman to have a child.'

'I suppose I did.'

'Did you think all that out for yourself? Now they read Freud and D H Lawrence and their rights stop short of the children. They're not in such a hurry to make trouble for themselves. . . . See?'

'You mean Edward has left off believing in the things he used to believe in and that he's too old to collect a new set?'

'That's what I meant.'

'It's not only that. Do you remember the new heaven and the new earth we were all to have after the War?'

William had moved to the next bush. There was nothing further to be said about either Edward or Violet and his trees needed pruning.

Catherine rested her forearms on her knees. A thrush was singing. She wondered why people wanted so much . . . why they were always trying to improve each other and the world. A thrush in a green garden, cool sheets at night, the knowledge that your children were sleeping safely under the same roof. . . . Why want more?

But she wanted more. She wanted her children to be people of importance. She wanted complete understanding with her husband. She wanted to be sure she was of some use in the world and behind all those wants she was a mass of petty, foolish vanities and desires, many of them so cheap and silly that she hardly liked to own she needed them.

William whistled as he went on pruning. Far up the garden the thrush sang.

CHAPTER FOUR

I

William was working in his greenhouse. He had three of them, all without heat, and all in a ruinous condition. If they had a little money he could have repaired them, put heat into them, and made them pay. But there was never any money and now, with the children's schooling to be thought of, there would be less money than ever.

There was none for holidays, for theatres, for new clothes for Catherine, or new curtains for the house. There was no money for anything but the barest decencies and necessities. When other members of the family showed him the new piano, gramophone or car which had been that year's acquisition he felt sore that he, in his turn, had acquired nothing. He disliked his home, its lamp-smoked ceilings, smudged walls, and faded curtains. Only his gardens and glasshouses were tolerable.

He could contrive to grow better tomatoes and chrysanthemums than anyone he knew. His poultry also produced more and larger eggs. The others either had to buy these things or go without them.

He worked steadily, potting up chrysanthemums. The dull midsummer day hesitated on the brink of rain.

He wished he had more pots. Perhaps this year he would be able to sell enough tomatoes to buy one or two more casts. Last year they had spent the money on fruit for jam, this year the trees were coming into bearing. He would strike more cuttings of the late white chrysanthemums. It was no good growing coloured flowers. Most of those he sold went into churches or onto graves.

Adam drifted in and stared. He liked the smell of the greenhouse as he liked everything about the garden. The smell of dried earth and decayed leaves in the upper house, where William was working, the smell of damp earth and acid tomato foliage in the lower house, the dark tanks full of water . . . the colour of the broken shards of earthenware . . . the smell of the dry moss William was putting in the bottom of the pots . . . all these meant something to him, they appealed to him in a way that no book had done or ever would.

Edging in closer he watched his father. He would have liked to put the crocks in the pots, they made a jolly pattern, always different. The dry moss made him remember the day in the woods when he had run about and found banded snail shells, primroses, mauve and white violets, and black-stemmed ferns. He had picked so little moss that Catherine had made him carry the wet, heavy sack down through the woods to the car. The sacking had hurt his hands and scrubbed the backs of his knees.

He leaned against a pot and upset it with a crash. William leapt towards it.

'Not broken! My God! That's lucky for you. Why can't you look what you're doing?'

'I don't know, Father.'

'Why haven't you got anything to do?'

Adam stared resentfully. He had got something to do. He was learning to pot up a plant. He didn't know that he was learning, he only knew that he was occupied and happy.

'I don't know, Father.'

'Then get out.'

Adam hesitated. He wanted a trowel. He was making an edging to his garden, an edging of white stone. He wanted to ask, but he was afraid that William would say no. Bill would have asked, because Bill never seemed to notice when William or Catherine were angry. He was simply angry back again. Adam was afraid. He stared at the trowel.

'Get out, can't you?'

Adam took the trowel and ran. Catherine, digging out ground elder in the bed under the glasshouse wall, looked up and saw him.

'Adam. Did Father say you could have that?'

Adam ran on.

'Will . . . iam!'

William didn't answer. He was working against time. There was more to do than he could manage. At any moment someone might call him out. That was one of the joys of a doctor's life. Let her shout. If she wanted anything she could come to him. Catherine pulled herself to her feet and went round to the greenhouse. Her face was anxious, frowning.

'Oh, Lord! What is it now?'

'Did you say Adam might have that trowel?'

'No. I'm blowed if I did. Make him bring it back.'

Catherine went down the garden with her hand fork. Adam was really working. He had cleared a space of waste ground and picked out the stones, he was busy fencing it in. He was making a trench and stamping the stones in thoroughly.

'Adam!'

He looked up, and put his trowel behind him.

'You mustn't take Daddy's trowel. He can't work if you do. Take the fork. And don't leave it out all night.'

She thought: 'I must remember, at tea-time, to see that he doesn't. For he will.'

Adam never put anything away when he had finished with it. His mind never seemed to reach forward to the fact that he would need it next time. He was genuinely aggrieved if the thing were spoilt or broken.

She put the trowel back on the glasshouse staging and took the big fork.

'What do you want that for?'

'For the ground elder.'

'Where's the hand fork?'

'I lent it to Adam.'

'What on earth did you do that for? How do you expect him ever to learn anything if you give way to him like that?'

'I wanted him to finish what he is doing.'

'What I want to know is this. When are these children going to learn what is theirs and what isn't? Nothing's safe from them.'

Catherine went to the door. 'I do tell them.'

She knew it was a grave defect in her own nature that property meant so little to her. She simply didn't care about 'things' except at the moment that she was using them. She couldn't make herself angry about a chipped cup or a lost book or a trowel that had been left out in the wet. They mattered, but they mattered very little in comparison with the fact that Audrey or Adam had learnt to wash up the cup or read the book or used the trowel. She tried incessantly to be careful and methodical because things, once lost or broken, couldn't be replaced. There was no money for them. And William hated it.

She could see, too, that it was bad for Audrey and Adam. They both liked to possess 'things' but couldn't be at the pains to take care of them. To Audrey and Adam their parents were wealthy people to whom everything was possible. Why should they take care of anything? There were more of the same kind in the shops.

'They must learn,' she thought. 'They *must* learn. They will be poor when they are older. And they will have to begin on so little.'

II

William went on potting. Catherine and the children were a disappointment. He would have liked Catherine to have been a social success and to have been very attractively, but inexpensively, dressed. He wanted to be proud of her. But Catherine looked haggard, and her clothes were shabby and carelessly put on. In company she was silent and self-conscious. At home she was either working at top speed to catch up on the day or utterly tired out at the day's end. Tired, and full of half-expressed fears and worries about the children and her management of them.

Why worry? The children looked well. They were handsome and well grown, and she dressed them suitably. But they didn't shine at anything, they were indifferent and backward at games and their company manners were, at inopportune moments, deplorable. They were so much worse than their home ones. Audrey was clever, beyond doubt, and Adam sometimes drew gracious and surprising things, but they were not friendly, either to himself or to anyone else. They lived lives of their own.

William felt that Catherine had become a stranger to him. Sometimes he wondered if they wouldn't both be happier if they decided to break off and give it all up. The sourness, the disillusionment, the mutual disappointment were poison to both of them, yet they held on.

Marriage was a wrestling match. Jacob had wrestled all night to detain the angel on the mountainside. For Catherine as yet unproved, unknown, he still wrestled. Until he knew her he would hold her, weary though each of them might be.

Catherine went on digging up flowering ground elder. She had been told that the best way to kill it was to dig it up whilst it was in flower. She tugged at the white, worm-like roots.

It was a pity that she and William fell out so often over questions of discipline. The children seemed to come between them rather than belong to them both.

William saw life in terms of top dog and under dog. Catherine in terms of individual liberty. William wanted the children to respect him because he was their father. Catherine wanted them to respect him because he was William, a person deserving of respect. To William his children were his own flesh and should therefore have like natures; to Catherine they were acts of an incalculable God, created in the likeness of relations she had far rather they didn't resemble.

To Catherine they were a transitory part of her life. Soon, too soon, they would be gone, and she would be unnecessary to them. They took up far too much of her time, she saw hardly anything of William, and they were eating her youth; but she poured herself out for them whilst they were there, the more readily since she had no other interest.

Time ran away so fast! Yesterday they were babies, tomorrow they would be gone.

William couldn't see that. Sometimes he was jealous. He would catch hold of her roughly, and kiss her in front of them, holding her with both hands behind the shoulders. Catherine hated to be kissed in the presence of her children. She would wriggle out of his arms, patting her hair and giving her clothes a shake, like a fastidious cat coming in out of the wet. Her love for William was one of the very few things she didn't want them to see or share.

III

Bill lay on his stomach on the grass, making an arrangement with blocks of wood and plasticine and cardboard. Bill's fingers were a pleasure to watch. They were so capable. Audrey, hunched up, a book on her knees, her fingers in her ears, sat intent by his side. She was changing rapidly from a chubby child into a weedy little girl. She had begun to develop features and her face had thinned.

Catherine sat at rest, watching them. When she simply looked at her children, when she was not obliged to interfere or correct them, her anxious mind was at peace and she was able to love them.

Bill stood up, square and stocky in his cotton tunic, he walked round his finished work, made sure that it was all as he had intended. The interest went out of his face. He turned his back on it and stumped away across the lawn, looking for something fresh. Bill was very like William. Adam would have carried the finished work about for the rest of the afternoon. Bill didn't care if anybody saw it or not.

He came over to Catherine.

'Must I help you?'

'No, you mustn't.' Bill's face fell. 'But you may.' Catherine pointed to the tangle of dirty white roots and flagging leaves. 'Get your barrow and take that to the bonfire.'

'Say please.'

'Please!' Catherine watched his broad back and sturdy legs as he moved away. Bill was different. He owned and ran himself. Audrey and Adam had been indifferent but dependent. Bill was neither. He was an obstinate person and had a flaming temper, but he was easier to control.

Bill trundled back with his wheelbarrow. Catherine went on digging. Out of the corner of her eye she watched him push the tangle well down, weight it with a grass root, heave the barrow out of a crack between the stones – grumbling under his breath – and stagger off with it down the garden. Halfway up the path a stone got under the wheel. The light, toy barrow jerked and went over. Audrey looked up from her book.

'Hullo!' Her voice was cynical. 'What d'you think you're doing?'

She went to the rescue. Bill turned on her a face of fury.

'G'way!'

'Leave him alone, Audrey. Bill doesn't like being helped.'

Audrey stretched herself, yawning. She liked helping people. She thought Bill an unpleasant person.

'All right. I don't want to help him.' She came and stood over her mother. 'Do you like weeding?'

'No.'

'Then why do you do it?'

'Because I don't like weeds.'

'I suppose I ought to help you!'

'I suppose you ought.'

Audrey pulled up some of the creeping Jenny which, every summer, spread out from under the lupins. She looked at the dirt on her fingers, sighed, and pulled up one or two roots of groundsel.

Bill came back with the empty wheelbarrow. He jostled Audrey to get at the weeds, stepped on her skirt and leaned across her.

'Get out, Bill. You are a nuisance.'

'G'out of my way!'

'Don't!' Catherine rubbed the back of her hand across her forehead. 'Audrey! Move up a little! Do try and work together.'

Audrey moved, grudgingly. She could help her mother, quite as well as Bill.

'Look! What a lot!' Bill tugged, hot-faced and important, at his full barrow.

Adam came in through the door of the vegetable garden.

'Come and see what I've done!'

He waved the garden fork.

Audrey jumped up. If Bill were going to walk about all over her, she had just as soon be with Adam.

Catherine went on tugging at the ground elder.

'All right. I'll be there in a moment.'

She wiped her hands and got up, slowly. If Adam wanted to 'show' it was necessary to go at once and inspect, or he would be too discouraged to work next time. The afternoon went so fast, she thought, and there was so much weed. It looked as if an energetic hen had had a dust-bath in the corner where she had been working, no more.

She walked down the path. Adam's garden wasn't rectangular, but the stones were fairly well sunk in and the patch was well cleared.

'Can I have some flower roots, Mother?'

'Later. They'd die if you moved them now. Look . . . move that stone a little bit this way. It'll make the garden a much better shape.'

Adam sighed. That was like Catherine. Everything he did came unfinished the moment she looked at it. He so much wanted her to praise him, and her praise was so difficult to get.

'Why would the plants die?'

'Because it's the wrong time of year.'

Audrey's face suddenly shone. 'Why not vegetables . . . vegetables to eat?'

They went over to the herb border, dug up mint, parsley, and thyme, transplanted a broccoli plant or two. The clock struck four.

Catherine went back to her garden. Bill sat on his barrow, waiting for a load, and chewing a grass blade. When Bill spoke he was amazingly faulty in grammar and construction, but when Bill worked it was difficult to remember that he was only four, and years younger than Adam.

Bill thought in action. Adam's thoughts were so deep that it took him a long time to get them even as far as words.

CHAPTER FIVE

I

Adam was going fishing. Fishing days were long and glorious. Quite early, before breakfast, he had dug in the marrow bed for maggots. Then he had looked out the tackle and the old army haversack and put them on the table in the hall. Now he was going out to get oranges, bloods if possible. He wondered if Miss Trenchard, when she heard he was going fishing, would give him an Ogo Pogo eye to put in his cheek on the way down.

He walked slowly. There was no hurry. He would go all round the village to get there. Market Square, the main street, Bull Ring, Costard's Pond, Golder's Close, the jitty, every street and separate group of houses had its name and Adam knew them all. He knew that the little place had twenty-two shops – butchers, bakers, barbers, and greengrocers, drapers, sweet-stuff shops, hardware shops, shops which sold some of everything. There was the watchmaker across the close, under the church tower. The finest clock in England, the old man said their church had. Adam loved the deep note of the tenor bell, on which the hours struck. It thrilled him inside with a tremor half fear, half joy, so that he hardly knew whether to put his hands over his ears or to stop and listen. But there was no time to stand in Golder's Close this morning, looking up at the church, as out of a stone well of houses.

He dawdled past old Dowell's workshop in the Bull Ring, which was always full of wracked gate-leg tables, worm-eaten wheel-back chairs and tallboys and chests-on-stands which had seen hard treatment. He liked to nose in at the door and watch Mr Dowell at work, gloomy and quite silent, except when a furniture owner came and he talked about flowered oak and veneer, and the sins of neglect and ignorance which had been committed on the cripple under his care.

'Oh, my!' he would groan. 'What a shocking job! They never ought to have treated it like that. Oh, dear, now! I'll do what I can. Oh, dear! What a shocking bit of work.'

Beyond the Bull Ring, in the main street, Mr Costard's horses were bringing in the hay from Walter's Hook. A month back he had seen the wagons in the wheelwright's shop, getting a spring coat of purest yellow and clear scarlet. Now they were swaying up the street behind the horses, already a little dusty with hayseed. The horses slipped and struggled on the tarmac, their brasses rang.

The door of the baker's shop was open. He could see Mr Lion, his black hair powdered with flour, putting the soft white loaves into the oven on a long shovel. There was a cricket by the oven all winter. It sang so loudly you could hear it the moment you went into the shop. Further down was the hardware shop where William sent him for pounds of nails and damp, heavy parcels of putty. The feel of the putty in his hands always gave him an odd sensation. He wanted to do something with it, though he knew at the back of his mind that it was too soft to work up, like clay, into new shapes.

At the end the of main street the road gang were tarring the road. He stood still. He envied them with all his heart. They were all young, all strong . . . brawny fellows in stained dungarees, with tarry hands and sunburned necks . . . loud, jovial, and friendly. They were full of noisy jokes which a passer-by could understand.

The man who pushed the reeking tar boiler wore a tiny cardboard 'boater' and a pair of paper spectacles. Whenever he spoke the others laughed. They worked very fast, spreading the tar with a spray and brushing it along with wide black brushes. Their thigh boots clumped stickily, their faces were red with the sun. Adam wished that he were the one with the comic hat and the spectacles.

The sun warmed his shoulder blades through his grey flannel shirt. The sixpence in his hand was hot, the rim cut into his palm, the surface clung greasily. He opened his hand and looked at it, guiltily, remembering the oranges.

II

Adam watched the line sink through the muddy water, the green and white float settle, bobbing, on the surface. He liked catching fish. Sometimes they caught roach, sometimes perch, more rarely a brown trout, washed down out of the park by the brook. Quite often he caught nothing, but he was happy even then.

He was fishing. No one would worry him to go and do anything else. Catherine never let him sit still when he wasn't occupied. 'Mooning,' she called it. But fishing was a sacred and masculine occupation. She left that alone.

Adam would sit, watching the green-and-white float till every line on the water, every crack in the bark of the willow tree, seemed to pass into him and belong to himself.

The swing bridge, curved like a slice of melon, hung open. Across the canal the stream tumbled down a ridge of stone beneath the leaning willow. Every now and again, with a long sigh, the breeze turned all the leaves over. They showed their silvery undersides like leaping fish. The grasses all around him bowed over with a sound like silk and the water of the canal shattered, and then rocked gently back to blue again.

Irene ranged the hot meadow with Audrey and Bill. Audrey was picking moondaisies, sorrel, and ragged robins, a great sheaf, nearly as heavy as a baby. There would be dreadful trouble presently, when Audrey had to lug them up the canal path and balance them on her handlebars all the way home. Already she was beginning to wish that she had left them in the meadow. Never again, now they were picked, would they float and swim and reflect the light in the middle of the running grasses. They were tousled, no longer beautiful.

Bill leapt the open field drains, to and fro. He ran round and round in circles, like a happy dog. His cotton shirt and button-on shorts were new. His behind looked so round in them that everybody spanked him. When he met a stranger he backed into a corner and said, with an engaging smile: 'Don't 'it me!'

But the roundness was hard and firm. He had a chest like a barrel, wide hands with square-tipped fingers, a wide, flat face.

Bill was rapturously contented, he was always that or in a boiling rage. Whenever he was in a rage he hit whatever was nearest. Usually it was Adam whom, secretly, he adored. Adam set his teeth and didn't hit back. Irene liked Adam. He never took a mean advantage. She rejoiced when Catherine picked Bill off and administered justice, whilst he battered his mother's shins with his hard little shoes.

Catherine never gave Bill his deserts. He was so normally happy, so easily occupied, that she gave him his head. She never really wanted to 'it Bill. Irene's fingers often tingled.

Irene looked at Adam's back. She wished she were fishing, too. Irene never came back without a fish, if she were given a fair chance. But Audrey and Bill made such a racket. Somebody had to keep them away from the banks.

She looked at her wrist-watch and called them back to the pile of mackintoshes and the lunch basket. Galantine sandwiches, oranges, jam puffs. It was easy and cheap to achieve luxury on a day in the fields.

They ate slowly, because days in the open are infinite and there is no need to hurry. Clouds led each other like sheep along the eastern horizon behind the railway embankment.

'Too bright for the fish,' said Irene.

Adam didn't care. There was still a long mellow afternoon when, his lips sticky with orange juice, the cracks in his hands smarting with it – but not enough to be painful – he would sit and watch other people watching floats. Comfortable, elderly fellows with baskets and beer bottles, railway porters off duty, ex-policemen, and the publican from the Locomotive Inn. Peaceful people who didn't talk, but who understood one another. They didn't expect to get much from the canal, it was fished too often, but, like Adam, they were contented, and the meek inherited the earth.

They had finished, all but two pink cakes, solitary on their open paper bag. Irene said those must be left for 'manners'. It was bad for them, she thought, to gobble up everything on a day like this. They'd find someone, on the way back, to give those cakes to, sooner or later. They all liked that. It was fun to see some surprised child grab the bag and run, as if afraid they might snatch it back again.

Suddenly Audrey jumped up.

'Oh, look! A barge! A barge!'

Down the canal the many-coloured bow of a barge parted the water. It came so slowly that at first it hardly seemed to move. An old brown mule and a pony, their draw-ropes decorated with blue and white wooden beads, were coming in a slow measure, like a dance.

A step, a step . . . a halt . . . a step . . . a step . . . a halt. Every so often the slack rope hit the water and then tightened in a shower of drops. A girl with burnt yellow hair ran, swinging her broad hips, to open the iron field gate. It shut with a clang, and Adam ran to rescue his rod.

The girl came abreast of them. She smiled down from the towpath.

'A fine day. A beautiful day,' she said, in an unexpected, warm, and friendly voice.

'Proper weather for travelling,' said Irene.

The girl waved at them over her shoulder and went on. The barge slid past very quickly, though it had seemed so long in coming. The children raced up the bank to catch sight of the shining brasses in the cabin, the large painted water jug, full of moondaisies, on the roof, and the dog sitting on the cargo of coal. In the stern, one hand on the thin, raking tiller, stood a man in a blue shirt, eating ham and boiled cabbage off a plate on the cabin roof.

The reeds hissed, the ripples danced, the canal fell silent. Over the alders at the bend a plume of smoke stood up from the chimney of the cabin stove. The children ran back down the path.

Audrey and Bill threw themselves on the mackintoshes beside Irene.

'Tell us about the judge who wouldn't pay for his wife's monument!'

'Tell us about the man who sold his brother!'

'And the man who was killed by the gipsies.'

'One at a time,' said Irene.

Adam straightened his wet line and replenished his hook from which he had torn the bait as he snatched the line away through the long grasses.

Audrey chewed a grass.

'Tell us about the man who killed the other man as they were both driving home in a trap. Doesn't his ghost go up and down the road still?'

'They used to say so.'

Irene didn't believe that story as she had done a year or

two ago. It didn't seem right to expect ghosts with so many cars up and down the road.

'Tell us why nobody lives in the house by Saxon camp.'

'Well, they say somebody comes and knocks at four o'clock every morning and when you go down to look there isn't nobody.'

'I should lie in bed.'

'Ah! That's the worst of it. You can't lie in bed. Something draws you. There's a something about the knocking won't let you lie still. You have to go. You've got to go down, all in a tremble, and open the door. And then . . . nobody.'

'But why does anybody mind if it's nobody?'

'Well, nobody won't sleep there.'

'I like Saxon camp. I think that's a silly story.'

'That's as may be. You go there at four in the morning and see for yourself. All I say is that nobody won't live there.'

Bill wasn't listening. He was blowing squeaks on a grass blade. Audrey was putting the second rod together.

'But suppose there was a knocking at our house at four in the morning and Daddy was out. Would Mother put the sheet over her head or would she . . .'

'If it was four o'clock at our house it'd be somebody to see your father. But this knocking isn't a knocking. It's a ghost.'

'But doesn't it do anything but knock?'

'And quite enough, too,' Irene concluded, opening the tin of bait. 'It's no good your putting a line out. It's too bright.'

'I'm going to put it in to see.'

Audrey liked to let her fishing run itself. In her experience you caught just as much fish if you hung your line in and left it as if you sat and brooded over it like Adam.

When she had wedged the butt of her rod securely in a tree root she ran off with Bill to a clump of alders. There were two stooled ash trees amongst them, easy to climb and ride. They vanished, shouting.

Irene went over to Adam. That was Audrey and Bill all over – never two minutes at any one thing.

When she was here beside the canal she was happier than she had ever been anywhere else, but already it was the happiness of memory. She and her father had come there often when she was little. He had taught her all that she knew about the ways of fish. But her father hadn't been down there for two years now, it was farther than he could manage, and a girl couldn't go fishing by herself. She didn't really want to go any more, she came for Adam and the other two. When they were down there they all belonged together, to one world. It was then that she was most fond of them. To her, as to them, the river valley was the most beautiful place in existence, yet already she was longing for something else.

The children were dear little things, but there! You couldn't talk to them. There was something wanting in life, she hardly knew what.

III

Audrey's float drew under. Irene watched it, half tempted to let it alone. Then she got up. Audrey was a nice little thing, even if she didn't trouble to fish, and the children prized the muddy canal roach enormously, whoever had caught them. She tried to free the butt of the rod, then began to haul up the dripping line.

Adam watched her.

'Got one?'

'Quiet! I'm not sure. Yes! He's there.'

'Big one?'

'Umm. Wait a minute. There!'

She held up the flapping fish at the end of the line before she unhooked it.

'What is it?'

'A trout.'

Once, two years before, they had caught a trout, but they had had to throw it back because it was too small. This was a fair-sized fish.

Adam picked it up. He looked at its brown back, its gleaming belly.

Audrey and Bill came running across the field.

'Oh! A trout! Whose line was it on?'

Audrey danced round Bill.

'It was on my line. I know it was. It's mine. I shall have it for breakfast.'

Adam stepped back. 'You weren't there. We caught it.'

'It's mine. It was on my line. It isn't fair.'

'Now then! Put it down, both of you.'

Audrey's hands had closed over Adam's. Her thumbs pressed down into the yielding, slimy surface of the fish. For a moment they tugged and wrestled, pushing each other.

The fish slid out from between their fingers and shot into the grass.

'You've spoilt it!' Adam cried on a rising note.

'I've not. I shall eat it. It was on my line.'

Irene picked the fish up by the tail.

'It's not fit for nobody to eat. You won't either of you have it now it's been pulled about like that.'

She swung it, a wide underhanded throw. The trout gleamed through the air and fell with a splash into the double ditch that ran beneath the alders.

'It was my fish,' Audrey cried. 'It's not fair!'

Adam said nothing. He was filled with intolerable grievance. She'd done nothing for it. He'd sat still all the afternoon, whilst she'd done nothing but run about and make a noise. And now she'd dragged the fish away from him, spoilt it, lost it.

Irene picked up his line, began to reel it in.

'That's enough. If you're going to quarrel we'll stop.'

'That was your fault,' Adam turned on Audrey.

'It wasn't. It was my fish. I was in the right.'

'You'd no need to rush at it like that. You could have shared it. You didn't either of you catch it. If you can't behave better than that I'm not going to bring you down again. There's no pleasure in it. Stop it, both of you, and pick up your things.'

Bill's round face drew up into a knot. 'Must we go home now?'

'No. We'll go round by the lock. But no more fishing.'

They trailed off, carrying their baskets. Usually it was the final treat, to go down to the lock and look deep down

the weedy sides at the evil, black water, far below, to come back
by the osier beds and through the winding path across the
meadow hay. But now all that was spoilt, as Irene had said,
there was no pleasure in it.

Bill was miserable because he hated a row, especially
the sort of vague, unfinished rows that Audrey and Adam
had. If they had fought it out he wouldn't mind it nearly
so much. But now they would smoulder for days. He began
to cry.

'Oh, I don't like it!'

Audrey stood still. 'Bill! Don't be an idiot!'

Irene held out her hand. 'What is it, ducks? Shall I take
your basket?'

'Oh, I don't like it! I don't like it!'

Bill looked from Audrey to Adam.

Audrey shuffled her feet in the dust. She was still sure that
she was in the right about the fish, but already her quarrel
with Adam was a load of misery. If only he could have said that
it was her trout! Then she would have shared with him at once.

'Oh, Bill!' she said. 'Don't cry.'

It was Adam's fault. Adam had made all this trouble.

The three of them stood still upon the sunny path, looking
at Bill.

Adam said nothing. The enormous cloud of his disappointment filled the heavens and blotted the earth. The
whole day had climbed to the climax of the trout and then
there was nothing left to look forward to.

'Take my hand, Bill,' Irene coaxed. 'We'll give you a hop,
a skip, and a jump.'

Adam dawdled along at the back whilst Audrey, helping Bill and carrying the heaviest of the baskets, was already beginning to feel better.

He looked at her back. She was in the wrong, she knew it. That was some consolation.

First his island . . . then the trout . . . she took everything.

He thought of his island, its dark trees, its still pools. All at once he was there, catching trout innumerable though his feet plodded on the dust of the canal path. He forgot Audrey.

CHAPTER SIX

I

Audrey and Adam seldom quarrelled in front of Catherine. She looked so perplexed and unhappy that they felt uncomfortable. The person in whom they both put their faith and their dependence became no older and no wiser than they were. So they hid their quarrels and only under extreme provocation ran to her for justice.

'You're wrong,' was her invariable judgement. 'If you quarrelled you're both wrong.'

She would find them occupation at opposite ends of the garden.

The rivalry between Audrey and Adam worried her. There was room for both of them yet, although their interests were as different as possible, somehow they always managed to run at the same thing. That this up and down tussle, this running fight, was a necessary prelude to any real friendship between them, never occurred to her. Violet had been so much older than she had been, had married so young, that no argument had ever been possible. She assumed that two different and very positive people, who had not yet learnt to see anything

196

outside their own point of view, were going to live amicably together because they belonged to the same family. She didn't understand that jealousy and admiration, contempt and an almost maternal affection, can live together in the same mind and be felt for the same person.

So she combed the countryside for interest. She took them to the tileyard and the water mill, tramped long winter miles to meets of basset and otter hounds, organised paper-chases and picnics.

'Why don't you leave the brats alone?' William would ask wrathfully. 'If you leave them alone they'll jolly soon amuse themselves.'

'But they don't. They quarrel and scream and spoil things and fall out with Bill. They simply get bored.'

'Do them good to be bored. They'll never learn if you spoon-feed them.'

Catherine didn't believe him. It was not good to be bored. It was a state of mind out of which nothing good could come. She wondered if he knew what it was like to have two leaden, sullen children hanging about you on a busy morning. Once or twice she smacked them out of sheer exasperation and with a resulting improvement in their spirits.

Catherine doggedly set herself to make them useful to themselves and each other.

'If you won't play, you shall work,' she said.

She spent terrible afternoons in the carpenter's shop with Adam, who wept profusely before he learnt how to drive a screw and, having learnt, abstracted William's pet chisels for the purpose of using them as screwdrivers. She set Audrey, writing under the injustice, to darn Adam's socks and make Adam's bed.

'It's not fair,' Audrey said, with tears in her eyes. 'Because he's a boy! Why shouldn't boys make their own beds?'

'Boys have to go out to work all their lives. You may have a house of your own. Besides, you can't do things only for yourself. It's so dull.'

'I shan't marry,' said Audrey.

Having lodged her protest, she settled down with some pride to the work which Catherine set her. The long morning's cooking with Irene she really enjoyed.

Adam and Bill feigned severe stomach-ache over her cookery. Audrey learned to lie low and pounce at them at the end of a meal.

'I made that. Yah!'

'It's making me feel sick!' Adam would complain, whilst Bill laid a hand on his diaphragm and heaved realistically.

'Then why did you have two helpings?'

William would chuckle. He was beginning to notice and like his daughter. She was a competent little thing.

But Catherine wasn't satisfied. She felt that they wanted something, undefined, which she had failed to give them. She revived a little when she found that her experience wasn't an uncommon one.

'I don't know what they want,' said Hilary's mother. 'They have any amount of fun. They're always out, and they have their ponies, and lessons with a cricket coach. But they're just as grumpy and surly . . . I'm tired out with them, and I told them so. I told them they were a pair of exceedingly nasty children and they could get out of my way.'

'And did they?' Catherine asked, interested.

Hilary's mother laughed. 'They did! They knew I meant it. In another minute I could have hit them. Dissatisfied little wretches.'

She stood at the top of her paddock, one foot on an upturned bucket, smoking. The sleeves of her jumper were pulled up, a wisp of hay clung to her grey jodhpurs. As always she gave the impression, when stationary, of not being at rest.

'Oh, what a day I've had!' she continued. 'Up at six this morning to feed my ghastly hens, and drag the water up to them and collect the eggs. Then breakfast with my wretches and two hours coolie work in the house. Then out for an hour to exercise the ponies. And then Beauty played up. Started sidling about all over the road and refusing to pass a heap of stones. You know what it is if you once give in to them? I had to take Edward off her and send him home on Hopeful whilst I had it out with Beauty. Little beast. She knew I was tired and she fairly took it out of me. She's a nice pony, there's no vice in her, but she can be tiresome. I got her home just in time for lunch. And then the boys ran at me to say they'd lighted a fire in the paddock and might they roast potatoes. In the paddock! With the grass as dry as tinder after a month's drought and a whole stack of new hay in one corner. My winter's feed! So I ran and stamped it out. Then they said I always came and spoilt everything, and now there was nothing else to do for the rest of the day. I told them I knew what they were going to do, and that was keep right out of my sight for the afternoon. I haven't spoken to them since.'

'When they say they don't know what to do it always makes me feel like a jelly fish,' Catherine confessed.

'Jelly fish! You aren't a jelly fish, you're a doormat. These infernal children make doormats of us. Nobody took all this trouble with us. And our people didn't have to work like we do. Look at you . . . look at me . . . we work. We're always teaching them to blow their noses and wipe their feet on the mat and pick up all the litter they leave lying about. I don't like work. I'm not used to it. I can't give myself up body and soul to children, and ponies, and hens. I've got to enjoy myself as well or I'd just as soon be dead. And I get so tired that sometimes I'm bothered to know how I'm to keep going.

She took her foot off the bucket.

'Since you're here I'd be thankful if you'd come and help me feed my mouldy hens.'

They tramped round the enclosures filling zinc water troughs, freeing hens from trap nests and pouring grain into patent hoppers.

'I hate hens,' said Hilary's mother. 'A duck's a fool and knows it. But a hen thinks it knows such a hell of a lot. If I wasn't making twopence ha'penny each for graded eggs, I'd sell the lot tomorrow.'

'It isn't the work I mind,' said Catherine. 'It's just that it seems to be taking one round and round in a circle. It's the same as it was five years ago. The children aren't any tidier or any different. We work just as hard and things don't get any easier. We simply seem to be getting nowhere.'

'Where d'you expect to get? That's life, isn't it?' Hilary's mother swilled the last of the water out of her pail. 'Or if it isn't life it's all that you and I are going to get, my dear, so make the most of it.'

She yawned, and swung her bucket.

II

Impossible to know what Robin's mother thought. Eagerly, a little more faded, a little more untidy, she ran from one enthusiasm to another.

The huge, ramshackle vicarage was full of foreign students, slow South Germans, French boys from Rennes, polylingual Swedes. Robin was nursed, minded, and finally tutored by representatives of nearly every nation in Europe.

He was inured to nut sandwiches, raw carrots, diets of orange juice and lettuce leaves, milk treatments, raw meat treatments, cold baths, sun bathing and his mother's prentice hand at psychoanalysis.

Through it all he continued steadily to be Robin. A silent, secretive, but pleasant-tempered child who went out indifferently with any one of his father's pupils, accepted the diet of the moment, and was neither conspicuous nor detested when he mixed with other children.

It was no good asking his mother why he was contented. It was simply because he was Robin, and not because of nuts or Freud or daily doses of Coué.

He had no enthusiasms. Catherine, looking at him, thought she had never seen a child who looked so like the product of a public school training before he had even come to the beginning of it.

Catherine went to tea there with a feeling of relief. Everyone there was so tremendously keen on something which seemed to matter at the moment. Sitting on rugs in the sun beside the tennis courts, everyone talked, argued, discussed, and laid down the law. They applauded modern art, condemned modern civilisation, tore up and re-arranged the map of Europe, hotly debated the cause of Indian nationalism, and were very advanced and liberal and progressive.

The talk gave Catherine, while it lasted, the illusion that everything was going at a great pace towards some definite goal, and that the world was a stimulating and exciting place. Afterwards, driving home with William, it seemed strange to think that it had been just talk . . . amusing but rather silly talk which led nowhere and influenced nobody. But she continued to go as often as she was able, because this light spate of opinions carried her away from her own preoccupations and doubts. She went the more readily because Audrey and Adam were happy in the company of Robin and showed, when they were in his garden, the agreeable selves which strangers so rarely saw.

CHAPTER SEVEN

William was driving home through the glaring August evening. The day had been long and the work had fallen awkwardly, but he wasn't tired now that it was over. He was tired whilst he was hurrying, but the fatigue was psychological. Once the rush was over he became a whole man again.

As he thought back over the patients he had seen that day he was filled with an immense pity for them. They worked hard, and the bewildered patience on the faces of the older ones showed that the motive and the meaning of their work was gone.

Their work kept them, but it wasn't enough. In years past there had been anxiety and penury often enough in the countryside, but the countryman had no doubt as to the value of his work or as to his place in the scheme of things. Now that assurance was gone.

No wonder the younger men went into motor works to tighten nuts or to spray cellulose paint onto mass production cars; no wonder that the girls drifted into shops and factories. The drain of the big towns was being more and more felt in the emptying countryside.

A man, bicycling towards him, suddenly held out his arm

and signalled. William, with a return of fatigue and irritation, slowed up.

'Yes? What is it now?'

The man pulled out a handkerchief and wiped a hot face.

'A smash, sir. At the Green Man.'

'What kind of smash? Know any details?'

'There's a young fellow hurt. There's a girl and an old lady, too.'

William sighed. 'All right. I'll get along there.'

He always carried a bag of emergency dressings now. He felt, bitterly, that he had had enough to do with motor accidents this summer. No provision was made for dealing with them, and no one ever attempted to pay him for his services, mileage, material or time. He drove rapidly to the crossroads where he found an interested crowd, and in the heart of it, a baby car with its side buckled up, a scared-looking elderly lady sitting on the running-board nursing her wrist, a young man lying on his back on the grass, groaning, and a flamboyant young woman with torn stockings and a grazed shin hunched sulkily on the grass. A trade van, with a broken windscreen and dented radiator, was half in and half out of the ditch.

'It wasn't my fault,' the elderly lady greeted him. 'I slowed, and I sounded, and they ran right into me.'

'That's right, doctor. I seen it.'

'It wasn't her fault.'

'He run right into her.'

The young man groaned.

'Just look at my stocking!' said the young woman.

William bent over the young man, unfastened his raincoat and proceeded to examine him.

'Stand back, can't you? Has anybody sent for the ambulance?'

'Yes, doctor. It's coming, right away.'

'Oh, doctor! I hope he isn't badly hurt.'

William looked at the elderly lady. Her car was new. It looked like a broken toy.

'I'm afraid so. I fancy there's a good deal of internal damage. It's difficult to judge the extent without a thorough examination.'

He opened his bag and took out his hypodermic case, selected the morphia and a syringe. A decent kid. A pity you couldn't mend the human body as easily as you could push out the dented panel of a car! The waste of it.

'Oh, doctor! I've hurt my leg, doctor. Just look at my stocking!'

William stood up and drew the young man's clothes over him.

'Put a coat under his head and shoulders, some of you,' he said. 'Steady now . . . and a greatcoat over him.'

There was nothing else that he could do; they might be able to do something in hospital, if he got over the shock well enough to stand an operation. He thought it unlikely. He went over to the girl.

'Oh, my leg!'

'Gravel rash,' said William, without interest. 'Simply gravel rash.'

He had no patience with her, sitting there and whining about her spoilt stocking whilst the boy lay groaning without help or sympathy. She flung away from him peevishly, and William left her. He hated her cheap prettiness, her cheap scent, her cheap self-pity.

'I'll see to you later,' he said.

The elderly lady had a fractured wrist. Her arm was blue, her hand already swollen. She looked from her hand to the boy on the grass with frightened eyes. It was all so sudden and so horrible. One minute she had been driving along, carefully, proud of her new car and her new freedom, and now . . . all this wreckage and pain. And none of it her fault.

'I'll have to put this up on a splint,' said William, rummaging in his bag. 'You must have it X-rayed and properly set as soon as ever you can.'

A Ford van slowed up and stopped, a milk lorry stopped, a motor-bicycle and side-car stopped. Men cycling home from work leaned on their handlebars and stared. Children pushed in closer, sucking sweets.

'Get back, can't you?' William said wrathfully.

All these people, crowding and pushing and goggling, and not one of them able to help.

The milk lorry moved on and William saw the girl had gone with it, beside the driver. She hadn't waited to see the boy into the ambulance.

'It's all right, doctor. We got her address.'

'He was just giving her a lift. She don't come from about here.'

William finished his bandaging and stood up. The ambulance arrived; a policeman, mopping his forehead, had at length materialised and was taking notes and warning the crowd off the skid-marks on the road and grass. An AA scout appeared and walked round and round the baby car whistling dolefully.

'Whew! Hi! Hi! Hi!'

The ambulance throbbed gently, the ambulance men lowered away the stretcher. The accident was now complete in every detail. If only there had been a little blood it would have been a perfect example. The crowd pushed, sniffed, whispered, and breathed heavily through its nose.

William helped the stretcher into the ambulance.

'Steady with him. He won't stand very much more. I shall be back at my house in about a quarter of an hour if the house surgeon likes to ring me up.'

He went back to the elderly lady.

'What's the damage?' he asked the scout.

'Chassis's bent. Just you look. Her steering must have gone. Better get her onto the grass and ring up a garage.'

William turned to the car's owner.

'Were you going far?'

'I was going to spend the weekend with friends at Beaconsfield.'

'Have they got a car? Can they come and pick you up?'

'No. Yes, I mean. Oh, dear! They're not very great friends – I think I'd rather go home.'

The thought of arriving, helpless and dishevelled, in a strange house, almost overcame her.

'How far have you come?'

It turned out to be no great distance.

William looked at his watch. 'If we're ringing up the garage to fetch your car we might as well hire one to take you home at the same time.'

'Oh, if you would! I'd rather be home.'

'You'd better come back with me.'

William wondered how she'd stand the journey. He'd talk to Terence Healy, get him to drive slowly. He packed her into his own car and drove her home.

He hailed Catherine, who ran down from Bill's bedroom, discarding her flannel apron on the banisters as she came.

'Look after her for me for a little while,' he said. 'She's had a bad shaking. Stay there till I get out of the surgery.'

Catherine went in timidly, then stood still and smiled. It was impossible to be shy of such a pathetic, frightened person.

'Oh! Do take your hat off. I'll do it for you. And here's the other cushion. That one feels as if it was stuffed with bricks. Look . . . slip this under your arm. Now . . . you'd like a cup of tea, wouldn't you?'

'Oh, please! Nothing to eat, just tea.'

She smiled apologetically at Catherine.

'I'm so sorry. So much trouble.'

'Oh, no. Besides . . . this is doctor's house, isn't it?'

'I must look such a sight. Oh, dear! That was what that dreadful girl said. "Look at my stocking." She didn't care what happened to her young man. Oh, dear! What a nightmare! I wish I was home.'

'Is it very far?'

'Oh, no . . . it won't take an hour. I couldn't possibly go on. I couldn't turn up in somebody's house like this. Agnes would have such a shock.'

'Shall I ring her up and tell her?'

'Oh, would you? Bring me the book. I can find the number.'

Catherine gave the message, interrupted by excited, bird-like cries of perturbation from the other end of the line.

'She's well out of that,' she thought, as she hung up the receiver. 'Agnes sounds like a hen canary. I wouldn't be ill in her house for a pension.'

She came back. The little woman looked at her.

'My dear! What a charming room.'

'I like it.' Catherine looked ruefully at her faded chair-covers.

'It has a most wonderful *feel*. I noticed it the moment I came in.'

She closed her eyes.

'I don't think you ought to talk.'

Catherine was anxious. The people she knew didn't talk about the feel of a room. It struck her as being odd.

'I am tired . . . now you mention it. I won't talk.'

Catherine sat still. A doctor's house was strange. People fell into your life for a few minutes, you were intensely sorry for them, belonged vividly to their lives and troubles. Then they were gone again, and quite often you never met them any more. She felt sorry for this little person.

'Are you sure you want to travel? We could easily manage . . .'

The stranger's eyes flew open. 'Oh, *no*. So much trouble. There's no need. Besides, I want to be home.'

'Of course you do.' Catherine tried to keep the relief out of her voice and hated herself for being relieved. She heard Terence Healy's car chattering at the surgery door.

'That's Terence. I'll lend you a rug and some cushions. His car isn't . . . you'll travel better with cushions.'

She helped William pack her in and watched the car drive off.

'Poor little soul!'

'I've just rung up the house surgeon. That boy died.'

William sighed. The folly and waste of the whole business oppressed him. Catherine came close to him, let him put his arm round her.

'I know . . . the whole thing seems such an awful shame.'

William shivered. 'I hate motor accidents. They give me the horrors.'

Catherine came closer, she kissed him. Then she looked at the disordered sofa, the dirty teacup and the dusty foot-marks on the drawing-room floor. She ran to make good the damage.

CHAPTER EIGHT

Irene was out. Twice a week, when she had washed up the lunch plates, cleaned the sink, washed the scullery floor, fetched in the coal for the kitchen fire and put out the tea tray, she was free for the rest of the day.

She twitched at the hem of her coat as she walked across the square. She hoped that it covered her frock. Catherine gave them brown uniform so that an afternoon frock, our mother said, was unnecessary. No one would know.

But they did know, everyone knew, that she had no afternoon frock. She was growing, too, and even with skirts getting so short she was afraid that hers weren't long enough. When she stooped she was nervous lest the piece at the back, where her stockings left off, should be uncovered.

She hurried down the jitty, crossed the court and looked across the kitchen through the hanging sheets and shirts. Our mother was ironing.

Irene dropped into a chair on the opposite side of the table and leaned her arms on it. She was glad to sit down. These thundery September days the soles of your feet got it, something awful. She wondered if it was worth it, going on.

She pushed her money across the table. Our mother's

face lighted with a look of relief. Irene's money made such a difference to the family budget. She counted it, dropped it into a tea-caddy and gave Irene back half a crown.

'She do pay you regular, that's something,' she said, with a sigh.

She thumped the iron down on its rest and shook out a white pinafore.

'Ah, now, our mother . . . couldn't I have an afternoon frock? I could get the stuff that cheap . . .'

'Nothing's so cheap as nothing. You don't have no call to get an afternoon frock.'

'I feel a fool coming out in this.'

'Well, you don't look one. I'd be the fool if I bought you another. And summer nearly over at that.'

Irene sighed. She knew the rest. Our father had been laid up with his chest over a month last spring, and Maggie wasn't old enough to leave school, and Frank and Ernie didn't pay nothing in no more, being married.

'Ah, now! Mightn't I take another place . . . nearer Oxford? I'd make a bit more there.'

'Now you're not going to Oxford yet! I won't have it. You're not old enough. You wait till our Maggie leaves school, can't you?'

'I don't get nothing out of it . . . not here I don't.'

'She feeds you well and she don't worry you. You might be a lot worse off.'

Our mother shook out the pinafore and began to pull out the lace frills. Her eyes had a hard look. She didn't want to part with Irene.

'You don't want to leave me, not yet,' she said in a dull voice.

She poured out a cup of tea from the pot on the hob.

'That's what you want,' she said. 'You're tired. I get days like it myself.'

Irene drank her tea. It was hot and black and sweet. A year was a terrible time to wait . . . but it would be our Maggie's turn then. She felt she couldn't sit in the hot kitchen any longer. Our mother was right, yet she felt at odds with her about it. Our mother seemed to think a year was no time at all.

'Where are you going?'

'Just out for a bit. It's that hot.'

'I can't help it with all this ironing. You'll be back for your tea, I reckon?'

Irene nodded. She went out up the street and along the empty road in the warm, lowering weather. They'd get a storm before long, she wouldn't wonder. That'd freshen things up. Her skin prickled, her coat was too hot. She couldn't take it off and show the brown frock. She took off her tam-o'-shanter and swung it in her hand. Presently she waved it.

A boy of about twenty, in blue dungarees, was bicycling down the road. He jumped off and stood leaning against his bicycle.

'Hullo, Irene.'

'Hullo.'

'Who told you I'd be coming along this way?'

'I didn't need telling.'

'You look hot.'

'Oh – ah.'

'You don't need to work so hard.'

'It's not the work . . .'

'What is it, then?'

'I'm tired of this!'

The boy's face clouded.

'Ah, now! Don't let's have that again.'

'Have what?'

'You know.'

'I can't help it! It goes on so. She's good enough to me, poor dear, but I'm doing myself no good here. Sometimes I think when I've got to do that old scullery floor over twice every day I'll be sick. Always in a mess of mud from the drying yard.'

'Don't go away. You don't need to do that.'

He looked at her, unable to find words. He wanted to say how much he needed her. She had only to wait . . . only to wait a little longer. He wasn't, thank God, on the land. One day he'd be a master plasterer, working on his own.

He couldn't even put out his hand to touch her, out there on the road, where anyone might be working, behind the hedge, in the fields. His eyes travelled all over her, from her shining hair and troubled face down to her dusty shoes. She was perfect.

Irene looked away, troubled. 'I'm to wait till our Maggie's left school. If only I was in good service I could put a bit by. I don't like myself here. . . . It's not that I want a lot of good times. I'm not getting myself nowhere. I've learnt all she can teach me.'

Tom nodded. He could understand that. Irene's eyes were hot with frustration and weariness. Tom was no help, she thought. He expected too much of her. She wanted to come to him to grumble and let off steam, she wanted him to put his arm around her, crush her up tightly and tell her not to be a fool. But he was no use . . . he simply admired her. Steady as he was, it was he who was dependent on her.

'All right. I don't mean it. Only everything got on top of me today. The stove smoked, and that old Eb brought in a whole basket of spinach to be picked over for lunch, and two of Bill's shirts come down off the line and got all over black. I don't have no luck, somehow.'

They moved off together down the road. Tom looked left and right. The fields were empty. Gingerly he put his arm round her. They walked on slowly, intensely aware of each other, looking straight ahead down the long road.

Over the hills the sky thickened until presently there was a roll of thunder.

CHAPTER NINE

When Catherine looked back on that summer she realised that it had been a summer of changes. Several things, slight in themselves, had conspired to change the current of their lives.

It mattered that Violet and Edward had gone to live in Cornwall, it made a difference that the living in their village should have fallen vacant soon after the accident at the Green Man, and that the little lady of the motor accident should have pulled strings to get the living for her nephew. It was important, she considered, that he should live in a village where there was a good doctor, for he and his wife had many children, and William was a good doctor. It mattered, too, that Jane should have married.

All these changes gave Catherine a more normal focus. Audrey and Adam ceased to have so dreadful an importance.

Jane, having gone to the Dolomites, had come back with a husband. She was defiant about it, almost aggressive. It wasn't in accordance with her declared principles.

'However,' she had written to Catherine, 'we are both agreed that we give it up if we are no longer in love with each other.'

'Which is sensible,' said Catherine.

William laughed.

'Don't you believe it. It's a pose. Would you leave me?'

'Why not . . . ? If I really wanted to.'

'Huh! You'd never leave me.'

Catherine knew what he meant. Men were much more conventional than women. He meant that she wouldn't face the scandal . . . the resulting loss of status. He little knew how furiously she still longed to shake off all her responsibilities, bang the door, and run.

'I don't know much about modern music,' she went on, following her thoughts a little further, 'but I know that I shouldn't care to be shut up in a top flat in Chelsea with a piano that never stops.'

'Her Peter sounds a tedious sort of ass. Everything must be subordinated to his art . . . isn't that the catch word? Where was he in the War?'

'At a perfectly good public school, getting swished for cutting games. You forget. Children grow up.'

'And Jane's to go on with her job so that he can go on with his music . . . which is too modern to pay. I admire Jane. She has the courage of her convictions.'

'Courage, yes. Convictions, no. Jane doesn't reason. If she's been told anything loud enough, or read it in a really popular book, then she takes it in and goes on believing it . . . and never sees any other side. She can't. She isn't made that way. She's like Violet. Have you ever caught Violet thinking?'

'Violet! Good God! No.'

'Neither does Jane. Her ideas are newer, that's all. She doesn't think.'

'Just as well, probably.'

'I wonder what Peter's like? Jane probably will walk out on him, one day. If the time ever comes when she's had enough of him she'll go. She's quite pitiless.'

'I like Jane,' William insisted.

'Violet's fussing over whether they ought to recognise Peter or not.'

'Peter *will* worry!'

'She's cooling down now. She's worrying about the people at the bungalow. Apparently Edward will talk over the fence to the ones next door. She thinks they aren't quite nice . . . as if they were meat which is beginning to go off. And Edward has built a fowl-house at the bottom of the garden.'

'Good. I hope his hens smell.'

'Oh, yes, and the men scratched her walnut overmantel when they were moving in so she didn't tip them and they were abusive. And marmalade is twopence a pound dearer there than it is at the International at home.'

'And you say Jane is like that woman!'

Catherine didn't answer. She wandered round the surgery, looking at the well-known rows of bottles. Brown, pale yellow, crimson, purple and orange fluids in them made them stand out against the whitewashed walls. The old gilt and black labels, Aqua Rosae Dulce, Tinc Tolu, Tinc Sennae co, Tinc Guaicol, dated from William's father's time. William could have found his way to any one of them in the dark. The places had never varied. Nothing in the surgery was new except the little boxes of endocrine extracts and the new serums for inoculation in one corner, and the new knowledge in William's head. The leeches and the pill-rolling machine had gone. Perhaps the bottles were doomed, too.

The place had a cold smell, like a dairy. It was half underground. Outside the window long trails of reddening virginia creeper shut out the light.

Catherine thought, 'I must go out and clip that off, it keeps out half the afternoon sun.'

It was cold here, on a wet day, but there was never a fire in the surgery, even in the winter. There never had been one and William would not have dreamt of having one started.

Catherine fingered a pile of white bottle-wrapping paper on the desk.

'I saw Sebastian on the road today,' she said.

'Sebastian? Are you sure?'

'Yes. I don't know what he was doing. He wouldn't come on here.'

'Hadn't time probably.'

'Partly. He didn't want to come. He was . . . surly.'

'Did he stop when he saw you?'

'He had stopped. He was changing a tyre.'

William grunted. He didn't believe Sebastian was surly. Nobody felt conversational when they were changing a tyre on a wet day. He held a wrapped bottle towards the lighted spirit flame.

'He looked so odd. Not exactly dirty or untidy, but his clothes were badly put on. He looked queer.'

Catherine knew that if she had told William that there had been a woman in the car he would have put all the queerness down to that. Well, of course . . . it was possible.

219

'I thought at first, until he spoke to me, that it wasn't Sebastian.'

'Why?'

'His face has changed a lot. He looks at you differently, William . . . I wonder what kind of a job Se has really got? You know how importantly Violet talks . . .'

'Talks like a silly woman . . . and a boastful silly woman.'

'I wish we knew more about him.'

'Why don't you write to Jane? She's his sister, she probably knows more about him than Violet does.'

'I don't think he goes to see her much. You see . . . Jane's got rather a good job. She makes quite a lot.'

'I don't see why that should stop Sebastian going to see her.'

'It would. He's that sort. He can't stand second best.'

William rammed a cork into a bottle.

'Then you'd better leave him alone. If he won't come to us you can't make him.'

PART FOUR

CHAPTER ONE

I

Catherine lay in a warm hollow of the sand behind a rock. The sea, streaked purple and green, danced under a strong wind. She wondered at her own happiness.

She had dreaded this holiday in Cornwall, ever since Violet had asked them. She had not wanted to come back with William and Bill to this place where once she had been so happy. Happy and miserable as only youth can be in the unreal years between fifteen and twenty.

'I have changed,' she thought. 'I shall never feel anything as strongly again.'

But if she had changed the little port itself had changed so much as almost to inhibit memory.

It had burst into an eruption, a series of bungaloid blemishes, on each side of the old town. Edward and Violet lived in one of these new bungalows, a makeshift affair of concrete blocks and galvanised iron, with interior walls of asbestos sheeting. The shops had become sophisticated, the beach crowded. Yet still, in spite of all the changes, its charm had persisted, and William had felt it, too.

The harbour was busy at all hours. The coastwise traffic, as often under sail as under steam, came in to load granite, china clay, or salted fish. The fishing fleet came and went with a constant bustle of cleaning down ship and baiting trawl. On the quays the nets were tanned and hung on high rocks to dry, crabs were boiled in an iron pot over an open fire, and in the boat-builder's shed a new rowing boat was slowly taking shape.

William and Bill loved to dawdle down the quays with her. It was much more interesting to watch someone else at work than to sit down to be amused. They had started, quite early, to walk down to the beach, but half the morning had been over before they got there.

The tide was low. A yacht, which had been shored up for the winter, was having her scroll-work picked out in gold leaf. An elderly sailing vessel was having her hull scraped free of barnacles and touched up with patches of red lead before being given a final coat of tar. Men in seaboots were stamping about the slimy bed of the harbour, overhauling rowing boats, repairing ropes. The gulls screamed and swooped all round them, quarrelling over stranded fish guts, swinging up in mazes of pattern, sharply white against the budding trees and grey houses.

Beyond, at the pier head, they had lingered to watch the pollack and rainbow fish, moving through the weed under water as clear as plate glass, had loitered till the chill wind of early May had driven them round the headland to a sheltered beach of coarse shingle where a rapid stream emptied itself into a cleft between the rocks.

Catherine watched William and Bill pottering about the rock pools. She thought:

'That's just by the strip of sand where they caught the big conger on the night line.'

She didn't call out to them. William and Bill simply wouldn't have been interested. It meant nothing to them. They were so little interested in what she told them that she began to wonder whether all the things she could remember had really happened, though she could still see the huge, limp conger, speckled with sand, hanging down at each end of the barrow in which it was wheeled triumphantly up the quays.

Every rock and pool was the same. There was the place where she had baled out a little green gurney in a bucket, and the big pool where she had gone prawning, years later, with Oliver, and he had cut his hand on a sharp edge of rock.

Oliver. Once it had seemed to matter so much that he and the others were dead. She had felt bitter, grieved, and desolated. She wondered, nursing her chin in her hand and thinking of Sebastian's face as she had seen it that day on the Birmingham road. Sebastian was younger than Oliver ... would Oliver have been different? Oliver had been so sane, so full of a quiet happiness.

She couldn't discuss Oliver with William. William couldn't be expected to understand the boy and girl relationship, so young, so free of any kind of thought for tomorrow, which had existed between them. Friends? Not friends, certainly not lovers. The thought of loving Oliver was laughable, beside William he paled and went out. Yet there had been something ... the comfortable something that exists between people who have known each other very young. There was nothing to explain to Oliver, because he knew all that there was to know already.

She stood up, shaking the sand out of her skirts, and went across to William. He stood, puffing at his pipe and watching the sea. Bill had run away, carrying on, as he went, a conversation with Mingo and Mungo, his two monkeys. No one had ever seen them, for they didn't exist. This made them peculiarly and privately his own. They were covered with silky dark hair and had pink hands and feet and sad, wise eyes and long, prehensile tails. They were graceful and lively, they scampered about with their tails arched over their backs, and sometimes jumped off the ground with all four feet at once. Bill loved them and was happier with them than in any other company.

But William, unless he was occupied, wasn't happy alone. She thought, as she stood beside him, that they'd seen a good deal of each other in the last fortnight . . . more than they had seen for a great many years. And it had been a success. It was a surprising thing that she could still be good company for William.

'Good holiday,' said William suddenly.

'Yes . . . and I rather dreaded it.'

'Why?'

'I thought you'd be bored,' she prevaricated, 'or that Violet would find Bill a nuisance.'

'Bill's a thundering good kid. I don't see how anybody could find him a nuisance.'

William looked down at her ruffled hair. He wondered

what was going on in her mind. He never knew what Catherine thought. That was what enchanted him. And when she wasn't worried or tired, what good company she could be! The two of them, just muddling about together, interested, but not disturbed, by Bill.

'This is a fine place,' he said. 'Plenty going on and yet you can get away by yourself if you want to.'

'It's changed, though.'

Catherine looked across the water at the town beach, still speckled with newspapers and orange peel after last Saturday's crowd.

'A good thing they do come.' William liked to see the crowds strung out along the beach at weekends. It was his belief that the new motor traffic was saving the towns from tubercle and the villages from inbreeding.

'Not that it does the place any good,' he went on. 'One of the fishermen was grumbling at it this morning. They come down and mess up the beach and bring their own food with them. Families used to spend a week or two down here, deal with the shops and go to the entertainments, and hire out boats by the week. Now they come for two or three hours in a charabanc and spend nothing.'

'There's no money for long holidays.' Catherine picked up a flat stone and flipped it across the rocks into the dancing water. 'They're like us, they have to take what they can get.'

They stood silent, looking across the bay because the day was perfect and there was no need to talk. Catherine thought that the world was out to take what it could get. A good time!

The little port had done its best with a cinema, a charabanc service, a series of little dress shops. The confectioners' windows were full of cheap coloured cakes, filled with cream. Everybody wanted something bright, specious and amusing. They didn't believe in it, even whilst they tore, and grabbed, and shouted . . . but neither did they believe in anything else. The good time wasn't real, behind it was a sense of worry and dislocation. She and William had that feeling, though they had no chance to live noisily.

She thought how valuable William was because he didn't want to grab, and because this holiday hadn't been tawdry and crowded, but a real chance to know each other. All these years, she thought, and we haven't even begun. He gets much more out of life than I do.

William took his pipe out of his mouth.

'Confound it!' he said. 'Here's Violet.'

His voice was flat with dismay. Catherine laughed.

'William! If you can't change your face, for the love of Mike go off and hide it. Oh, look! She's coming because she thinks she ought. She hates sand in her shoes.'

They both looked at Violet, plodding dutifully against the wind. She had the strayed, disconcerted look of the resident who finds herself on the beach.

William shrugged his shoulders. 'You deal with her. I'm going to talk to Bill.'

Catherine went to meet her sister, who stopped, gratefully, when she saw her coming.

'How you can! Standing about in all that wind!'

'It's all right under the rocks. Come and sit down.'

She felt grieved because the peace of the morning, and her companionship with William, had both been broken into.

Violet put her shopping bag on the sand and sat on it, tucking her skirts tightly round her knees. She had never quite got used to the sight of her own stockings.

'I felt so sorry for you, out on the beach. Such a poor holiday. But it's fearfully cramped, up in the bungalow, and I've nowhere to take you. If only we'd been in our old house we could have gone round the shops in the morning and there were such a nice lot of people to see in the afternoons.'

'This is what we like. No telephone, no responsibility. William and Bill are having the time of their lives. I love it. It's so casual.'

'A lot too casual. You ought to be here in August. It's revolting. Crowds of young men with nothing on but flannel shirts open at the neck and grubby flannel trousers. Girls in bathing dresses, dripping wet, pushing through the shoppers in the High Street . . . and couples sprawling all over the beach behind every rock. They think nothing matters because it's Cornwall.'

'It isn't only Cornwall,' said Catherine. It wasn't any use trying to explain William's attitude towards the seaside crowds. To Violet the August people were as incomprehensible as savages.

'No, it isn't. That's what I came to talk to you about. About Sebastian . . . and Jane. You can't talk in the bungalow, you never get the sitting-room to yourself, and those people next door listen over the garden fence. I wish Edward wouldn't encourage them. . . .'

Violet pulled off her gloves and rubbed the backs of her hands where the stitching had marked them.

'It's about Sebastian,' she repeated.

'But he's still in the same job, isn't he? I thought it was a good one, on the engineering side of the . . .'

'The Eeseefroot Ice Cream Company. It never was a good job. I didn't tell you. I hoped he'd get another. He simply goes round to tea shops and places and puts in new ice cream machines and soda-fountains. Then he goes back every few months to see if they're working.'

'It's better than no job at all. They may give him a better one.'

It was hard on Sebastian. He had always had a passion for machinery. His qualifications had been excellent, but there were too many young engineers with excellent qualifications.

'I don't think there's any hope for it at all. He's lucky even to get a job like that. They picked him out of forty others. I wanted him to come down here to us instead. Touring about like a commercial traveller! But he wouldn't.'

'No . . . I shouldn't think he would.'

'Oh! Se's obstinate. I know that. But I'm worried. Last time I saw him he looked so slovenly. Tired . . . and careless . . . and hard. He's bitter about it.'

'Has he seen Jane?'

'Jane's too full of herself to worry about Sebastian. Jane's got her cake and she's eating it.'

Violet turned one of her gloves inside out.

'Even if Jane took a decent interest she couldn't do anything. You know what Sebastian is. You never get a word out of him. I don't know where he's living half the time . . . he hardly ever writes. You don't know your own luck . . . having your children not grown up yet. All that work . . . and what for? Look at Jane! Look at Sebastian! Could anything be less like what we intended?'

Catherine took a handful of shingle and let it run through her fingers. As usual, Violet didn't want advice. She was using Catherine as a waste-paper basket for worries. But this time they were real.

'It's not only Jane and Sebastian,' she said.

'That's no consolation to me. You know what Jane's flat is like. The most awful set . . . up to all hours talking so that you don't know which way to look. Young men in dirty pullovers trying to look like that dreadful person in *The Constant Nymph*, and girls who can hardly get their lips apart for paint . . . people we shouldn't have looked at if we'd seen them the other side of the road.'

'I think most of it is quite bogus. They're all very young.'

'There's such a thing as being too charitable. Jane's asking for trouble and one of these days she'll get it. Oh, Catherine! If only she could have had a nice, respectable, comfortable house like we used to have, so that I could go and stay there sometimes. I can't go and stay with Jane. She makes me feel a fool, she doesn't even want me.'

Catherine put her hand over the one that held the glove.

'Jane's just taken up with what she's doing. She's young.'

'You talk about being young as if it was a disease.'

'It's a hateful time. Everything's so real. You're going to do so much. And then, somehow, you don't. I'm sorry for Jane. . . .'

'You needn't be. Jane's sorry for me. Jane's very pleased
with herself. She makes me feel an interfering old fool. And
I'm not old. I'm only forty-five.'

Violet took her hand away from Catherine. 'You'll know,
one day,' she said. 'You can't understand . . . yet.'

Catherine was silent, because she did understand. Not
to know when you weren't wanted till the thing was made
brutally plain . . . how pitiable! She wondered whether she, in
her turn, would know when to stand back. Perhaps no parent
ever did, because when parents interfere out of love they don't
know that they are interfering.

'It's all gone wrong,' Violet said, with a hurt simplicity.
'I can do nothing with either of them.'

She sat limply, looking at her own knees. The tide was
turning, the waves sounded gay, rhythmical, on the outer
ridge of rocks.

II

As they climbed the steep slope to Violet's bungalow they saw
Edward going in. As always, Edward remained an unknown
quantity. They rarely saw him, for except during the evening
or in very bad weather he was seldom indoors. He drifted
about the quays in an old snuff-coloured jacket which hung
away from his thin back, a pipe in his mouth, a stick under
his arm. He leaned his elbows on the pier or walked for long
hours upon the cliffs. When there was anything to be done in
the garden he worked there, ignorantly but very patiently,
in a slatey soil and on a slope which needed all the persistent

rains of the West Country to keep it moist. He fed his hens, pumped up the water and cleaned the family boots as methodically as if he had done nothing else all his life. But his face, fallen, old, and disappointed, struck Catherine afresh every time she saw him. Sometimes as he looked at Bill, busy, happy and shouting, she surprised a look which startled her . . . a look as though Edward were sorry for him, because he was happy.

Catherine sighed as they went into the hall. She found the bungalow oppressive. The distempered walls were still streaked with the winter's damp, and Violet's suites of furniture looked large and incongruous in the small rooms. They were an obvious misfit in that tawdry house. The overcrowded sitting-room and the pictures which crammed the walls were a pathetic attempt to impress Violet's past standing upon her neighbours. The whole house was clean, stuffy, and in a chronic condition of neatness. Violet spent hours in polishing the heavy furniture and making crochet lace to edge the linen window blinds which kept out most of the light. The atmosphere of a solid town house was carefully preserved. But it was possible to hear every sound from one end of the bungalow to the other . . . a water pipe whining in the bathroom, a door rattling, William knocking out his pipe. There was no privacy.

The weekly letters from Audrey and Adam lay on the hallstand. Catherine carried them into lunch with her, and put them beside her plate. Violet looked curiously at her.

'Aren't you going to open your children's letters?'

Catherine laughed. She knew so well what to expect from

those painful compositions beginning: 'Dear Mother, I hop you are quite wel . . .'

'It's all right, there won't be anything in them.'

'You don't take much interest in your children,' said Violet, moving Bill's chair so that it shouldn't knock against the leg of the table.

It didn't seem necessary to answer. William was chasing a queen wasp, Edward was turning the beef over with a puzzled air, wondering which side he ought to begin, Violet was frowning at a smudge on a spoon.

Interest? Catherine hardly knew. When the children went to school their lives, for those lost months, ran underground. She didn't know what was happening to them. She divined that Adam, who was developing in every way except that required by examiners, was happy enough, and that Audrey, whose reports were always satisfactory, had failed to fit in. No one told her these things, Audrey and Adam least of all. How should they? But she knew that other girls puzzled Audrey and hadn't her interests. Audrey was a person who clung to her own point of view, she might be bullied but she couldn't be coerced. She learnt conduct very slowly. No. It wasn't likely that Audrey would be happy.

Suddenly Edward spoke.

'Nothing in them! No, there wouldn't be. They never tell you anything.'

He looked across at William, who was dropping the dead wasp out of the window.

'A man who has children is a fool,' he said. 'Look at us . . . look at the money we've spent on them . . . and look at us now.

Money . . . hundreds of pounds . . . thousands. Everything they wanted. And look at us!'

He passed the plate to Bill, who looked appealingly at Catherine.

'Mother! Might I leave the fat?'

Catherine nodded, making a face at Bill to ensure silence, but Edward hadn't heard him.

'What good has it done?' he said. 'That's what I want to know! Money wasted.'

'I wouldn't say that,' William argued. 'There's a lot in education. These kids who're leaving schools now, they know their jobs well . . .'

He started a long dissertation with examples and anecdotes. But Edward had fallen silent again; he went on eating his beef whilst Violet, frankly puzzled, tried to take a polite interest in what William was saying. Vaguely, she felt that William was clever but that Jane, had she been there, would have understood better what William was trying to say.

After lunch Catherine stayed behind to help Violet clear away and polish the table, William drifted out into the garden in the wake of Edward and his pipe. He leaned his elbows on the wall beside him and looked down at the sunny harbour.

'This is a grand little place,' he said. He felt grateful to Edward.

Edward started. 'Eh! It's a poor place enough. It's not the house I meant to have. It's badly built.'

He searched in his pockets for the matches.

'It would have been all right if I could have retired ten years ago,' he went on. 'I should have retired in good times then, when I was doing well. But I was squeezed out in the War. A man can't begin again at my age.'

'It's a fine little place, though,' William persisted. 'With the sea, and the river, and the ships . . .'

He thought that he would like to retire to just such a place as this.

'What? Oh, the place is all right. But it's no use to me. A man don't want to retire because he's useless.' He puffed slowly at his pipe. 'I've thought of buying a dog sometimes, but there'd be no room for a dog in the house. A dog brings the mud in.'

He looked across the harbour.

'I always liked a dog,' he said. 'A dog don't talk, it don't have opinions, it don't want you to agree with it. A dog thinks you're a fine fellow, and there's an end to it.'

William agreed with him. He liked a dog, but there was no room for a dog in his own house full of children.

'There must be plenty of other retired people down here,' he suggested.

'People? I suppose there are. I can't say I make friends. I don't need them. The ones I cared for all died or moved away long ago. I don't want new friends. They don't want to be troubled with a dull chap like myself . . . I can remember when I thought myself a fine chap . . . doing well . . . and with a couple of smart children. It's not so long ago either. It don't seem long.'

William said nothing. He had never felt that he was a fine fellow, he had never thought about himself at all, except when he knew that he was enjoying himself more than usual, or that he was more than usually tired. He knew, on the contrary, that he wasn't doing at all too well, that he was still paying off debts, that years of heavy expenditure lay ahead of him, and that Catherine was the only capital he had ever made out of life. Even Catherine was a doubtful speculation. And the children . . . ?

'There's no profit in anything one does,' Edward concluded bitterly. 'As for the children, as far as I can see we might just as well never have had 'em. What good have they ever been to me?' He moved off towards the gate. 'Hundreds of pounds . . .' he murmured finally.

William sat where he was, puffing at his pipe. He had never had any sentiment about his profession; as his father's son, it had been forced upon him. He had never, till now, understood how important it was to him. He had always been efficient, always interested, but this new feeling was another matter. His profession, his deep association with the lives and feelings of other people, this healing of bodies, which was so largely a healing of minds, had come to be the most important factor in his life. It was more important than Catherine.

It had been a good holiday, but he wasn't sorry that he was going home. There was that 'waster' baby which might, or might not, be doing better on the food he had ordered for it, poor wretch. He wondered if they had got a bed in the sanatorium for that girl yet, and how that unusual case of diabetes was doing on the new treatment. Even two weeks was too long to be away. He felt that if it ever came to parting with all these people, with whose lives and misfortunes he had been intimate for so long, a great deal of the meaning would go out of his life. They mattered to him. He had used his intelligence on their behalf, felt compassion for them, had for them that inexplicable love of the protector for the protected.

Catherine and William spent the afternoon upon the cliffs. The day had already the flavour of departure. Tomorrow's early start, tomorrow's long day's driving occupied their minds.

'It's a mercy Bill's old enough,' Catherine said. 'Once we couldn't have done this.'

She looked gratefully at Bill, trotting indifferently ahead.

A kestrel rose out of the hollow of the cliffs, a fishing smack, far out on the bay, shook out her sails to catch the evening breeze. They heard the chug-chug of her oil engine as she went about, hunting for the wind. Catherine looked at William, at William's shabby grey flannels and deplorable hat. She felt sorry that his holiday was over. In the long year it was almost the only pleasure he had.

'We're selfish beasts,' William said suddenly. 'We've enjoyed this holiday. . . . But look at Edward and Violet!'

'They don't enjoy themselves.'

'They do not. What's it all about, anyhow?'

'That's just it. If only they'd have it out . . . snap at each other . . . be done with it. But nothing happens. There's just a dreary feeling. You sit in the room with them and feel as if the roof would lift . . .'

'They might get more out of it, after all. I bet I would.'

Catherine walked on beside him. William, she thought, had nothing, in all these years of work he had made nothing that she and the children hadn't spent.

238

'Suppose we get like that, one day,' she said.

'Oh, no, we won't!'

'I'm frightened,' she insisted. 'You work so hard, do so much. You get nothing out of it. And at the end . . . when we've done with the children . . . when we're old.'

William stopped.

'Look here,' he said. 'It's time you stopped being frightened. You're not going to worry about me. You needn't . . .'

'But when you want to retire . . .'

'I'm not going to retire. I used to think I wanted to, once. Now I know I never shall.'

'But you said just now if you were Edward you could get more out of it . . .'

'So I could. But I shouldn't care for this sort of thing for ever. A bungalow's all right on a holiday, but I should want a small house with everything very nice about it. I don't want a makeshift.'

'You can certainly hear far too much in that house. We could do all right in an old cottage.'

William threw an arm round her. 'No, we won't. I'm not going to see you struggling round a cottage without any maids. You won't worry me to retire, will you?'

'I won't. But I don't want to feel that you can't retire, because of me. If you've always looked forward to it I'd much rather you went on planning for it. . . .'

'No. It wouldn't be fair.' He gave her shoulder a squeeze. 'Besides, I don't want to.'

Catherine looked at him. She would have lived on anything, anywhere, if he had wished it. It was only what he deserved. She saw why he didn't wish it. Two-thirds of the reason was that he wouldn't give her less than her due, but the deciding third was the fact that he didn't want to part with his work, which he loved, and which had become part of him.

She thought, 'What a grudging little wretch I've been. I've resented having to give up and work for him and the children. I thought I loved them, but really I've only wanted to make a good job of them. I've been cross with Audrey and Adam . . . frustrated and angry when they wouldn't develop the way I wanted. I've pulled and dragged and worried at them and at my jobs. I've resented William because he didn't know what I wanted. I've felt tied and bound. I've whined like a puppy on a chain.'

She wanted to tell William that she loved him, but she kept silent, for to tell William would make him embarrassed and derisive.

CHAPTER TWO

Catherine sat on her heels by the gas fire in Jane's living-room, making toast. The table was pushed back and Jane, in a short green tunic, was springing conscientiously about the room. The nails on her bare feet were manicured and polished with a pink paste, her fingernails were cut to points.

Outside the window a raw November morning broke reluctantly over a blasted heath of chimney pots – thousands of them, dirty brown and red, like burnt heather. The noise of the traffic beat at the shivering window-panes, the furniture quivered now and again, sparrows chirped in the guttering.

The room smelt of fresh coffee and stale cigarettes. In the kitchen the Westphalian student on an educational passport, who made the excellent coffee and cleared away the cigarette ends, was singing an air from Offenbach. Peter wasn't up yet, and wouldn't be, for an hour or two, but his music loaded the piano and hung over the edge like an impending snowfall in a thaw.

Catherine watched Jane. It was amazing how she kept it up. Every morning at eight she started to practise, barefooted on the painted floor. She went up and down, dutifully, between the two kaleidoscopic pictures on the pistachio-coloured walls. At nine she appeared, dressed in her street clothes, for breakfast. By half-past she was out of the house on the way to catch a district train to one of the half-dozen schools she visited in the course of the week. At six o'clock she returned from a day of alternately dancing and catching trains to spend the evening reading and copying out Peter's score whilst the Westphalian student – who had her own methods – did her obscure but efficient marketing. By eight o'clock Peter's set had begun to drift in, and went on drifting in till after midnight. They sat upon the floor, on the table, on the window-ledges. The room was blue with cigarette smoke, loud with conversation.

There was also music.

Jane and the student Hansi ran about with cocktails and coffee cups, talked incessantly, seemed to know about everybody's work and their exact (varying) relationship to everybody in the room. The walls of the room were blobby with condensed human breath by the end of the evening.

Peter sat on the floor by the gas fire, a lock of straw-coloured hair falling into his eye, his hands in his pockets, treating his set with a kindly insolence. He never moved from that position. If people wanted to talk to him, that was their affair.

As soon as it was all over, Jane and Hansi piled cups and cocktail glasses into the sink, emptied the ashtrays, opened the windows and dragged the furniture back.

'Dear Jane!' Peter would say, looking at her through half-closed eyes from his place on the floor. 'Such a good housekeeper!'

'*Ach!* But only leave it!' Hansi would protest. 'It is nothing. Tomorrow I will do it.'

But Jane couldn't leave it, any more than she could go to bed without having a bath and trimming her fingernails. Often it was three o'clock before her door closed for the night.

Jane dropped to the hearth beside Catherine and held out her hands to the fire. She didn't look comfortable on the floor. She sat with a straight back, as though she was in a chair.

'Why do you let so many of them come in at night?' Catherine asked, standing the toast on edge against the fender.

'Because it's so good for Peter's work.'

'But most of them know no more about music than I do. They only want to talk about themselves.'

'They all know interesting people. It gets Peter known. It doesn't do to be out of things.'

Catherine took a fresh piece of bread. She didn't think that Jane's set were particularly valuable. They were Bohemian because it was an effective pose, because they had jobs which bored them . . . because it gave them something to talk about. She wondered if any of them could substantiate their claim to knowing famous people.

'Peter's been asked to play at two studio parties next month,' Jane went on. 'I know. . . . They don't pay anything. That's not the point. It gets him talked about.'

She stood up, pulling herself up by the mantelpiece. It struck Catherine that Jane had no longer the face of a young girl. Her vigorous young body was that of unspoilt youth, but her face was a dateless mask. Even that mask was etched with lines round the mouth and eyes. There were hollows under her cheekbones. All Jane's set, with their ceaseless chatter about youth, about living their own lives, about expression, had that macabre, sullen look. It made Catherine feel that her own face was conspicuous, naked. She had, and expressed, too many unfashionable feelings.

Jane stretched herself.

'It's all life,' she added unexpectedly. 'One has to live. I couldn't go through life half asleep, as you do.'

'I have beautiful dreams,' said Catherine, turning the toast.

Jane shrugged. 'You're sentimental and thoroughly dishonest,' she said kindly. 'You've never looked straight at anything in your life.'

Catherine grinned. Standing as she did between Violet and Jane she could see the point of view of both generations. She wondered, as Jane went off to dress, what Jane thought she was about.

Jane was no artist. Her dancing was efficient, but something vital was lacking in the result. It was without joy, without any kind of passion. There she was, working hard and living a most uncomfortable life, not for any joy she took in it, but for the sake of a set of principles.

That those principles were of a fundamental silliness did not alter Catherine's growing conviction that Jane was admirable, solid, and bourgeois.

Rebellion of the arts, freedom of sex life, the social regeneration of mankind through the tacit refusal to do anything which gave the doer a moment's inconvenience . . . to these things Jane was bringing the same earnestness which Violet had lavished on the upkeep of her house, the teaching of a narrow social code, the preservation of an absurd set of conventions.

Catherine wondered if Jane had ever, in the old sense, been in love with Peter. She talked six times of Peter's work to once that she talked of Peter. There was no tenderness between them, little apparent friendship. They talked baldly of the business side of the arrangement. Jane was there to increase Peter's income and make his work possible. Peter was there to provide a background for Jane. There were no forbearances or small courtesies between them. They wrangled publicly and with the utmost firmness and good temper, and spent little of their free time together.

She snatched the toast back, aware that she had let it catch fire.

'O-oh!' cried Hansi, coming in with the coffee pot. 'But you have burnt it. See . . . it does not matter. Myself, I will eat it.'

To waste any food at all was crime unspeakable to Hansi, but she wouldn't let Catherine or Jane eat burnt toast, whoever had burnt it. She was there to give her services in return for learning English. Good. She would fulfil the last letter of that contract.

Catherine stood up. She wondered if she ought to insist on eating the toast, which she liked to eat black, or whether to do so wouldn't hurt Hansi's feelings.

In the next room she could hear Peter's bed creaking as he turned over to light the first cigarette of the day. She wondered why she disliked him. Perhaps it was because his name wasn't really Peter but Reginald, and because he lived on an allowance from his perfectly sound manufacturing family in the West Riding. An allowance carefully calculated as far enough short of the subsistence level to keep him at work.

Peter really did like noise, disorder, interminable conversations and meals at all hours. He worked at his music because it amused him. When it didn't amuse him he stopped and didn't begin again until the inclination returned. Office hours were not for him. On some days the flat rang with his complicated dissonances, on others it would be silent whilst he slouched out into the sunshine to waylay one or other of his set or to hunt for the lacquered and inlaid tea trays which were his other passion.

He really didn't mind whether he arrived or not, though it amused him to let Jane talk about his significance. And he had, Catherine decided, a keen, shallow intelligence . . . a cruel intelligence without emotion. He thought Catherine a fool but paid her the compliment of admitting that she was not without physical attractiveness. Catherine felt that this was why she hated him.

She was far happier at breakfast with Hansi and Jane. There was a slippered ease in being simply three women alone together. Only a married woman can appreciate woman's society at its true value. They sat talking, their elbows on the table, the pleasant smell of hot toast in their nostrils.

'I wish you weren't going tomorrow,' said Jane. 'You always go just as soon as you come. You've nothing to do when you get down there.'

Catherine laughed. Useless to explain to Jane that she felt any need to get back to William and Bill, or felt blank without them. Jane would have said, 'Then you ought to leave them oftener.' Jane put herself in pawn for nobody.

'You know,' Jane answered her thoughts, 'it would do you good if you got right away from them for a bit . . . struck out on your own.'

'I am on my own.' Catherine wondered how she could explain that her life, so trivial, so humdrum in appearance, was a complicated and intensely interesting job. 'It would bore me to have a job.'

'But you ought to do things that bore you.'

'That's a flat contradiction. Why?'

'Because you ought to live.'

'But I do live.'

Jane was silent. Catherine wasn't living in accordance with Jane's principles, therefore she must be wrong.

'O-oh' said Hansi, putting down her cup. 'But she lives! You English . . . you are so funny. If anyone does not think quite the same you say, "She does not live." But I say: "I like it, but it is not wrong because you do not like it. For you it is wrong, for me it is different." But you English . . . always you must be right.'

Jane took her dispatch case from a chair.

'That's all very well. Catherine's life is very bad for Catherine . . . and for Catherine's children too. Why . . . what on earth will you do with them in three or four years' time if you go on being like you are now?'

Hansi laughed and started to collect the cups.

Catherine looked thoughtfully from Hansi to Jane. Hansi was eighteen, Jane was twenty-five. Already in that seven years, there was a difference of outlook. Jane was defiant, challenging. Hansi was tolerant, without enthusiasms, inclined to shrug her shoulders at the world.

'Why, what do you expect me to do with them?' Catherine asked, lighting a cigarette and ruffling up her hair.

Jane looked at her in despair. To her Catherine was a nice child who had wilfully refused to grow up. Catherine had never run mad over her work, indulged any of her physical appetites, or had an 'affair'.

'What you want is a lover,' she said finally.

'I have a lover.'

'Oh, William!' Jane's voice was disgusted.

It flashed across Catherine that Peter and Jane had simply refused that duel of the sexes, that running fight in which she and William had been for twelve years engaged and which they were still pursuing, urgently, to some end which never came in sight. She laughed, leaning both elbows on the table and looking up at Jane.

Jane looked at her watch. 'I must go!' she said, and went out, abrupt and efficient. They heard her heels clicking on the stone stairs.

Catherine looked at Hansi. They were rather a puzzle . . . these young men and women from Rennes, from Lyons, from Mainz and Heidelberg and Tübingen, from Oslo . . . cool, hard-working, disillusioned and friendly.

'What shall you do when you have finished your course?' she asked Hansi as the German girl rubbed up the table.

'Me? I shall teach. I do not want to, no. But it is the best thing for me.'

Catherine nodded. That was so. After all the talk of new careers for women the bulk of them still had to choose the three old professions of nursing, secretaryship and teaching. She wondered a little about Audrey. A beautiful vagueness still existed in the minds of headmistresses as to what their pupils were to do when they left school. Their responsibilities ceased with matriculation. She wondered . . . would Audrey take the bit between her teeth like Jane or would she be like Hansi . . . on whom nothing seemed to make any impression?

Jane's attitude was a flat refusal. Beauty, Jane said, was all nonsense. Beauty was nothing, expression everything. All love, not physical passion, was sentiment. Physical sensation was life, the one thing of which you could be sure, all else was illusion. Jane said she was a good animal, and did a great many things which were not natural to her in order to prove that thesis.

Catherine yawned. She had always been passionately aware of her own body . . . hot turf to lie on . . . the cigarette after a bathe . . . the deep bliss of a hot bath . . . that apotheosis of physical sensation through which she had created Audrey, Adam and Bill . . . these things were good. But to be shut up in them for ever . . . to have no more than that . . .

And Hansi said nothing, refused nothing, expected nothing. She simply worked with a cool, quiet common sense.

In his room Catherine could hear Peter stirring. It was one of his active periods. Presently he would come in, slouch without greeting her to the piano, hurl handfuls of music on the floor till he had found what he wanted, and then settle down for the rest of the morning.

Catherine stood up. She would go out. After last night's protracted conversations she felt that her ears needed a rest.

She remembered, as she pulled on her coat, that she had come to London to speak to Jane about Violet. It was impossible. In that atmosphere you couldn't speak about Violet. It was hard for her to understand Jane and Peter, impossible for Violet. It was far better that Violet should stay in Cornwall and feel miserable than that she should come to London and feel a fool. It was better to be lonely than to be laughed at, and Jane certainly had a trick of making both herself and Violet look ridiculous.

She wondered, stepping down the interminable stone stairs, whether presently Audrey and Adam would find her ridiculous. If they loved her very much they wouldn't mind – but did they love her as much as that?

She thought, I wasn't here to think of Audrey and Adam, I came up because of Violet, because she keeps on writing about Jane. I was a fool, you can't arrange other people's affairs for them. Jane doesn't want Violet, she can't even see that Violet wants Jane.

She stepped out into a weak sunlight.

Violet couldn't do anything with Jane even if Jane wanted her. They were so far apart that they couldn't help each other. She wondered why she no longer disliked Jane . . . at herself for making her in some kind of way, a friend.

PART FIVE

CHAPTER ONE

I

The years drifted down on Audrey and Adam, impalpable as dust, yet slowly changing them before the critical eyes of Catherine and William. They had no indiscriminate admiration for their children. William, in the beginning, had not admired them at all. He had been quite frank about their status as dreadful inflictions, as they grew older he accepted them on their merits, and on that footing alone.

Catherine loved, but didn't admire, and as always, love made her caustic and gave an edge to her tongue. Because she loved she drove, she exacted, she looked for perfection. To persons in their teens she was more than a little tiresome . . . that craze of hers for wanting everything finished.

Slowly, after the manner of the adolescent, Audrey and Adam built up a wall of reserve, different from the unscalable wall of childhood, but more lasting. They had to have some kind of protection against her, they couldn't let her know too much. They were neighbours, Catherine felt, but not intimates. She didn't quarrel with the arrangement, she believed it to be the only one possible between any group of persons. People might cry out that they wanted to be understood, but it wasn't true. To be too well known is a disquieting experience.

Adam had cried out one day, between anger and tears . . .

'You don't understand me!'

'No, thank God!' William had retorted.

Adam had stared at him, rebuffed, but he had gone off to think.

Catherine sometimes looked at them and wondered. She had kept the bond which, tacitly, had been made between them. Persons they had come to her, persons they left her control. She wondered if she would have been wiser if she had bound them down. They were so amazingly silly, so crude and callow. They had the most distressing lapses into early childhood, combined with the queerest flashes of middle-aged wisdom. They were so unfinished, so unbalanced, and so very much their own.

'Why worry?' William repeated. 'They've got to learn off their own bat now.'

But Catherine, who had urged them up into trees and five-barred gates, who had sent them out onto the roaring high road alone on bicycles, and dragged them, shrieking, into the brook to learn to swim, stood dismayed before the spiritual risk.

'They'll be all right,' William insisted.

'Why? Other people's aren't . . . always. Why should ours be?'

'They won't if you fuss over them.'

Catherine sighed. It was her nature to fuss. If anything actually went wrong she was cool and more capable than usual, when everything ran smoothly she fretted.

'Let them alone,' William advised.

So Catherine let them alone and was at once confronted by the paradox that the child who is let alone runs immediately to look for you. For they were growing up to be excellent company.

When she was with Audrey, Catherine was happy and at peace. Her mind and Audrey's were component parts. This was the more strange in that Audrey wasn't at all the daughter she would have chosen . . . she had expected different things of Audrey. She had wanted her to have a fine and original mind, to fulfil all those dreams and ambitions which she herself had been forced to forgo. Audrey who liked to follow Catherine round the house, not to learn, but to show her quicker and neater ways of doing things, Audrey who loved organised games and enjoyed her dinner, Audrey who was efficient, good-humoured and capable at moments of a broad, rather coarse wit which enchanted William, had become extraordinarily good company.

Gradually, Catherine had learnt to expect Audrey to be merely herself and not to force her to develop unnatural gifts. She had always allowed Adam to be himself . . . why was she less just to her daughter? It seemed that a son could develop in any direction he chose and remain a wonderful act of God, but a daughter who failed to fulfil her mother's requirements was guilty of the combined vices of Goneril and the unjust steward.

It didn't occur to her at once that Audrey had been forced down into the mould not without some bruising of the fabric. . . .

There had been her natural tendency to make friends older and more intelligent than herself . . . .

This had been considered side; she had learnt to drop that, the penalties were too severe. Audrey was now one of a group of what she described as 'cheerful souls', people whom she could like, without engaging her affections at all deeply.

Audrey was never likely to hurt herself more than once with the same tool. She couldn't get what she wanted? Good. She shut a door and ceased to want. Catherine, watching Audrey, had changed her school. Audrey was happier, but her line of reasoning didn't vary. She continued to be one of a group of cheerful souls.

Catherine admitted that she was right. Quietly, and with her usual logic, Audrey was taking the road to happiness. It wasn't a road Catherine had taken, or ever could take. Catherine's progress was a continual running and falling, and getting up again, surprised, and progressively a little less hurt. Audrey walked with a stick and kept to the middle of the road.

She watched Audrey with some amusement, allowed her to edit her clothes, her conversation, and her amusements.

'Why do you let the child talk to you like that?' William asked. 'It's none of her business.'

'If she doesn't do it now she'll do it later, when it really matters. Let her say what she thinks . . . I don't want to lose touch with them, William.'

'I don't like that hat she's chosen for you. It's unsuitable.'

'I know it's too young.' Catherine took it off and looked at it doubtfully.

'It's not that. It's a beastly hat. It looks like a pudding basin.'

'Let her choose them, William. It's only what she would have liked to wear herself. Vicarious enjoyment. She's always in school uniform.'

William shrugged his shoulders. He liked a hat which looked worth the money he'd paid for it. The wretched thing had nothing on it but a tuft of game bird's feathers.

He was proud of his daughter. A nice child . . . not exceptional, but clean-looking and straight-backed, and reasonably intelligent. Some day, well in the future, she would make some nice chap a very fair sort of wife.

She wasn't Catherine, of course. He never suspected that Audrey knew she wasn't Catherine and privately disliked the priority that Catherine and William gave to each other over any of their children. The day had not yet come when she was to look on that priority as inevitable, without resentment, but it was already causing her to look tentatively towards marriage as a possible experience.

Audrey was of her generation. Her sex education had been neither fortuitous nor over-insisted upon. She simply knew what everyone else knew, and there was an end of the business. She thought that it was one of the things over which too much fuss was made. It wasn't in Audrey's character to make a fuss.

But marriage, all things considered, had its points. It was more permanent than most careers, and more various. She meant to have a life of her own, to keep herself and be independent, that came first. Only if it ever came to marriage, she wouldn't feel that she was being called upon to make a sacrifice.

That was another thing about which too much fuss was made. If you did a thing there was probably some good reason why you did it, so why run round talking about sacrifices? Making a noise and drawing attention to yourself!

She loved Catherine and William, deeply, with a hidden love, whose unshaken loyalty would last the rest of her life, but she didn't consider that anything which they did for her or for each other was a sacrifice. Their limitations were a natural result of the life they lived, the standard which they had set for themselves and the income upon which they had to support both that standard and that life. Any further limitation was imposed either by their love of each other or of their children. Audrey was quietly learning to give love as well as to accept it.

II

Catherine wasn't as happy with Adam.

Adam was developing from a boy into a youth after whom people turned their heads to look ... especially women. Catherine was afraid that he knew it. Women would do anything for Adam. Irene always mended his bicycle tyres, but she made Audrey and Bill mend their own. She said it was good for them. Adam always got more ice cream than either of the others. Audrey said that Miss Trenchard simply looked at him and the spoon slipped. His tennis and his dancing were alike deplorable, yet he never lacked partners.

Catherine distrusted Adam's looks. They would make life too easy for him. She was hard on Adam. She had to be, or there was every chance that he would sit down and let himself be pushed. It wasn't easy, for Adam treated her beautifully.

He listened when she talked, agreed with her opinions, chose her presents which he knew she wanted, and waited at the foot of the stairs for her when they came away from parties . . . and kissed her hand when she went to bed at night.

He kissed her hand!

In Adam it wasn't absurd. It was his attitude towards her. He had none of Bill's robust scorn for women, he had a slightly whimsical air of respect that was almost courtliness.

Yes. It was necessary to be hard on Adam.

The harder she was the more charming he became. She wondered whether it was because she was hard to please and gave trouble. Also, she criticised.

Adam would bring Catherine a drawing.

'Look!' he would say. 'I did it for you.'

Catherine would look. She didn't for one moment suppose that he had done it for her, but she was intensely interested in what he had drawn.

'It's good. I like those bare trees. But the roof's out of perspective.'

Adam would snatch it back and go to his father.

'Rotten! Why can't you look at things? Did you ever see a roof like that?'

Adam's eyes would look large, dark, and hurt. It wasn't a criticism of his drawing. It was a personal affront.

'Take it away and do it again,' William would insist. 'You can't leave a thing like that.'

Adam would do it again, though it was no joy to him. He had to do it again if he wanted approval, and approval was what Adam craved. He was learning to discriminate. He disliked those who said, 'Yes, beautiful, how clever of you. Put it down over there and I'll have a look at it in a minute.' They simply wanted to get out of being bothered as quickly as possible. But Catherine and William really cared . . . Catherine could see the dawn of that understanding in Adam.

It was a pity, she thought, that Adam hadn't a competence. She could see him, a pleasant bachelor, in chambers, with a few choice books, a collection of prints, and the most comfortable armchairs in Europe. For Adam was an admirable host, delightful, but never very deeply involved with anybody. As it was he would have to begin life at seventeen. And he had no money sense at all.

He was absurd about money. He still thought that everything he wanted ought to be his immediately. If he wanted a wireless set he thought it ought to fall from heaven, complete with self-changing batteries. The first few days of the holidays he would look grimly at Catherine and remark at intervals:

'The Barretts have gone to the seaside.'

Or:

'The Simpsons have got a yacht of their own.'

'How nice,' Catherine would say brightly. 'That must be a pleasant change from the suburbs of London.'

Or:

'Thompson takes a gramophone back to school with him.'

'My dear ass,' Catherine would explode, about the third day, when the bill for extras had come in. 'Do you or do you not realise that your father works extremely hard and that he gets very little in return for it? You've had a lot of extra pocket money, you've run up a bill for fives balls and the Lord alone knows what you've done with all the pencils and india rubbers you've had this term.'

'I lost them.'

'Quite. I should also like to call your attention to the fact that as soon as you leave school you will get a small fixed sum on which to feed, clothe, and lodge yourself. If you spend it all in advance . . . what do you think will happen to you then?'

'I don't know, Mother.'

'Get your brains to work and think. You aren't Simpson or Barrett or Thompson. You're the extremely lazy son of impecunious parents. You're going to have to work like blazes if you ever want to have a wife and a home of your own.'

Adam frowned. He wished she wouldn't say blazes. Women didn't say that sort of thing any more now. It was going out.

He coughed gently.

'Won't there be quite a lot of money when you're both dead?'

'Not a bent ha'penny.'

Adam looked hurt. He had at least, Catherine reflected, learnt to read. Quite suddenly, like his power of speech, his power for grasping the written word had come, released by some new necessity for excitement and beauty which he concealed as deeply as he could.

Like Catherine he read Shakespeare 'for pastime', smuggling Audrey's school editions away upstairs as fast as she brought them home. He read *Julius Caesar, Romeo and Juliet* (strange choice) and copied out long passages of *A Midsummer Night's Dream* in his unformed, difficult handwriting. Catherine found them at the back of his drawer, crammed behind his shirts, and put them back again. She wondered what use these gifts and graces would be in the slack hands of her lazy son.

She hadn't noticed that he had become independent. The change had been so gradual. He had learnt to use his hands. He and William would lay bricks, cement, prune trees, bud and layer, strike cuttings. Adam could now use a putty knife or a pointing trowel, he was no longer at a loss with saw, chisel, and plane. When he was alone he muddled about the beautiful old villages of the Cotswold border with a camera strapped on his back. He liked to record the wide streets of comely stone houses, stone bridges, straddling heavily, old doorways, the wavy line of old roofs.

CHAPTER TWO

I

It dawned slowly on Catherine that her children had inherited a countryside. To Catherine, brought up in a busy seaport at the gate of the most beautiful scenery in the West, Oxfordshire was poor, rough, and remote. She couldn't understand the attachment of the children to their commonplace fields and slow brooks, to the village and the house.

The fields – Church End, Costard's Lease, Manor Close, Clark's spinney where the bluebells grew, Jericho spinney to which the Christmas holiday meet always moved off first ... the bathing pool by the mill upon the Cherwell ... the leaning willow with the wild currant bush upon its crown where they had once found a clutch of duck's eggs ... the hunting bridge, deep in the fields, where they ate supper on summer fishing nights ... the canal with its locks and lock-keeper's houses ... the old common ... the long dewberry hedge on the way to Jericho, a farm without a road ... the mill and the friendly miller, stooping to open the door in the mill wall that they might see the iron wheel throwing up the black, bitter-smelling water ... the farm kitchen, high and dark, going from floor to rafters, where Audrey had made butter . . . the trout ponds, still and shining under the fir trees, where Adam had learned to throw a fly. . . . All these they had inherited, these had become part of them.

The house, too . . . to them it was a friendly place, full of lofts and workshops and outhouses and stray garden corners that nobody wanted. The house was their own. Catherine remembered Bill's astonishment when a friend of his checked a heated chase on the threshold of the living-room with: 'You beast! To run in there where I can't get at you!'

There was room for each of them to have a separate bed-room, a cache for property not in common. But a separate sitting-room they would not have. They preferred to gravitate to the living-room, where Audrey would use the armchairs as pin-cushions and cover the floor with scraps and threads of cotton, Adam would print off photographs or draw, and Bill would sit with his feet on the sofa, playing a cheap ukelele to the accompaniment of an ancient gramophone.

Outside the house lay the village, where they knew every-body, and many of them always wore the same clothes. There were certain chronic bowlers and characteristic cloth caps that they would have missed as much as they would have missed the carrier's white-faced horse, or the grocer's white horse that someone, on an election night, had once painted in Conservative stripes.

They liked best to climb the church tower, up the belfry stairway, worn and polished a greasy black by generations of ringers, the steps thin in the middle and canting at unex-pected angles. They liked to stop at the ringer's loft where the clock pendulum wagged against the wall and the bell-ropes dangled like lambs' tails. Above the loft were the bells themselves and the oaken wheels, rising out of a bed of oak sawdust. They could lean across the railing and 'buzz' a bell till their ear-drums were shaken by the deep booming. Above, from the leads, they could see the whole place lying map-like at their feet.

There it lay, the cars crawling like beetles upon the main road, grotesquely foreshortened people coming and going with shopping baskets and parcels for the post. You could see a woman in her backyard pegging out washing, two men singeing a dead pig, a child on a sunny doorstep nursing a cat upside down. Old Mr Bowyer going up to the white bee-hives to feed his bees, the hound from the Friend at Hand stealing something from the butcher's. Children running, screaming, and singing 'Draw a Pail of Water' in the school yard, old Mr Mayhew going for a walk in his long green ulster, with his hands behind his back, the maid at The Willows looking out of the top window . . .

And all around everything a ring of country broken by three lovely spires and diversified by the lace-like beauty of trees not yet in leaf.

They would lean their chins on the parapet, clasping their hats, and gloat. They knew no other place as they knew this place – they would never again know every house, every person, and every tree as they knew the houses, people, and trees in the place in which they had grown up.

Already that heritage was on the verge of becoming a background – a memory. Only Bill was still a child. Audrey and Adam no longer looked on the garden as anything but a place to sit or work in. To Bill only it was still wonderful.

He liked to sit on the nine-foot gate, commanding two streets, and strictly forbidden. Bill's convenient memory often allowed him to be up there. He was – literally – on calling terms with every door across the street. He knew far more than Catherine or William would ever know about what was going on in the village. He liked to sit up there beside the hawthorn hedge under which, in the days when they were still interested in funerals, had been buried Tibby's redundant kittens, a dead hedgehog, and a bird or two. A little farther on was the Lady Sudeley, which always carried such a crop of apples in August when there was no other fruit, and beneath her untidy branches, scarred with the marks of Bill's climbing feet, were the Alpine strawberries, netless and left to be plundered.

None of them could remember the day when it had been a ragged triangle of harsh soil, streaked with clay and thick as a plum-duff with stones. They thought the trees and the raspberry canes and the sacred onion bed had always been there, the brick marrow bed under the wall and the sharp-smelling groups of currant bushes.

Sometimes Catherine wondered if this intense local feeling was any drawback to them. They had been away so seldom, seen so little else. Other parents seemed to drift about in the holidays – Scotland, Brighton, the Engadine – somehow they managed. She wondered if it were her own fault that she could not. She wondered if she had not, on the whole, lived with her children a little in the atmosphere of a dream . . . they had lived a life so quiet and, according to some standards, so old-fashioned.

Jane had said that she lived in a dream. Perhaps for once Jane was right . . . her life had changed as slowly as a tree grows. She could never have said from day to day: 'Here is a difference in the height,' or 'There will be a new branch here', but when she looked back, when she tried to remember the past, then the change became apparent. She could not tell at what moment she had begun to strike roots in the new soil, nor trace her return, from a new angle, to William. She had nothing, by any ordinary standards, to show for those slow years.

Then she saw that she need not consider her own point of view, because to Audrey and Adam those years were broken and chequered by a hundred trivial incidents – squabbles and reconciliations, small gifts, treats, disappointments.

II

She had Jane a great deal in her mind during the summer that Audrey was to leave school. For many months she had had a feeling, vague and hard to define, that Jane was living under a strain, that there was hidden trouble. She was put out, but not surprised, when Jane arrived unexpectedly one week-end at the beginning of the holidays.

Catherine was glad, when she got her telephone message, that she had the house and garden to herself. Audrey and Adam had gone to a tennis tournament and would be home at some hour – not to be foretold – when it would be over. The light evenings on the tennis court spun out indefinitely; it was unthinkable that they should leave before the finals, though it was unlikely that they would be in them. So someone else was bringing them back. Bill had bicycled off, under protest, to play cricket. Football was Bill's game. He would charge, muddy and valiant, in the face of the heaviest forward line that could fairly be put in the field against him, but he drooped and became self-conscious the moment a bat was put into his hands. There was no camaraderie, for Bill, in a ghastly game in which one was compelled to stand in the limelight to be bowled at. A game which one played in white flannels and for which it was necessary to part one's hair! The flat green cricket fields, bordered with willows, the white figures dotted on the grass, and the long golden afternoons had no charms for him.

William was away, on the farthest edge of the round, deeply engaged in a difficult confinement.

So Catherine walked the mile to the station and met the train, and walked back with Jane over the old common.

'Oh,' said Jane, 'isn't it quiet!'

She pulled the hat off her sleek head. They walked slowly. Soon they had lost sight of the railway, the river, the road. The fields were drying after a spell of rainy weather, the grass smelt bitter under their feet. Their footsteps made dark marks in it, and there was a sound of horses tearing grass at the bottom of the pasture and swishing their tails against their flanks to keep away the flies.

'Peter's gone to Munich,' she volunteered.

Catherine wasn't surprised. Peter often went off some-where at a moment's notice.

'Won't you stay here while he's away?'

Jane laughed.

'He'll be away some time,' she said drily.

They sat down on a stile at the top of the hill. There was a draught of air here, delicious against hot arms, it flowed up and over on to a stubble-field. Jane swung her long legs idly, looking out ahead of her.

'I'm going to sell the flat,' she said. 'You might as well know. It's been arranged rather a long time . . . I've known since the spring.'

'You mean he isn't coming back?'

'Just that. I think Emilia really will be able to do more for him than I could. She's not very young. A widow . . . an Italian. Her husband was a Jew. She knows all the right people.' Her voice trailed off.

'Who's Emilia?'

'He met her last spring at a party. We've seen quite a lot of her. It's all right. She knows what she's doing . . . and I think Peter's absolutely right. It'll be a wonderful thing for him, and naturally Emilia wasn't going to have any half-measures, even if I was.'

'But you . . . what are you going to do?'

'There's a lot to do. Clear things up. Sell what we don't want. He just left everything. He would.'

She swung herself over the stile and stood up.

'I've got engagements for the autumn,' she went on. 'I don't know if I shall keep them . . . I'm tired.'

Catherine looked at her. I bet it hurts, she thought, it hurts even if it's only a friend who leaves you for somebody who can do more for them.

She looked back in her mind across the years. She saw Jane dancing conscientiously in her green tunic. Jane catching trains, Jane running round with cocktails and sandwiches . . . and Peter (who was Reginald) sitting passively in a corner, accepting small attentions from his guests. Yet it was Peter who was gone and Jane who had obstinately remained behind.

Jane put a hand on her arm.

'I couldn't have gone to stay with anyone else,' she said. 'But you don't pry. You don't sympathise. I'd like to stay for a bit, till the collapsed feeling goes off. I didn't know I should feel like this, when it was all over. I feel like a squeezed orange.'

'Stop as long as you like. You must feel . . .'

'That's just the point. I don't feel. I wouldn't care if I simply hadn't minded. I thought I didn't. But I've gone numb . . . about everything. Do you think it'll last?'

Catherine could only shake her head. It was no good offering Jane any conventional advice about rest and diversion. Jane saw through that sort of thing at once.

'That's another thing,' said Jane. 'Don't tell them at home. I'm tired. I don't want all that yet.'

They walked on in silence over the bright stubble, the village rising into sight along the crest of the hill. A flight of wood pigeons, their wings clapping in the stillness, got up out of the field. Jane looked at the village.

'It's wonderful to come down here to you. Everything is always the same, and nothing ever happens. How you can!'

Catherine laughed. How you can! Violet's phrase. Well, she could and she did. But did nothing . . . as she had so often thought . . . ever happen? Struggles with money, struggles with physical fatigue . . . Adam to push on, Audrey to hold back, William to conciliate and understand . . . Bill to manage . . . Bill was so masculine. If you wanted him to do anything you had to stalk him upwind like a stag or indulge in the most exhausting battle of wills . . .

She thought of Terence Healy after he had finished tinkering with the magneto of their ageing car. William had thanked him warmly. He knew as well as Terence that a new mag was indicated, but the thing couldn't be done that quarter.

'Don't mention it,' Terence said grimly. 'It's been one long pleasure.'

III

The house was dark after the sun. Jane went away to change and wash. Catherine lingered, shaking up cushions, putting away books and papers and scattered scraps of material, emptying ash-trays. The living-room, by this time in the afternoon, always looked so frowsy. She moved the roses on the dresser into the middle of the table, pulled out a faded one, shook up the hearthrug.

A car's wheels gritted in the dust of the market square. She saw Audrey and Adam get out, heads were pushed out of the car windows, voices called out in the clear stillness, called again as Audrey and Adam answered, looking back over their shoulders as they ran into the house.

They burst into the living-room: 'Are we late?'

She looked up. They stood together in the doorway.

Adam looked sleepy, pleased with himself. He had greened one knee of his flannels. She thought automatically that she must send them to be cleaned at once. Then she looked at Audrey.

Audrey's youth hit her with a blow that was almost physical. Audrey was flushed, happy, her eyes shone, between her parted lips her teeth were white and even, over the soft line of her face, her round chin, there was a glowing, dewy look that seemed to come from something outside herself and that covered her as the dew covers a flowering apple tree.

Catherine's heart hurt her as she looked. Youth was so lovely, and it lasted such a little while.

'Had a good time?' she asked mechanically.

'Quite.'

'She drew Robin,' Adam said. 'She'd never have been in the semi-finals if she hadn't.'

'I've had a lovely, lovely day,' Audrey said. 'We've been playing ever since half-past two.'

Catherine picked up one or two rose-petals which had dropped on the table as she pulled the rose out. She knew that Audrey's lovely day had had little to do with Robin.

Upstairs she heard Jane's door open and shut again, her footstep on the landing. It flashed across her that she didn't want her to meet Audrey like that . . . looking so young and alive.

'Run up the garden path, both of you,' she commanded, 'bring in the deckchairs. And go and get tidy for dinner.'

She followed them up the garden and picked up the fruit basket and hand fork and the garden gloves which she had left lying when she answered Jane's telephone call. It would probably rain again in the night.

She stopped Audrey as she came back, carrying a couple of chairs.

'Where's Adam?'

'He's gone down the garden to look for fallen apples. You forgot to give them to Irene for the pudding.'

'Cousin Jane's just come.'

'Jane? I've never met her . . . have I? She doesn't come in the holidays.'

She thought a moment.

'Oh, yes, I have. I didn't like her when she used to stay here. I wonder why?'

Catherine remembered Jane switching her skirt out of Audrey's fingers . . . she remembered Jane's hard, cocksure youth. Jane had patently disliked Audrey when Audrey was a child. But people changed in their relationships with their changing ages.

'Oh, well. Be decent to her. She hasn't had much of a time.'

'Of course I'll be decent to her.' Audrey shrugged her shoulders at this apparent slur on her manners. 'All right. I know what you mean. I'll keep Bill out of the way, and so forth.'

She ran in, swinging her chairs . . . tall, strong, and quite unwearied by a long afternoon's hard exercise.

CHAPTER THREE

Catherine found that between Audrey and Jane there was a kind of armed politeness. Audrey behaved very prettily . . . leaving the conversation to Jane and William at meals, spending tedious hours at tennis-quoits with Bill, and doing extra dusting and sweeping in the mornings so that Catherine might play hostess to her guest. Yet it was perfectly plain that Audrey was being sweet, reasonable, and polite in order to please and help Catherine, and not at all because she liked Jane.

It was, unexpectedly, Adam who was the success. He hung round Jane in the mornings and told her, yet once again, all those laboriously funny stories which his family already knew to exhaustion. He showed her his garden, his carnation cuttings, his rockery. He also brought her his mending.

Catherine stared when she found Jane sitting in the garden, contentedly stitching up a tear in Adam's raincoat. She ran Adam to earth in the vegetable garden, arguing with Bill on the subject of whose garden the Lady Sudeley actually came in, and claiming first right to the apples, which he proposed to dole out to Bill as a favour.

'What on earth do you mean by giving your mending to . . .'

'Oh, that's all right! I thought it would save you the worry of finding out.'

'Save you? Save yourself, you mean! Of all the unmitigated . . .'

'It's all right. She likes doing it.'

Into Catherine's mind flashed a picture of Adam, sitting on the hall floor, Ellen and Audrey doing up a boot apiece.

'You'd better go and get the steps and pick those apples,' she said, changing the point of attack. 'There are far more there than we shall ever eat. I'm going to sell some of them.'

'Sell our apples?' Bill's voice was indignant.

'Who said they were your apples?' Catherine countered.

'They come in my garden.'

'Now look here, Mother,' Adam argued. 'You see those stones that I put in? That's the edge of my garden . . . and they go right round the apple tree . . . don't they?'

'The apple tree doesn't belong to either of you. You don't prune it, you don't winter wash it. All you do is to knock the boughs about getting at the fruit. It's time you stopped squabbling and grew up. If you want to make sure about the apple tree you'd better ask your father.'

The boys both vanished in the direction of the potting shed to get the ladder. They knew better than to say anything to William. They knew well enough that he endured the irregular patches of asters, lupins, marigolds, sprouting broccoli, parsnips and herbs at the garden end . . . with their accompanying litter of neglected tools, muddy jam jars, and battered tins . . . only because the herbs grew so well there and because Adam had a green hand with delicate cuttings. Carnations grew in his garden under his and Bill's brutal treatment which had failed to respond to William's skilled handling.

Catherine picked up fallen apples into the lap of her overall. Audrey was out. She had gone to spend a day on the river with Hilary and Edward and their lanky cousin, Veronica. Adam and Bill were presently going to the dentist with William, and Jane was going to stay where she was.

Jane seemed to be in a hazy condition of mind in which she was quite contented to drift.

'I can't think what she sees in Adam,' Catherine had said to William.

'He reminds her of Peter, I should think,' William had retorted.

He was annoyed with Peter. He was even a little annoyed with Jane, whom he liked. It was all very well for people to talk, as Jane and Peter had done, about the perfect freedom of either party in a marriage to discontinue the relationship whenever they thought fit. He didn't like the casual way Peter had drifted out, as though he was leaving furnished apartments.

He had put this point of view to Catherine.

'Jane doesn't see that,' Catherine said. 'She doesn't feel she has any claim on him. That was the idea.'

'You always said she'd be the one to clear out.'

'I know. Peter looked so supine. I always rather wondered if Jane didn't simply collect him in the first place.'

'He's been collected again. However, I notice he always

manages to get himself collected by somebody who's going to do him a bit of good.'

'I think his people might do something about it,' he added.

'I don't see why they should. They dropped Peter years ago. The father told him to get out and his brother can't stand them. The old man gave Jane a hideous diamond brooch for a wedding present and he sends her a cheque at Christmas. Besides,' she continued, 'Jane's quite capable of looking after herself.'

'That's not the point. They ought to do something.'

Catherine had dropped the argument as hopeless, but the thought of it was in the back of her mind as she went back to Jane. She sat down on the grass at her feet, looking over the fallen apples.

'Jane,' she said, 'has anyone written to Peter's father?'

'Why, no. I've hardly thought of them. We haven't seen them for years. I did go up there, once, for a weekend.'

'You never told me.'

'It wasn't interesting. It was all very rich and stuffy. Huge meals, a house with a great billiard-room . . . never used . . . and lots of glasshouses. You know the sort of house. Pictures in gilt frames and turkey carpets and massive awful furniture. Everything very ponderous and very well kept. A great shiny car at the station with a manservant to put a rug round your knees, and a fire in your bedroom and the sort of maid who tiptoes in with the early morning tea and shuts the windows and pulls up the blinds ready for you to dress. The most repulsively comfortable place I've ever been in. They wouldn't understand what Peter's done.'

She went on, neatly and efficiently, with the mend in Adam's raincoat.

'Why did you let Adam give you that?'

'He didn't exactly give it to me,' Jane said indifferently. 'He was wandering about with it, bleating, and looking for you. I like doing it. It's a rest.' She threaded her needle. 'You really ought to make Adam more efficient. He could do so much more if he liked. You don't manage him properly.'

Catherine sat still, with an apple in her hand.

'Being efficient didn't help Sebastian.'

Jane looked up. 'Catherine . . . what has happened to Sebastian? You saw him.'

'We didn't. That's the queer part. You know Violet came up to see him . . . after he had the smash with the car and got turned down.'

'The smash was his fault, wasn't it? Wasn't there an idea that he was . . .'

'He ran her into a ditch on a straight road, with no traffic about. Still . . . it does seem a bit rough . . .'

'Rough! You're either doing a piece of work or you're not doing it . . . especially when there are two or three other people waiting to take it if you fall out of it. But that was Sebastian all over. He had to have what he wanted . . . or nothing.'

'Still . . . Violet came up and we went down one day to see him. He'd never answered her letter saying she would come. We wandered about all over the Berkshire downs till at last we found the place . . . a garage at a crossroads where he's been working. There was a man outside, tinkering with a car, and nobody else in sight. He directed us to Se's cottage. I saw the man staring after us when we had gone on.'

Catherine went on sorting apples as she talked. She was frowning a little.

'We found the cottage, outside a lonely little village . . . hardly a village, no shops, no pub. The cottage was a dingy little place across a track, over two fields. We had to trail up, Indian file. You know the sort of place . . . white lace curtains with coloured edges in the windows, and a blistered front door and . . . oh, yes . . . dirty-looking fowls. There was a girl in the garden, pegging out one of Se's shirts. There was a wind blowing and the wet sleeve had smacked her in the face just before we got there. She stood, wiping her face with the back of her arm and looking at us. The moment I looked at her I thought we'd been fools to come.'

Jane stopped stitching. She laid down her work and looked across the garden at the overgrown stocks round the sundial.

'Violet didn't notice anything. She never does. She walked right up to the gate and asked for Sebastian. The girl took her arm down from her face and looked at William. "I'm sorry," she said, "he's out." She wouldn't look at Violet. She looked frightened, and worried, and defiant. She must have been pretty in a dark sort of way before she got haggard and draggled. Violet just stood there. "When will he be back?" she said. "I don't know," said the girl, looking at William and twiddling her wedding-ring. "He didn't tell me that." "I can't go all the way back without seeing him," Violet said, looking at William too. So there we stood and argued it with her and the girl said nothing and the fowls squawked and Se's shirt blew about on the line and at last we got Violet to come away. And Se's never written a word to us since, good or bad. Violet cried in the car coming back, but only because Se had gone out when he knew she was coming . . . oh, yes, and we stopped to take in petrol at the garage on the way back. The man had to go inside to get change. We heard him talking to someone in the back of the garage, and then they both shouted with laughter. It was that bit that hurt me most . . . that and the girl's face.'

'Is Se working . . . really working there?'

'I don't know. If he is . . . it's all right. William said the girl was the right sort . . . I thought so, too.'

'Is she . . . what sort of girl is she?'

'I don't think Violet will be pleased . . . William thinks she will suit Sebastian better than anyone like ourselves would have done. . . . She must be a decent sort to live in that ghastly cottage and wash his shirts and feed fowls and generally work at everything.'

Jane sighed. 'I tell you what I think. I should imagine she thinks the world of Sebastian and isn't a bit taken in by him.'

Catherine looked up at Jane, who didn't notice the look. It struck her as a thing Jane wouldn't have said a year or two ago.

'William said,' she suggested, 'that perhaps it was good for Sebastian to be allowed to get on with mechanical jobs and nothing else, and to go about the house without a collar and wander down to a pub if he feels like it. That girl would take everything he did as a matter of course . . . and pick up new tricks like a clever dog if Sebastian wanted to get on again.'

'You only saw her for ten minutes.'

'Why don't you go and see them yourself? Sebastian won't mind you.'

'I don't know. I'd thought of going, then it seemed cheek.'

'It was cheek . . . for us. William and I both felt like that.'

'It's rather the impression that Sebastian gives . . . always. He won't be helped and he sees red if he's pitied.'

Jane cut her cotton and folded her coat.

'I'd hardly thought of Se for years. All this time . . . except for you . . . the others haven't seemed to matter. But this last week, since I've been alone, I've been thinking about him. We used to be able to talk to each other, when we lived at home. Have you ever noticed how few people there are to whom you can really talk? I mean to tell things. I haven't always liked Se, but we know what the other of us means.'

'I suppose so,' said Catherine doubtfully. She had never been one of a family. She put the sound apples back into the lap of her overall. 'Half these apples have got earwigs in them. I wish you would go down and see Sebastian.'

Jane laughed. 'Catherine, you've got the most untrained mind I've ever met!'

CHAPTER FOUR

I

Catherine and Audrey were sewing in the garden. Sometimes the family split up like that.

William and Adam and Bill were laying bricks, all wearing dungarees and all very busy and important. Bill was mixing the mortar, Adam was laying the bricks with the aid of a spirit-level and William was going round the result with a pointing trowel and cursing himself and them, quite impartially. The work was to be a frame for seedlings on the outside of the over-full glasshouses.

William was perfectly happy. Adam was happy because he was entrusted with an important part of a real piece of work, and Bill because he was slapping up mortar like a workman, getting in a mess and making his arms ache, and both were happy in addition because they were working with William. For Adam and Bill had, in the last two holidays, suddenly inherited a father. They weren't sentimental about it, they didn't even talk much when they were together, but William and Adam and Bill were one gang. They were comfortable in each other's society and not the least interested in each other's thoughts or ambitions.

For William, Adam and Bill had been suddenly transformed from perfect nuisances who dropped things, annexed tools, left glasshouses open, and trampled across flower beds, into willing and interested companions. It amused him to work side by side with Adam, to go out in the morning and leave him with something in the way of cleaning bricks or getting out a trench to prepare, to stop in the middle of the work and ask his advice, to draw little diagrams in the evening and push them across the table to Adam for his approval, he even liked to have Bill stamping and whistling about the place. He was aware that a pair of tiresome and unpleasant children had become a pair of perfectly good sons.

Audrey looked at the three of them, working together, and threw up her chin, giving her dry little laugh. Men! The creatures! There they were, being important, all by themselves. She sat a little closer to Catherine. She liked to be left alone with her, as much as she liked to be left alone with Adam, for they were friends.

Catherine was getting on a bit, but she still looked younger than most other girls' mothers, and she could make her laugh! Sometimes they would take a whole day off together and then, when they were far out in the fields, they would take off their hats and link arms, and sing, and chase each other down the steep pastures, and generally play the fool.

There was a fearful and perverse joy in doing this with Catherine, who normally had to be obeyed. But Audrey was beginning to have a very shrewd idea how far Catherine's authority extended. Once it had been absolute, but now it was a relative authority, based upon their goodwill. She might storm at that authority, but she sympathised with her and would always, when necessary, take her part. It was so easy to see that Catherine was often tired and puzzled.

Audrey edged her mouth with a row of pins and held her work up to the sun.

'I shall make them with a hip yoke and edge the legs with blue,' she recapitulated, for the discussion had been going on at intervals all the afternoon, 'and a jumper top.'

Catherine wondered idly why Audrey didn't swallow all the pins when she talked with a mouthful like that. It was a feat, like eating gravy with a knife, which never failed to make her shudder.

'Do as you please,' she said, 'as long as you let me wear a nightie that I can tuck my feet into.'

'Feet!' Audrey's voice was scornful. 'A lot of nightie stays round your feet all night . . . doesn't it?'

She pushed the pins into the material with an expert hand, shook it, and held it up again.

'I think these are going to look really smart,' she said confidently.

Catherine stretched herself idly in her chair. She was glad that Audrey preferred to make her own clothes. It had solved the problem of what was going to happen when Audrey was too old to be satisfied with the ones which she made for her. She was mending a three-cornered tear, several inches each way . . . in the back of one of Bill's shirts.

'I can't think why you bother to mend that,' Audrey said. 'Look at the hours of work you're putting into it! He can't wear a shirt with a great darn like that.'

'I don't see why he can't. It all goes under his pullover.'

'You know as well as I do that the next time that Bill goes to a cricket match he'll be certain to change in a hurry and find that that's the only clean shirt in the house. You won't notice it under his blazer, and then when he takes his blazer off to field it'll show up for simply miles.'

'It won't show very much when it's washed and ironed. Besides, I can't throw it away. It's nearly a new shirt.'

Audrey sighed. That shirt ought to be suppressed. You were judged by that sort of thing. Catherine never seemed to understand that.

Catherine went on darning. She wished that Audrey wouldn't always steer by what other people thought. She would run about the house in a creased frock, and with a hole in her stockings, and spend hours . . . or what seemed like it . . . in getting ready to go to tea. The days when she had had to drag an uninterested and repellent Audrey to other houses were long gone by, but she felt that it was time that Audrey developed a standard of clothes and behaviour which was constant, and not merely intended for public approval.

It was like her habit of stuffing half-worn stockings and frocks back into her drawer and getting her coat pockets choked with used handkerchiefs.

She turned the shirt round and began on the other side of the tear. Audrey laid down her sewing and snipped idly with the scissors at the grass edge. She wanted to talk to Catherine, but it wasn't easy.

'I wish I hadn't to go back to school this term,' she said.
'Why?'
'Such a lot of our form have left.'

'What are they going to do?'

'Nothing much. Stay at home, most of them. Or take courses in Domestic Economy.'

'Would you like that?'

'I don't know. I'm tired of school. I want to live. But I'd hate to just mess about.'

She stitched severely, for some moments, in silence. They told marvellous tales . . . some of the girls who were leaving . . . they left you with the impression of hurrying about in cars, doing an endless amount of expensive and exciting shopping, going to dances, touring the Mediterranean, staying at Juan les Pins, winning prizes for golf and tennis. At the back of her mind Audrey had a feeling that it wouldn't be as gorgeous as that . . . that most of them were 'telling the tale'.

'Some of them have marvellous times,' she said doubtfully.

Catherine went on with the shirt. She wished that she knew more about the world outside the four walls of her garden. Was it really so full of girls having marvellous times . . . now with the money market fluctuating like a fever chart and the country fumbling uncertainly through a crisis?

'You wouldn't have a marvellous time if you lived here,' she said.

'It's all right.'

'Not in a year or two. When Robin and Hilary and Edward aren't coming home any more . . . or even Adam and Bill. Not when all the other girls you know are doing something, somewhere else.'

'Can't I take a job . . . soon?'

'As soon as you're ready. You can't take a half-paid job . . .
we'd only have to keep you as well. What would be the good
of that?'

'Other girls take them.'

'Other girls can live at home. Wait. Another four years will
make a lot of difference.'

Audrey said nothing. It was like Catherine to talk casually
about four years as if it were four minutes. Middle-aged
people had no idea of time. Besides, she wanted to help.
Years more with everything to take and nothing to give . . .
She wanted to feel that she was doing something to keep the
household going, doing something to shift the burden from
Catherine and William.

'I want to get on,' she insisted. 'Look at the cousins . . . look
at Sebastian and Jane.'

'I know.'

'Why didn't they get more out of it . . . I thought they were
both clever?'

'Sebastian had the luck to be born at the wrong time and
Jane married the wrong man.'

Audrey frowned. She didn't think it was as simple as
all that. Why hadn't they done more? Why were Catherine's
generation content with such shabby lives? Catherine and
William lived dully in the heart of the country, Sebastian
was working obscurely, in a wayside garage, and Jane was
a prematurely old young woman listlessly arranging for a
divorce which seemed to have more to do with money than
with passion. There was the whole world to run at, full of marvellous things to do, to see, to acquire. If only you had enough

courage . . . if only you wanted them enough . . . and none of them did anything.

'It must have been their own fault,' she said. 'I can't understand why.'

'Everything is one's own fault,' Catherine agreed. 'I don't see that that makes it any easier. But Jane got what she thought she wanted and Sebastian didn't, and it seems to have worked out badly for both of them. But you can't call either of them failures . . . yet. I don't think Sebastian is one.'

'But he got drunk and wrecked his car and lost his job,' Audrey said crudely. 'And Jane's giving hers up . . . I don't like Jane, she makes me feel like eating lemons.'

Catherine pricked at the edge of her chair with the needle.

'When you get older . . .' she began tentatively.

'But why does being older matter? I'm older now than you were when you left school. I'm not a child . . . I think it's dreadful to be old. You leave off caring for things. You just take Sebastian and Jane as a matter of course. . . .'

'I think that anybody's life looks a little dull . . . to outsiders,' Catherine said. 'But it's interesting whilst you are living it.'

'Dull! But you are none of you going anywhere. Nothing happens.'

Catherine laughed. 'What do you expect to happen? Angels or earthquakes? The War happened to us. It was harassing and disagreeable . . . I don't think everybody even found it stimulating. And afterwards it was flat and tedious and everything was at odds . . . and still is . . . I've had quite a lot happen to me . . .'

'Yes. But you haven't made it happen. . . .'

Catherine looked at Audrey, sitting on the edge of her chair, bright-eyed and impatient. Audrey had these moods when Catherine felt as though she were driving a horse that was almost too spirited for her to manage. She thought:

'It's no good trying to explain . . . she's young . . . she's different from me . . . her life will be different from mine . . . She can't learn from me. . . .'

Audrey pushed her work away. She didn't think Catherine understood what she had meant . . . that she could feel with her that mood of utter dependence . . . of being forced to wait . . . which was worrying her. Then she turned, put her arm round Catherine's neck and dragged her head down till it rested on her broad young shoulder.

'It's all right . . . I don't really mean anything . . . don't worry,' she said.

She was filled with a sudden and quite irrational desire to protect Catherine, it was so strange and new that she sat staring up the garden with a pricking sensation at the back of her eyes.

Catherine laughed and lay still. She knew quite well what Audrey was feeling. Beneath her head she could feel Audrey's shoulder and her firm young breast. . . . How strange it all was when she could remember the small, striving infant in the hollow of her arm! This normal, sturdy, and loyal young woman was her daughter.

She was grateful to her for being what she was.

II

But when Audrey had gone Catherine understood that that gesture of affection had been designed to shut her out. Audrey didn't believe that she understood her ... she was sorry for her and thought her walled up in the complacency of a middle-aged failure.

A middle-aged failure. Somebody who had had nothing out of life. She remembered, as keenly as if it had been yesterday, the hard feel of the baked earth under her breasts ... firm, warm, and friendly, the day she had lain under the gorse-bush beyond the old common.

A failure. Young things were fond of that word. Older men and women shied away from it ... Was it from their own sense of loss, the assurance that something had gone out of their lives? Was it that or was it more knowledge?

Catherine thought that in her life there were no strong shadows or highlights, everything had become blurred from the multitude of shades of colour that she could define. It was difficult to say 'this is a success' or 'that is a failure'. Did she like Jane more now because Jane was no longer hard, defiant, and young ... or because there was actually more in Jane to like? Or because she herself was a failure and a negation?

She wondered. She knew that her will wasn't her own will any more. She went in and out, rose up and slept under circumstances of complete submission to the terms which life had dictated to her. And she was free. Because she accepted everything and made what use of it she could, because she had

290

no ambitions and no hopes, because her love for William and her children satisfied her emotions, she was at rest, centred in the 'now' which occupied her thoughts.

Yet as she sat there, it seemed as though a blinding flash of her own spring came back . . . spring with its hailstorms and shrill sunlight, its acid green leaves and massed, impertinent flowers, as though for a moment she was not Catherine but Audrey, eager to seize the world in both hands and wring out of it the last drop of the essence of living. . . .

She looked at herself with Audrey's eyes, asked herself, in Audrey's voice: 'Is that all?'

For a moment . . . one sweeping black shadow in her vision of Audrey's spring, she knew why the old hated the young.

'Is that all?'

All . . . after so many struggles, after so many tears unshed, and sorrows concealed lest they should appear ridiculous . . . simply one more shabby and elderly creature standing, with an unheeded warning, to impede the path of youth. . . .

She saw herself sitting, young, like Audrey, with Balzac's *Eugénie Grandet* open on her knees and exclaiming angrily, to her empty bedroom, 'I won't have a life like that! I won't! I won't!' and then closing that pitiful record of provincial meanness and squalor with a chill misgiving that indeed life . . . and especially women's lives . . . was very much like that. That night the candles of romance had given their first flicker. She had reviewed, ruefully, the women whom she knew.

But Audrey wasn't romantic. Her ambitions were quite concrete. . . . She prayed fiercely for a moment that Audrey might be one of the very few people who are capable of controlling their own lives. Then, firmly, she shut the door upon the young Catherine.

For Audrey she would not be too safe a guide.

CHAPTER FIVE

I

Audrey was in the kitchen helping Irene to cut sandwiches and make scones for a picnic lunch. This morning the house had seemed too full of people. There were hot days when she felt like that, and there was always one day in the holidays when she and Adam escaped together and talked themselves out.

Irene worked silently. Catherine said that Irene's temper got a little worse every month. Audrey thought that it was more than that, for Irene told her things that she was never likely to tell Catherine.

Irene's father was always out of work now. Audrey thought it was a shame that there was no dole for agricultural labourers. They called him Old Jesse, but he was only fifty-five, and though he had always been in work up till now his club money would stop pretty soon. Our Maggie never kept a place either. She'd had three in the last year. Irene said that our Maggie didn't like housework and simply played up in order to get notice given her. Audrey cordially disliked our Maggie . . . a sullen lump of a girl who took everything Irene gave her and gave nothing back.

Audrey sliced ham thinly, watching Irene cut bread and butter.

'We'll never eat all that,' she said.

'I know by this time what you'll eat and what you won't,' said Irene firmly. 'You won't have any of that left over.'

She hunted in a drawer for a paper bag.

'Next summer you'll be cutting them for yourself,' she added.

Audrey put the point of the knife into the mustard-pot.

'No, I won't. You'll be here still.'

Irene shook her head.

'It's true this time. I'm going. You'll find somebody else. You won't miss me.'

She kept her back turned to Audrey. She hadn't understood until it came so near the point how much she was going to hate parting from Audrey and Adam. She'd been with them so long. She and Audrey had worked together so often. The fun they'd had . . . just over nothing, shelling peas and eating one here and there, getting the stones out of plums and cracking them for the kernels. She still had the little blue vase with the white heather on it that Audrey had bought her for a 'philippine' for a double kernel. And that Adam . . . who was going to get him out of his scrapes now? A new girl wouldn't sneak his bicycle round the back way for him and knock the pedal straight and put a bit of enamel on the framework so that 'she' wouldn't know that 'he'd' knocked it about again. She wouldn't wash shirts for him on the sly or take him out hot buns in the middle of the morning . . . she'd even miss Bill. . . .

Audrey went on spreading mustard. She felt prickly and uncomfortable. She wasn't any good at saying things to people. She didn't want Irene to go . . . Irene was simply part of life . . . she had always been there. She would never feel the same to anyone else in the kitchen.

'Of course we shall miss you,' she said roughly. 'Nothing will be the same if you go.'

Irene shook her head. She blew her nose and looked round the dark kitchen. The new girl'd never be able to get as much out of that stove as she'd done. Lots of things would have to be replaced that she'd tinkered with and mended and never complained about. She hated the sight of the stone floor and the old slopstone sink with the split drainboard and the copper that smoked every Monday the wind happened to be in the west. She wouldn't have to wash bath towels and shirts and piles of kitchen cloths if she left here, or make her back ache kneading bread and scrubbing boards. That place she'd heard of they'd give her forty pounds a year and nothing to do but cook. But now it came to leaving . . . now that she meant to tell 'her' tomorrow that she would have to be off . . . she felt that she could hardly bear it.

'You know the people who were building those new Council houses down at Weston Underbridge?' she said, and stopped to blow her nose.

'Those little pale brick houses?'

'Yes. They've gone bankrupt. Trying to do it too cheap.'

'Wasn't Tom Hole working for them?'

Irene nodded again. 'He's got a job away . . . at Slough.'

She couldn't speak to Audrey about Tom. They'd been

walking out together four years now. It couldn't go on much longer. They couldn't go on waiting for ever.

'Nobody wants any work done here,' she added.

Audrey saw that that was true. Every penny was precious. In their own house they thought twice before asking anyone to mend a sash cord or a door lock or to do a little distempering and painting. These were things which anyone with a little patience and common sense could do for themselves, more, there was a certain pleasure in doing them. As for having houses built . . . or doing more than the most necessary repairs . . . that was impossible.

'Everybody's hard up,' said Audrey.

Irene thought that there were degrees of being hard up. 'If I can get a good place I can put by a little . . . besides sending some home,' she said. 'It's hard on our father, losing his job with the sheep. He don't like to just sit and look out of window after all these years. He's never thought of nothing but the sheep. Our mother says that when Ernie was born old Mrs Voss called down the stairs to him that he'd got a fine son, born just an hour ago. "Yes," says our father, "and I've got a fine lamb what's beaten him by fifteen minutes."'

Audrey laughed with Irene, partly because she wanted Irene to laugh, partly because the story was an old friend.

'That was him all over,' Irene went on. 'Always around after them. Sitting up with the ewes in the cold and wet, lambing time . . . always at it . . . folding them, washing them, driving them, changing pasture. They talk as if it was an easy, pretty job to be a shepherd, but it's hard work, and cold work, and work that never stops. It's work that gets a man down in the end, gives him rheumatism and sends his chest wrong. Even if they hadn't given him the sack he'd never have got through another lambing season.'

'They let him go down there, don't they?' said Audrey.

'They do. But young Mr Costard don't give heed to him like the old man used to do. Our father told him this spring not to put the lambs out up-field. The sheep'll be right enough, he said, but if there was to come a little more rain the lambs'll be up to their little bellies in muck. You've only got to keep the pens in front of the barn a little longer. But would he listen to him? No! He put them out and lost near a dozen of them. So our father don't go up there no more, he just hangs about the house till he sees that he's in our mother's way and then he goes out to stand on the street corner. And Costard's going to give up the sheep this winter, so they say.'

Irene went over to the stove and turned the scones on the girdle.

'It won't be Costard's without the sheep,' she said sadly.

'And it won't be this house without you,' said Audrey, packing sandwiches in the basket.

'It's no good. Even our mother sees I've got to go, now. She'll have to go out by the day, next winter. Our father won't like that. He's never let her do no outside work, not since they married. It's hard on her . . . after bringing up all of us. I can remember our mother pushing me and Frank in the same pram and carrying a full bucket of water at the same time. . . .'

'Yes,' said Audrey. 'I can see what you mean. You've got to go.'

She hoped that Tom managed to marry Irene pretty soon. She'd never thought much about Irene's private life, but now that she came to think about it she could see that it was asking too much to want Irene to stay where she was.

II

Adam was coming back with Audrey from the Old Common. They had gone out ostensibly to see if the blackberries were ripening on the long hedge by the stubble-field, though both had known well that it was far too early. It was only an excuse to get out of the way for a long morning.

But they had dabbled their feet in the spring and lain on the slope of the hill with their hats tilted over their eyes and their bare arms and legs grilling, discussing the characters of Catherine and William and Bill the aggressive as they directly affected themselves. Then they had talked, more seriously, about each other.

The relationship between them had changed, the rivalry between them was toned down by the fact that now they were no longer children but were definitely taking different roads, both because they were man and woman and because they had widely different natures. Each, privately, thought the other a little ridiculous and each, also privately, admired the other's qualities.

Adam both admired Audrey and was jealous of her. Jealous because she had the precocious mentality of a clever girl, and because she brought home reports which could be shown off to relations. Catherine and William never showed Adam's reports, nor did they ever worry him about them. He had supposed that they were not interested simply because they were his reports and not Audrey's, until one morning early in his summer holidays, when William had tossed the report over to Catherine with . . . 'Look at that! *That's* rather better!' and Catherine had given a sigh of relief. But he still longed for them to be proud of him. It wasn't fair that Audrey should find everything so easy. It never occurred to him that Audrey was deliberately planning her road in advance. Adam didn't plan. Things happened to him, as they happened to Catherine.

But Adam also admired Audrey, and for many reasons. She was loyal. Audrey, himself, and Bill, they might quarrel and abuse each other, but they hung together. The savour went out of things if one or other of them were away. He might disagree with Audrey, but he would stand up for her against anybody on earth. And he was proud of her, he liked to go with her to tennis parties and dances, he thought her slim throat, outlined by its long plaits, her fine wrists and ankles, the most beautiful things he had ever seen.

They dawdled down the long field together, taking turns with the basket. Audrey was chewing a grass. Her face was tanned with the heat, her lips were bright red, her teeth small and white. She moved easily from the hips, her cotton skirt swinging, the little hairs gleaming on her bare brown legs. She looked shrewdly at Adam, wondering how anything so purposeless and inarticulate was going to get anything out of life.

She told him, at some length, what Irene had said in the morning.

'*She* won't go,' said Adam confidently.

'Yes, she will. She means to go. She's got to get a better job . . . I wish I had a job instead of being at school. It's all rubbish my going on to college. There must be dozens of jobs I could get now. . . . If I could get my matric at sixteen' (her voice was a little shrill) 'I ought to get a job quite easily.'

Adam swung the basket. 'You could get a job next year as easily as anything. But when you're older . . . suppose you don't marry . . .'

'Oh, I shall marry,' Audrey said confidently. 'I used to think I wasn't going to because children are so awful. . . . Look how mother used to stew round after us and get all hot and bothered if she thought we weren't behaving properly.'

'You needn't have children. Everyone doesn't.'

'I know that, thank you. But I don't think it's the game. I shall have just one or two and manage them rather well.'

Adam bent forward and picked a harebell. 'Crumbs!' he said earnestly. 'I'm sorry for them.'

'I pity the poor wench who marries you.' Audrey's tone was acid. 'I wouldn't be her . . . not for a fortune.'

Adam grinned but didn't answer. He didn't mean to marry. Audrey was all right. A sister had her uses. You could say what you liked to her. But a wife!

'Here,' he said. 'It's time you took the basket.'

Audrey stretched out her hand.

'Besides,' Adam went on suddenly, 'it isn't every man that

can keep a wife. Look at Father . . . he doesn't get much out of it, does he?'

Audrey wrinkled her nose. 'You'd noticed that . . . had you? He'd have a much easier time without all of us. I wonder if he likes us? No, I'm sure he does. I like Daddy.'

Adam said nothing. He wasn't going to give away to Audrey how much he thought of his father. That was something he would never tell to anybody.

'It's all right for Mother,' Audrey went on. 'She likes it. It gives her somebody to boss.'

Adam looked at Audrey and laughed. 'What's the difference between boss and manage? What about those children you are going to manage rather well?'

He ran backwards down the slope, clapping his hands.

'You are like her,' he said. 'You are! You are!'

Audrey's eyes filled with tears. She stamped.

'I think you're odious! And I've not got to marry, anyhow, I shall keep myself. I don't want to boss anybody.'

'You can't start yet!' Adam stood looking uphill at her. 'I shall start when I'm seventeen.'

'It's not fair. Because you're a boy you get a much better chance . . . even if you are as idle as sin. Because Bill's a boy he can be a doctor. But I've got to put in years and years more . . . I've got to go back to school and be a prefect and keep order in prep and see that the lower third don't push each other about when they're changing their shoes.'

'I'll be a prefect some day. Our prefects are awful brutes. Gee! I won't half give it to the upper fourth when I'm a prefect.'

301

'I'm sure you will! I shall simply loathe it. I hate giving orders. I simply want to do my own job and not be interfered with.'

They came to the stile at the bottom of the field and sat down on it. The wood was frayed in places where the cart-colts had rubbed their necks up and down the top bar, and one or two long horsehairs were always caught in the rough parts. A certain kind of black caterpillar was only to be found on this particular stile, and there were always blackberry-stained bird-droppings round it in the summer holidays.

Audrey and Adam always sat here for a little while on the way home. In front of them was a steep field which had been down to clover hay and was now a vivid green aftermath against the farther edge of stubble. When they were at the top of that they would be able to see the church tower, tall and watching, and the enchanted feeling of being alone in the fields would have left them. The hollow between the hills was warm and sleepy.

Audrey sat chewing her grass blade and thinking, ruefully, about the coming term. She had to be responsible for the rest because she was senior, but it wasn't her job. Audrey hated to be responsible for other people. It struck her simply as interference.

Adam watched her, his chin in his hand. Something was dawning in his mind, a feeling of coming change that seemed to press against the walls of his known life as though presently it would crumble them away altogether, would leave him out in the open. In two years, with any luck, he would be leaving school. Two years was a tremendous time. Two years ago he wasn't much better than Bill who was still content to play solitary games which had no outcome and no meaning. In two years more he would be as old as Audrey . . . ready to look for a place in the world. Not much of a world, if what one read in the papers was true. Not much of a world if what one heard Catherine and William saying about Sebastian and Jane was true. Not much of a world when you thought of Irene's father and Tom Hole. Not much of a world if you believed Eb.

'I don't think jobs are very easy to get,' he said.

'I don't care,' said Audrey. 'I'll work. I'll get on. I won't be stopped. You'll see . . . I'll get on better than you do.'

Adam did not answer. Audrey probably would get on. She was vigorous and knew how to use her elbows. But he would have what he wanted, for all that. He wondered what it was that he did want. It had little to do with getting on and with getting money. He wanted peace and quietness in which to do the things that he liked . . . to improve at them . . . to get all the time a little nearer to the point at which he would feel that nobody, not even Catherine, could tell him to do them any better.

'You'll get what you want,' he said at length. 'You always do. People give in to you.'

'To me? They give in to you a great deal oftener. You look all helpless and sad, and before they can turn round you've got what you wanted and are off through the door with it without even saying thank you.'

Adam grunted. He hadn't meant 'things'. But Audrey always meant 'things'. When Audrey wanted anything it was always something she could hold in her hand . . . money, or food, or a frock. He never knew clearly enough what he wanted to ask for anything definite like that. When he got anything definite it never satisfied him, he began at once to look beyond. The things that he wanted most were states of mind . . . like complete understanding and accomplishment and little easy matters of that kind. He envied Audrey. She could always go straight for what she wanted and just grab it.

Audrey threw away her grass stem.

'I think it's rotten, being a girl. You can't begin low down in your job and work up. Where you begin, there you stop . . . unless you're really good. Unless you're unusually clever . . . or pushing . . . or original it never becomes a career. It's just a job . . . the same job. I couldn't stand that.'

'You could if you had to.'

'I won't have to.' She kicked the bar of the gate. 'Oh, I know what you mean. You've got to stick at what you can get these days. I used to think grown-up people had a great deal of money and could do whatever they liked. But they don't. Most of them haven't even the free time that we get. That's what I shall miss . . . not having my own time.'

'But they have more money . . . a lot more money.'

'No, they don't. You've got to pay away great pieces of it before you get any good out of it. You look at us. By the time father's paid taxes and insurances, and our school bills and all sorts of rubbishing things like toothbrushes and soap and gym shoes and fowl-corn and people to mend things we can't mend ourselves . . . there isn't much left.'

'Are we really hard up or is it just the way they talk?'

'Yes, we are. I used to think they were both pretty mean. But they aren't. All the more reason why I should get a job as soon as I can.'

Adam scratched his head. He had never thought of a job as a job . . . as a means of living, though he had often thought of what he would like to do.

'Eb says people don't want to work,' he quoted. 'He was grumbling about it out in the garden only yesterday. He says they only want to get off. He says they're always going into town on the buses and spending money on things they get no good of. He says they don't work round their gardens the way they used to do . . . they go in and crowd up and down looking in the shops or going to the pictures . . .'

'I like Eb,' Audrey said. 'He never goes anywhere, and yet he's perfectly happy. I think he's quite right. I don't want to rush about either. I just want to live.'

'Eb says they don't want to go on like he does. They've no use for work.'

'You needn't be virtuous about it. You haven't much use for it, either.'

Adam grinned, and got up leisurely to go. It was a pity that they had to go back. He had enjoyed being with Audrey. Probably they wouldn't get a day together for the rest of the holidays. He wondered if she was right that he didn't want to work. He wanted to work at his own time . . . in his own way . . . but he was beginning to see that that wouldn't be possible. Perhaps Audrey was right, and that both of them owed it to Catherine and William to take what offered, as speedily as possible, however unpalatable it would be.

'You know,' said Audrey. 'We've got to play fair . . . they're trying to give us a chance . . . as far as they can.'

Adam admitted that. Quite often, lately, he had found himself in agreement with Catherine and William. The things they did seemed to turn out to his own benefit even when the immediate consequences weren't pleasant. Quite often he found himself at the point of backing his father up.

'I hate Irene leaving,' said Audrey. 'It alters everything.'

'I like Irene, but it won't make all that difference. We'll get somebody else.'

'I feel as if this was an end of something. It's gone on for a long time . . . being just us. But now I can see that it won't always be the same,' she looked at Adam in a kind of panic. 'I don't want things to change . . . I know we talk about what we're going to do – but I don't want to change. I don't want to grow up.'

She stood up and looked round her at the green field upon which the shadows were beginning to draw eastwards for the long evening.

Adam looked down at her, not understanding. He didn't care whether he grew up or not. He would always be himself.

CHAPTER SIX

William was busy repainting his glasshouses. He sat at the top of the ladder on a sack stuffed with straw. Below him Catherine sat on the hot grass with her shoes off, her arms crossed on her knees. She knew very well that she ought to be picking plums, but it was wonderful to have an afternoon on which she need not hurry, and she knew that in a little while Audrey would be there to help her. Less and less, as she grew older, did Catherine care for doing things alone. Her old taste for solitude had almost left her.

She looked back over her shoulder at William. It was amazing how many things he contrived to do well – in the middle of his other work.

They had come to admire each other. They had both hated their jobs, but they had stuck to them until, miraculously, they had come not only to like them, but to be unable to do without them. By the same process they had come really to need and like each other; somehow a real friendship, a real need for each other had grown up behind their differences and disappointments.

There had been a period at which William's loudly declared opinions, William's habits . . . the very way in which

he had poked a fire or opened a letter or blown his nose
. . . had irritated her to the point of screaming. That was the
point, she supposed, looking down the hot garden, at which
most marriages broke down.

Theirs had failed to break down for two good reasons, they
both had to work hard and they were both, fundamentally,
realists. Neither of them supposed that because marriage with
one person had become irksome, marriage with another
would automatically become the ideal state.

But the ground wasn't all covered by the fact that neither
of them now expected very much, either from each other or
from anybody else, that they had ceased to wish to change
the world or to dominate other people's affairs. They had
common ambitions and a common purse . . . but that wasn't
all. Neither was it to be explained by the humdrum fact
that they were completely used to each other. Their marriage
was something lasting, something which, for no very definite
reason, she felt to be good, something far more than an
arrangement which satisfied them both.

She turned her head as Audrey and Adam came into
the garden. She saw at a glance that they had about them
that atmosphere which is created by two people in complete
understanding. She thought swiftly:

'I'm glad Audrey is the elder . . .'

She saw too that the cloud of dissatisfaction which had hung
about Audrey for the last few days seemed to have blown away.

Audrey looked at her. It was so still that when they came
into the garden a flight of goldfinches had sprung up out of
the seeding cornflowers, scattering little sparks of song.

How could William and Catherine go on like that. . . .

The things Catherine and William did had once seemed to Audrey perfectly right because they were done by Catherine and William, but now she questioned everything they did in the light of what she herself would wish to do.

How could they be content from day to day with things which seemed to lead nowhere? How could they be completely satisfied with the weak tea and thin bread and butter of life . . . when there was so much else. . . .

She dropped down on the grass beside Catherine.

'You haven't picked the plums yet.'

'I was waiting for you.'

'Then Adam must carry in the baskets.'

Catherine laughed. They went out into the kitchen garden together. The currant bushes smelt rank yet fragrant, the flowers had run to seed upon the sage bush. Audrey nipped off a sprig of rosemary and put it between her teeth. She whistled as she picked, and finally sang, clear as a thrush:

> Now we are together,
> Never mind the rain,
> Never mind the weather,
> Here we are again.

Catherine chuckled. It was ironic that Adam who loved good music couldn't produce a note, whilst Audrey and Bill used their voices only upon the most approved . . . and preferably the most vulgar . . . popular melodies.

'What were you doing . . . sitting on the grass?' Audrey asked.

'She asks *me* now,' Catherine thought. 'I've given up asking her.'

'Thinking . . . about Jane, for one thing.'

'I wish you wouldn't think about Jane. I don't like her.'

'You needn't think about her. I had a letter this afternoon.'

She put down her full basket and took the letter out of her pocket.

'There it is. Read it.'

'Why should I?' Audrey took the letter dubiously, by one, corner. Her face had its old look of bright contempt.

'She's done a thing I didn't expect. She's gone to Peter's father. They're rather rich . . . and pobby . . . his people. They have fat meals and go to bed at ten o'clock.'

'I shouldn't mind the fat meals.'

'You wouldn't like the fat life.'

Audrey shrugged her shoulders. She thought it was silly to pretend to despise the material comforts. Everyone liked good food, a soft bed, a warm fire. Why not say so?

'A fat life would do Jane good,' she said severely.

'I don't see why you hate her. You're rather alike.'

Audrey put down her basket and leant against the hot wall.

'I'm not!' she said angrily. 'As if I couldn't get my own way without being perfectly foul about it! Or find another way.'

She opened the letter, her face changing as she concentrated over what Jane had written.

Catherine wondered if Jane would have liked Audrey to see the letter. She felt as if she were giving her away to Audrey. But what would be the use of that? Audrey was too old now to have things hidden from her, not that she had ever attempted to hide anything very much.

Jane had written:

'I know you'll find it hard to understand. The fact is I am happy here and I'm comfortable. I don't want anything else. Did I say happy? I mean that I'm not bothered. Peter's father doesn't expect more of me than that I should look handsome, listen when he talks, and be out of his way two-thirds of the time. It's restful. I've nothing to do that I can't do so easily that I don't have to think about it. I answer most of his letters for him. He has a huge correspondence although he retired years ago. I agree with him about his garden, and his glasshouses, and the cooking, and the possible resurrection of the Liberal Party. I've no business to be here. I'm here because he thinks I have a claim on Peter. But I'm going to stay. I'm going to go on answering his letters and taking the dogs for walks and pottering down into the town in his huge, shiny car.

'It's wrong. The world's full of people who are not only hard up but actually in want. I ought to pull myself up out of the rut. But I've never done anything for anybody but Peter, and I don't really care enough to begin. That's the truth, Catherine. I used to think I cared enormously for my work, for music, for all the new world that the new thought was going to bring about. I don't care! I don't care what happens to anybody else. I'm tired.

'I suppose you will keep on – walking about country roads in the wet, and ironing clothes and darning socks and talking about table birds, egg averages, and medlar jelly, and the new people at Underedge. Either you have very much more courage than I have, or else you're a great deal stupider. In any case I give it up. Life's a disappointing game and there aren't any rules. I'm not going to play any more.'

Audrey took a ripe plum out of the basket and fingered its bloom.

'I don't quite see,' she said. 'Peter's going on with the work he was doing. He didn't even take Jane's work away from her.'

'Peter was Jane's work.'

Audrey bit into the plum. She thought that she could see what Catherine meant. Irritating, to have your work snatched away from you. But why sit down under it? She read on, the cold, jellied flesh of the plum warming in her mouth as she lingered on its sharp flavour.

'This is an astonishing place. The streets are full of men out of work. Simply standing, stoically, with their hands in their pockets. Not grumbling, not getting excited about it, simply standing. The car goes past in the wet and I look at them, and they look at me . . . and I wonder how they can. And then I go into a shop and find it very nearly empty. The girls stand about talking and polishing their nails, and yawning, simply tired out with having nothing to do. I feel as if I was doing something eccentric when I go to buy a new pair of stockings.

'I wish you could see the room I'm writing in. It has brown velvet window curtains and a turkey carpet and huge oil paintings in gilt frames, and shelves and shelves of books that nobody reads, and a mammoth roll-top desk with a typewriter on it. It's called the library. I work here – if you can call it work. There is a log fire, and two Sealyhams and a fat spaniel are heaving and grumbling in front of it. Every now and again, when I feel energetic, I stop writing and kick them a little farther away and tell them they're burning their eyes out. I'm glad they're here. I like dogs better than people. They're less disappointing.

'The tide's down here, too. The room is a little worn, a little faded. Nothing is ever replaced now. The old man keeps up all his charities. He says the house will last his time, as it stands. I like him. He's a mass of prejudices. He's illogical. But he lets me alone . . .'

Audrey looked at Catherine.

'She won't go on like that,' said Catherine, picking plums.

Audrey licked her fingers.

'I don't see why not. She'll simply stay there, get middle-aged, and potter about . . . taking the dogs for a walk. She's much happier there than she pretends. She wouldn't do it if she didn't like it.'

Catherine shrugged her shoulders. She had always thought that Jane was incapable of developing a new set of ideas, or even of adopting them. Perhaps Audrey was right, and that the comfort into which Jane had lapsed was really native to her, as was the solidarity, the purely bourgeois atmosphere.

'I'm sorry for her.' She looked at Audrey, trying to excuse Jane.

'I don't think you need be. She isn't a person anybody need be sorry for.'

Catherine looked at her daughter's face as she went on reading. Sometimes she felt Audrey was older than she was.

She looked at others objectively, judged them in the light of common sense, without emotion and without pity. Audrey was completely unsentimental.

'I did go to see Sebastian. I went before I came up here, after I had sold the flat. He was quite reasonable about it. We spent a long day walking and talking on the downs. He met me at Newbury. I didn't go to the cottage. We took buns and apples and simply lay on the turf. It was a hot day. Sebastian talked quite a lot. More than he has ever done.'

Audrey flipped the letter over. 'She doesn't say what he told her.'

'You could hardly expect that. I don't suppose they even told each other everything, or the whole truth about everything. I expect they were simply glad to have a whole day together. When they were kids she used to try to manage him and he hated it, but they were both feeling wretched and flat just then and they were glad to be together.'

Audrey yawned a little. The whole question of Jane and Sebastian seemed to her to be boring, shabby, and trivial. Why did Catherine want to trouble about it?

'He told me he was married,' she read on, 'quite casually, as if it was something that didn't matter very much, one way or the other. I can't understand that. Either a thing matters enormously, or you leave it alone. He says he's going shares in the garage; that there was more work there than you would expect, and when they've made enough he and the other man will sell out and move nearer to a town. I don't know anything about his wife. I believe her name's Edna and he picked her up in Sheffield . . .'

Audrey folded the letter.

'Picked her up is good!' she said, in a pinched voice.

Catherine laughed. Some of Jane's phrases were pure Violet, but Audrey couldn't be expected to know that. She thought it was ugly of Audrey to be so merciless to another woman.

Audrey handed back the letter. 'I don't see what there was to read in that,' she said. 'I can't think why you bother about Sebastian and Jane. They aren't worth it. Or why you think worrying does any good.'

'It doesn't. I can't help being interested.'

'In Sebastian and Jane?' Audrey looked at her mother. So that was how she lived . . . being interested in the lives of her relations . . . and in her life, and Adam's, and Bill's. It seemed to her a curious way of living. Having once pinned Sebastian and Jane down as specimens she had no further interest in them.

'I don't care about them a bit,' she said frankly. 'What's the use of caring when you can't do anything?'

Catherine thought that that was uncomfortably like Jane. She looked at her daughter. Audrey leaned against the wall, the wind flapping her cotton skirt round her brown legs and defining the beautiful line from the hip to the knee. Every line of her body was supple, graceful, young. She thought, I ought to dislike her for being so young, but I don't, it blinds me to what she is really like. I look at her to see what she is thinking, and I can only see how she looks.

'I don't think I expected you to care,' she said.

It struck her how differently Audrey looked at things. She

didn't think Sebastian and Jane were immoral, as Violet thought they were. She simply thought that they were dull. Dull and inefficient. Fumbling and impossible. As Jane had thought of Violet . . . as she and William had also thought of Violet and Edward. Pitiable people whom it was not much use trying to help. She became aware for the first time of the wall, not between parents and children, but between one generation and another.

'I know what you think,' Audrey said. 'You think I'm like Jane. I wish you wouldn't compare me with Jane – or anybody else. I'm myself.'

She worked her shoulders irritably, remembering many things. Catherine's eyes following her at a party . . . Catherine admiring, checking, forestalling her thoughts.

'Darling,' she said. 'I love you so much if you'd only leave me alone.'

Catherine thought . . . I always imagined I had . . . but she had the sense not to say it. How right after all, how natural and salutary that Audrey should withdraw herself from the person who had combed her hair and trimmed her finger-nails, cleaned her teeth and edited . . . in biting language . . . her table manners. How right . . . and how disappointing!

She went on picking plums. She had fought that battle with William, she wouldn't fight it again with Audrey. Complete companionship with your daughter . . . what folly! There were some things that even Catherine didn't have to learn more than once.

CHAPTER SEVEN

Adam was packing his own trunk. He was filled with a more than common sense of depression. He was happy at school, in the Alsatia of the upper fourth which is neither oppressed beyond measure by its seniors nor clouded by the blight of final examinations. Yet it was a wrench to leave home, to put off his home self and return to the school world which always seemed so impossible the moment the car had left the school gates.

In a few days Catherine and William, Audrey, the whole countryside, would have become in their turn a dream, which he might regret, but for which he had no real feeling. It was the changeover that hurt.

And this term Bill was coming with him.

Suppose Bill behaved to him as he did at home? Worse still, suppose Bill behaved to the Middle School as he behaved to him at home? There were awful possibilities in Bill. There were his stamping rages in which he tried to scatter all before him . . .

Worst of all, Adam's school self was a different self from his home one. Suppose Bill came back and gave a comic broadcast of Adam at school! Nothing was more likely. Quite a lot of it, though it would move William merely to reminiscent laughter, would give Catherine a fit. Quite a lot of it was his private life which he was in no hurry to share with Bill and Audrey.

What about looking after Bill? He could see Bill telling him wrathfully to 'get out' and that 'it was his own (several adjectives) business' . . . in front of a whole gang of small rats in the lowest forms. All of whom would have to be put painfully in their own places, afterwards.

He liked Bill all right, but the thought of having him at school made the palms of his hands hot and sticky. He burst out into a perspiration at night when he thought of all the things that Bill might do. Bill would not have recognised tact if he were to meet it on toast.

At least Catherine and William had never said, 'Won't you be glad to have Bill at school with you?'

Bill sat on the edge of Adam's bed and watched Adam pack. School with Adam would be a dubious joy. He didn't want Adam to edit his amusements and be caustic about his expenditure. It was a poor job to have to follow on after a brother who had made some kind of tradition of his own.

He just wasn't going to be like him, and that was that! And he was going to choose his own friends, and that was that, too! He was glad he was going to see Adam sometimes . . . and they could swop home letters . . . and Catherine and William would come twice as often. . . . There were consolations.

Deep down inside himself Bill adored Adam. He was fond of him, simply because he was Adam and for no other reason.

He left other people alone when they were lazy, or stupid, or fell short of any of his standards, but he wanted Adam to be always at the top of Adam's form. He had for him one of those unrecognised, faithful, and exasperated friendships which are at the bottom of all family loyalties.

Catherine came up with an armful of clean shirts.

'Have you packed your collar-studs?' she said absently. Catherine was always absent and unfriendly the last day of the holidays, when they wanted her most. There were so many things always to find and to repair, on that last day. She supposed that this time at least she had thought of everything, bought everything, and at the last there was a hooroosh all over the house because Adam had only one football boot or Bill had lost his sock suspenders.

She didn't seem to know that this going back was different from any others. She had no eyes for Adam and Bill, sitting in an atmosphere of tension at different sides of the room.

She collected the books off Adam's chest of drawers, put them into an empty drawer and shut it with a bang.

Adam winced. She needn't have done that. Now the room would look bare. He liked to forget he was going until he had actually gone.

'Have you put your own things away, Bill?'

Bill got up reluctantly. It seemed only yesterday that he had spread them all out at the beginning of the holidays, though he had been hounded up to dust them many times since . . . flicked upstairs by an industrious, important Audrey, scurrying round with a duster before she went to the tennis courts.

He wandered into his own room and began to pack them up. If he left them to Catherine to do she would put them all into the wrong boxes. Catherine never cared where anything went as long as it was out of the way.

Adam went down to the hall to fetch his shoes. In the living-room there was a droning noise. Audrey was machining knicker-linings for dear life. She, as usual, had a day more than the boys. Adam grudged her that day alone with Catherine. He stood in the doorway and looked at her.

'I bet you don't get those done in time,' he said.

Audrey looked up. Her tongue, which had been travelling from one corner of her mouth to the other, stopped and was drawn in.

'You packing? Can't I help?'

Adam shook his head. He took a mournful satisfaction in packing his own stuff.

'Where's the noble Bill?'

'Putting his things away.'

'Huh!'

They looked at each other with understanding.

'It'll be all right,' said Audrey swiftly.

Adam grinned nervously.

'I'm looking for my shoes,' he said; and dived out of the room.

Audrey went on machining. Poor Adam! Really, Bill . . .

Catherine had simply spoilt Bill. Just because his own way never gave Catherine any trouble, Bill had always had it. Besides, Bill could always make her laugh at the crucial moment when she or Adam were certain to say the one thing which precipitated punishment. She agreed with Irene that what Bill needed was to be thoroughly well spanked. Not whipped. Simply spanked in circumstances of complete ignominy.

From the fund of her own experience she drew the knowledge of what was likely to happen to Bill.

'Adam's a lot too nice to him,' she thought. 'I simply shouldn't worry about him.'

Bill's head appeared round the door.

'Can you find my footer shorts?'

'Aren't they in your drawer?'

'No.'

'Have you looked in the airing cupboard?'

'Yes.'

'Have you asked Irene?'

'She hasn't seen them.'

'Who wants them?'

'Mother. She's packing.'

'Oh, Bill! You are a nuisance!'

Audrey jumped up, raced upstairs and began pulling drawers in and out. At the back of her mind was the recollection of the fact that when Bill had had 'flu last holidays he had slept in her room. She retrieved his shorts from under a pile of woven underwear, laid aside for the winter.

'Here you are . . . sure they're big enough?'

Bill looked at them hopefully.

'Oh, well! They'll have to be!' Audrey encouraged him. 'Hurry up with them. I'll bring up your raincoat.'

All at once she was sorry for Bill. He looked smaller, as

though the thought of school had shrunk him. She ran upstairs with the raincoat.

'Here. Let me. I'll pack, Bill.'

She dropped on her knees on the floor beside Catherine. 'Why?'

'I'd like to do it for him.'

Catherine would forget something. She always did. It made Bill miserable if anything was forgotten. He hated to be told about it, to have to do without it till it had come from home.

'Go and sit down,' Audrey coaxed Catherine. 'You're tired.'

'I'm not. All right. I'll finish the machining.'

'Oh. Please not. I want to finish it myself.'

'All right. I'll leave it.'

Catherine went away downstairs. Audrey and Bill were left by the gaping trunk.

Audrey retrieved the clothes list from Adam's bed.

'Have you got your footer boots?'

'No.'

'Have you got your ink?'

'No.'

'Have you got your writing paper?'

'No.'

'Oh, Bill, you are a fool. Go and get them. Hurry. You ought to have had them ready.'

'Well, I haven't.' Bill was unabashed. He went away slowly, hitting the banisters with a ruler.

Audrey packed, quickly, methodically, tightly. She loved packing. Presently she stood up. Bill was a long time getting his boots. She went down to the dark cloakroom off the hall. Bill was sitting on a coffin stool with his boots in his hand, sniffing.

'Hurry, Bill. I want your boots.'

She could see the hunched, infuriated shape of his shoulders as he turned.

'Get out, you ass.'

Audrey hung in the doorway. She wanted to console Bill. She knew those moments of black desolation which come down on the bravest mind at the thought of an unknown future.

'If you'll only be quick with those things I'll make you some gingerbread,' she comforted.

Bill stuffed his handkerchief into his pocket. He didn't want gingerbread. He wanted the place he knew and the people he knew. He dreaded the hateful business of beginning a new school, and making all sorts of breaks, in front of Adam.

'All right,' he said gruffly. 'Only don't go and put a lot of nutmeg in it, like you did last time.'

Audrey turned round to see William standing behind her, an appreciative grin on his face. How much she liked him. She liked his old faded soft hat, his old black stethoscope, his clever hands with the broad fingertips holding the battered leather bag and a handful of carnation cuttings.

'Packing?' said William.

'It looks like it, doesn't it?' his daughter agreed, caustically.

Adam came down, drawn from his finished packing by the sound of William's voice.

'I say,' he blurted out, unable to control his anxiety, 'will you have Bill put in my dormitory or not?'

'Why?'

'We wanted to know.'

Bill came to the door of the cloakroom. Behind William's back he made an agonised face at Adam.

'What do you think about it?' said William, no expression in his face or voice.

'I'd like to leave it to you, sir.'

William laughed. Adam's 'sirs' were occasional, but they never failed of their intention or of their effect. Usually they meant that Adam thought William had missed the mark.

'I think Bill would a great deal rather be with something nearer his own age.'

There was complete silence. Adam and Bill were staring at each other, appalled by the look of relief they had surprised on each other's faces.

Audrey looked at William and ran away towards the kitchen. William went on into the surgery.

'What did you want to ask that for, you ass?'

Bill emerged from the cloakroom, like a wild boar from its den.

Adam looked aggrieved. 'I wanted to know.'

'Ass. Giving everything away like that.'

William, coming out of the surgery, had a dissolving view of two boys scuffling on the lawn. It broke up as he approached and he found them both feigning interest in something at opposite sides of the garden.

CHAPTER EIGHT

They went down, all of them, to the 'last day' tennis-party at Robin's house. The vicarage was empty of French, Germans, Czechs, and Swedes in this last week of the holidays. The day belonged, by tradition, to Robin and his friends. Life moved with a larger, slower rhythm there, on that last day. There were no discussions, no shrill, excited cries.

Catherine looked at them, a country collection of half-fledged girls in cotton frocks, and solemn youths in flannels, well-grown, sun-burned, and, compared with their elders, extremely silent.

A country collection, yet in their own way beginning to show the colour of a new generation, a generation which would be bound by something in common, as she and Hilary's mother were bound, and as she and Audrey were not.

She thought it was a sober colour. There was nothing fantastic about them. It seemed already a long time since every girl she knew had displayed a gash of carmine across the lower half of her face. These girls had a hard, undecorated trimness, they played with a businesslike satisfaction. They appeared almost prim . . . until you heard the unforced freedom of their conversation.

She walked with Robin's mother into the meadow beyond and round by the sheltering yew hedge into the vegetable garden. It was too cold to sit still, and they weren't needed on the tennis courts. Catherine hadn't come to be with her children, that was over long ago; she had come to be with Robin's mother, whom she liked.

'Your Audrey's a woman,' said Robin's mother.

'Not yet.'

'I know. We all say "not yet."'

'I didn't mean that. I don't want Audrey to belong to me any more. I doubt if she ever did.'

'Not when she was little? How helpless they were! We had to do everything for them.'

'It always struck me as a mean advantage. Oh! I don't say that we took it. But when you look back on all that, you can hardly expect them to be our friends yet, can you?'

'What a queer way to put it . . . I do see what you mean. We've seen them in a rather undignified light. But I don't want Robin to be my friend. He's charming to me. I think your Adam's charming too. Did you see how delightful he was to that stupid Nancy Clary? She can't play at all; she spoilt the whole set.'

'Adam plays pretty badly.'

'As if that mattered . . . in a boy!' She stopped in the door of the vegetable garden. 'Look at them. I do like them as they are. Funny, callow creatures!'

Catherine laughed.

'I know. . . .' Robin's mother made her old, childish gesture with her thin shoulders. 'That's my way of saying "not yet".

But we've worked so hard over them. We've put so much into it. You're lucky. You've still got Bill.'

'Bill goes to school with Adam this term.'

They looked across the lawn, a lawn darkly green under a menacing sky. Bill and Adam were a little out of the picture, on the edge of a senior and inaccessible group of youths. But they were quite happy about it. Bill had just told Adam a funny story, or more probably invented an improper and appropriate nickname for someone in the company. Struggling with repressed laughter, they looked straight into each other's eyes, after the peculiar manner of men.

It struck Catherine that the word friends, which Robin's mother used so freely, had suddenly become appropriate to Adam and Bill.

She thought . . . this is almost the last year when all of them will be here on 'last day'. In a very little while they'll be coming home at all sorts of odd times, or have gone so far away that they don't come home at all. They'll go into the towns, or on service abroad . . . to the Argentine . . . to Africa . . . to Malay. . . . The girls will go away too, and the ones who don't marry will come home every year a little thinner, a little more dried up, a little more consciously eager over their jobs. She shook herself. She thought: Don't be morbid. Why can't you live in the time you're having now, like any sane person. It is the only time you can live in.

'Are you cold?' said Robin's mother.

'Oh, no,' said Catherine quickly, as though it were impolite to confess that you could be cold in somebody else's garden.

'Come into the hall. There's a fire.'

She lingered over the word fire as though it were a sinful luxury, and indeed in that house it was, though it was only a couple of logs from the old beech tree that had come down last winter.

Catherine thought how fragile Robin's mother looked, with her air of elderly youth. The chest between the thin shoulders was so sunken, her hips were so narrow, the gentle pink and white of her face had dried like an immortelle. Only her innocent eager eyes were as bright as ever, but the expression in them had changed. Their air of frank interest had grown a little haggard. Enthusiasm was being swamped by anxiety.

They went into the dark hall and sat down beside the fire. It was pleasant to sit there in the smell of wood-smoke, old wicker furniture, and early chrysanthemums. Catherine was glad to be away from the voices in the garden, so soon the time would come when she would no longer hear them.

Jane was right, she thought. You are incurably sentimental and dishonest. You love sadness for its own sake. But that's not quite true. It will matter when it's all over. I shall feel it less if I try the edge of it now.

A car stopped, scrunching softly, on the gravel outside. Hilary's mother came in, pushing the door to with a finality, as though it were something distasteful that she was dropping for good.

'Well?' she said, leaning against it and looking at them.

Her air was quizzical, as though she knew them both so well that she found them faintly ridiculous.

Robin's mother patted a chair. 'Come and sit down . . . you needn't take them yet.'

'I don't know. I ought to. I've not nearly done with them yet. Oh, well!'

She gave a long sigh, half real, half comic.

Catherine looked back at her, over her shoulder.

'I'm tired,' said Hilary's mother.

She dropped into a chair and looked at the log fire, crumbling slowly in the tepid evening.

'Oh! I know I've said that before. I'm always saying it. But it's true. I'm never anything else but tired. You're tired. We're all tired. It's not only our bodies, it's our minds. I don't know which matters most. None of us say anything about it, but we all know it.'

Catherine pulled her hat off and let her head drop back against the worn velvet of the sofa. A group of players came up to the lemonade table outside. In the pause two voices . . . a boy's, faint and ingratiating, and a girl's, brief, cool, detached, came in through the open window. Robin's mother raised an eyebrow, she looked at Catherine. She seemed more interested by the tone of the dialogue than by what was going on in the room. She made a faint sound of assent, but did not turn her head.

'It's no good pretending anything else,' Hilary's mother went on. 'We're worn out. We've had years on the stretch. Plotting to make both ends meet. Scheming to get our young on in the world. I'm not squealing about it. I shall go on. You'll go on. But I used to pretend I liked it, that it was amusing. But it isn't amusing. It never was.'

Catherine put her hands behind her head. 'I think myself that the outlook is a bit grim,' she said. She thought, too, that it was better that everybody had come to admit it, instead of pretending that it was a gallant game in which they and their children were taking part.

Robin's mother abandoned the conversation outside the window and turned her head, her large amber beads clicking against her collarbones.

'But when there's so much to be done, how can one possibly stop?' she asked. Her voice was a shade fretful.

'If you can't do it you have to stop,' said Hilary's mother. 'I'm simply stating facts. There isn't a woman I know who isn't thoroughly jaded. We started doing too much in the War, we found we could do it, and we went on doing it. Now the bill is coming in.'

Catherine looked at the other two, leaning their elbows on their knees and looking at the fire. It was true. They were tired. It was written in the slope of their shoulders, of their backs, in the tiny lines which began to show around their mouths . . . and most plainly of all in their eyes.

'Yes, we're tired,' she said. 'I don't see that anything can be done about it. But we have done a job . . . of a sort . . . all that I dislike is the feeling that we're too tired for anything else, and that there *is* little else we can do.'

Robin's mother frowned earnestly. 'I've never felt like that, I'm sure that's wrong. Everything so terribly important. I don't know which way to turn first. But it's true that I'm tired. Deep down inside me all the time I know that I'm horribly, helplessly tired. It seems so weak and silly.'

'Weak, silly, but quite unavoidable.' Hilary's mother stuffed a cushion into the small of her back. 'That's the point. We are weak. I wonder why we all thought we should be able to go on for ever? The way we've been hurried all the time! It's indecent. No one should have to be hurried like that.'

'I'd be happier if everybody gave up pretending,' Catherine said. 'We've had such a lot of that . . . cheerful idiots yapping encouragement whilst we got on with the work. "Business as usual" in the War, the "good time" afterwards . . . wasn't it fantastic and wasn't it stale? . . . And this sickening constant cant about "personal freedom". Freedom! There isn't room in this world to get your elbows away from your sides.'

'It's a dreadful world for the children to come out into.' Robin's mother chafed her forearm through the thin silk of her dress, a dress so long familiar to the other two that they had given up even noticing that she was wearing it yet again. 'I've worked so hard at Robin. I've taught him to love peace for its own sake, to respect his neighbours' liberty of thought and feeling . . . and now I've got to turn him out into a brawling pointless muddle where there isn't as much chance for him to live a decent life . . .' She broke off. 'It's all *wrong*. We've done more for our children than anybody on earth has done for any cause in the last twenty years.'

She stopped speaking. In the silence the two young voices, cool and indifferent, muted and insinuating, continued their duet.

Catherine listened to them for a moment. 'I've given up believing that a good time's coming,' she said. 'I know a bad time's come. I wish they'd stop talking and do something about it. After all, none of us want very much. Security. A living wage. Hope for our children.'

Hilary's mother laughed . . . a hard jarring sound as though she realised the folly of even those demands, a laugh which seemed to make it impossible to continue the discussion. They sat silent, looking at the fire, which burnt secretly, with a small blue flame.

Robin's mother turned to Catherine.

'Listen to Audrey's voice!'

They listened.

'Who's the other one?' Catherine was smiling at the comedy of that duet in two tones.

'I'm not sure. Wait! Yes. That's Roger Stowgate.'

Hilary's mother gave a short bark of laughter. 'That very finished youth with the sleek head?'

'Hush!'

Other voices joined them on the gravel path outside.

'It's not only Audrey's voice. Listen to Robin. Listen to Edward. The tone comes out so clearly when you can't hear the actual words.'

They listened. Outside, under the heavy trees, a steady cool blast blew up under an overcast sky. Catherine thought that there was something of that coolness in the voices outside, a cold breath of common sense and rational thinking.

And then, suddenly, the room was full of the generation of their own flesh and blood whom, except for Bill, it was no longer possible to call 'the children'. They had, all three of them, a sensation of being invaded by something friendly but alien.

Audrey came over and sat down on the arm of the sofa. She touched Catherine's hair lightly, with the back of her hand.

'Why are you all so grim?'

'We were discussing the rottenness of things in general.'

Audrey laughed.

'Shocking . . . isn't it?'

Over her mother's head she looked across the room at Robin. Catherine saw the answering look in Robin's eyes . . . frank, mocking, infinitely friendly.

They are older than we are. Who had said that? Nobody had spoken.

She found herself answering Audrey.

'It seems shocking to us.'

She became aware that the silent Robin was struggling with an opinion. Politely, with great kindness, he delivered himself of his verdict.

'You see, you all expected such a lot.'

They were silent, all five of them, going home in the car. The summer landscape, without shadows, darkly green, flowed past in the car in a scent of blackberries and dead leaves.

William put one hand on Catherine's knee as he drove.

'Silly!' Catherine whispered. 'After all these years!'

William didn't answer. It was precisely because of all those years that he liked to be near her, to be able to touch her. Catherine was untidy, vague, socially inept. But she was a trier. Valiantly, in blind ignorance and recurring dismay, she had kept his house and brought up his children. Even if her efforts weren't always successful, it was for them that he loved her.

A cold light stained the edge of the sky. It seemed to come from underground, it had a magic quality.

Catherine heard Audrey move in the back of the car. She bent forward.

'Look!' she said. 'It's all perfectly flat . . . like paper. If you put your hand against that hill you would go through.'

Catherine turned her head. There it was still . . . that flash of Audrey's under-self.

She thought: If it were true, if we could drive straight through to the other side, then it could always be as it is now. But that can't happen. We've got to go on.

Audrey understood her look, she was happy because of the drowned light of the evening and because of the things that she and Catherine could still say to each other without speaking.

'Oh!' Bill roused out of a half-sleep. 'It's the last night!'

They laughed, all of them, at that.

'It's not funny!' Bill roared. 'Stop, can't you!'

'No,' said Adam, 'we can't stop.'

Why, Catherine thought, does everything have two meanings tonight? I must be very tired. I must go to bed early every night after they have gone.

She closed her eyes. You could still smell the evening, though you couldn't see it. A sad smell, not the smell of summer.

What would I do if I had it all to go over again? We've had hard times, we've been hungry, we've been starved for amusement and interest and friends. We've been desperately tired. I've sat down again and again and howled with

334

disappointment. I've made mistakes. I've been angry. I haven't often understood what I was doing for the children. But I've loved them. I've had a wonderful time.

Those who haven't had them can't understand. Fancy expecting your children to be grateful to you! I'm grateful to them. I used to think it would never be over . . . the bringing them up, the endless work. . . . But all the time I was enjoying it.

And now I must sit back . . . out of the way. Not grab nor claim, not try to insist on what they do and what they are.

Audrey's all right. She'll choose her own path. Adam's all right. Nothing that happens ever really gets at him to hurt him. And Bill? It would be ridiculous to worry about Bill. . . .

Of all the things I once thought I had, I have only my own thoughts left.

Audrey's face drifted across the sleepy darkness of those thoughts, then Robin's when he had given his opinion.

'They will be happier than we were. They expect less.'

Happiness for one's children! Another folly.

She leaned, in the dusk, against the rough tweed of William's sleeve and thought that at last, even that wish had left her and that it was beyond her, in such a world, to plan happiness for her children.

And with the loss of that, the last of her ambitions, she lay still, and was content.